# IN THE SHADOW OF DENALI

## Also by Tracie Peterson and Kimberley Woodhouse

*All Things Hidden*
*Beyond the Silence*

## Books by Tracie Peterson

HEART OF THE FRONTIER
*Treasured Grace*

SAPPHIRE BRIDES
*A Treasure Concealed*
*A Beauty Refined*
*A Love Transformed*

BRIDES OF SEATTLE
*Steadfast Heart*
*Refining Fire*
*Love Everlasting*

LONE STAR BRIDES
*A Sensible Arrangement*
*A Moment in Time*
*A Matter of Heart*
*Lone Star Brides* (3 in 1)

LAND OF SHINING WATER
*The Icecutter's Daughter*
*The Quarryman's Bride*
*The Miner's Lady*

LAND OF THE LONE STAR
*Chasing the Sun*
*Touching the Sky*
*Taming the Wind*

STRIKING A MATCH
*Embers of Love*
*Hearts Aglow* • *Hope Rekindled*

SONG OF ALASKA
*Dawn's Prelude*
*Morning's Refrain* • *Twilight's Serenade*

ALASKAN QUEST
*Summer of the Midnight Sun*

*Under the Northern Lights*
*Whispers of Winter*
*Alaskan Quest* (3 in 1)

BRIDES OF GALLATIN COUNTY
*A Promise to Believe In*
*A Love to Last Forever*
*A Dream to Call My Own*

DESERT ROSES
*Shadows of the Canyon*
*Across the Years* • *Beneath a Harvest Sky*

HEIRS OF MONTANA
*Land of My Heart* • *The Coming Storm*
*To Dream Anew* • *The Hope Within*

LADIES OF LIBERTY
*A Lady of High Regard*
*A Lady of Hidden Intent*
*A Lady of Secret Devotion*

WESTWARD CHRONICLES
*A Shelter of Hope*
*Hidden in a Whisper*
*A Veiled Reflection*

YUKON QUEST
*Treasures of the North*
*Ashes and Ice* • *Rivers of Gold*

• • • • •

*House of Secrets*
*A Slender Thread*
*What She Left for Me*
*Where My Heart Belongs*

www.traciepeterson.com          www.kimberleywoodhouse.com

# IN THE SHADOW OF DENALI

## TRACIE PETERSON
### AND KIMBERLEY WOODHOUSE

BETHANYHOUSE
*a division of Baker Publishing Group*
Minneapolis, Minnesota

Published by Bethany House Publishers
11400 Hampshire Avenue South
Bloomington, Minnesota 55438
www.bethanyhouse.com

Bethany House Publishers is a division of
Baker Publishing Group, Grand Rapids, Michigan

Printed in the United States of America

Library of Congress Cataloging-in-Publication Data
Names: Peterson, Tracie, author. | Woodhouse, Kimberley, author.
Title: In the shadow of Denali / Tracie Peterson and Kimberley Woodhouse.
Description: Minneapolis, Minnesota : Bethany House, a division of Baker
    Publishing Group, [2017] | Series: The heart of Alaska ; book 1
Identifiers: LCCN 2016034522 | ISBN 9780764219474 (cloth : alk. paper) | ISBN
    9780764219238 (trade paper)
Subjects: | GSAFD: Christian fiction. | Historical fiction. | Love stories.
Classification: LCC PS3566.E7717 I5 2017 | DDC 813/.54—dc23
LC record available at https://lccn.loc.gov/2016034522

Scripture quotations are from the King James Version of the Bible.

This is a work of historical reconstruction; the appearances of certain historical figures are therefore inevitable. All other characters, however, are products of the author's imagination, and any resemblance to actual persons, living or dead, is coincidental.

Cover design by Dan Thornberg, Design Source Creative Services

Kimberley Woodhouse is represented by The Steve Laube Agency.

17  18  19  20  21  22  23      7  6  5  4  3  2  1

This book is lovingly dedicated in memory and honor of:

*Cassidy Faith Hale*

(March 14, 2000—September 16, 2015)


So young. So vibrant. So fun.

I wish I'd had more time with you.
More hugs. More laughter.

The past few months without you have been so very
hard as we've walked with your family through this
journey. But even through the heartache, there is joy.

Joy in the memories.

Joy in the knowledge of where you are—
No more tears. No more pain.

Joy in the anticipation of seeing you again—
and praising our Lord forever.

Joy in the lives touched and changed on this earth
by you—because you dared to shine your light.

You've inspired us all.

Your light—*His light*—is still shining.

I'm gonna let it shine . . .

# A Note from the Authors

We are overjoyed that you have chosen to join us for yet another journey into our great country's history. Again—as with our other collaborations—we'd like to reiterate that while this novel is rich with historical detail about Curry, Alaska, its incredible Curry Hotel, the Alaska Railroad, Talkeetna, Denali (Mount McKinley), and the people who lived and breathed this little bit of history—please remember that this is a work of fiction. While many real people are used in the story, their personalities and dialogue are from our imaginations. Please see the Dear Reader letter at the conclusion of the book to find out more details about the amazing research for this series and the author liberties that were taken.

We (Kimberley and Tracie) are passionate about Alaska. Kim's family lived there for many years and Tracie has spent oodles of time in that great state as well. On our last book tour together, our readers told us over and over how excited they were for another Alaska book. So here it is.

Curry, Alaska, and the grand Curry Hotel were very real indeed, although now the only way to see it is through the lens of historical photographs. At mile 248 on the Alaska Railroad today there are interpretive signs and a few lost remnants of Curry. The historic Curry Lookout is the only remaining piece still standing of this fascinating part of Alaska's history.

To give you a glimpse into this time and setting, we'd like to share an excerpt from the Preface of a book written by one of the team that was the very first to summit the tallest mountain in North America, Denali, back in 1913. Hudson Stuck's passion for Alaska, its peoples, its lands, and its mountains is commendable to this day. And one hundred years after the publication of his book, we would see the author's wish and desire come to fruition as the Great Mountain was rightly given back his true name: *Denali.*

From *The Ascent of Denali* by Hudson Stuck (Scribner, 1914):

Forefront in this book, because forefront in the author's heart and desire, must stand a plea for the restoration to the greatest mountain in North America of its immemorial native name. If there be any prestige or authority in such matter from the accomplishment of a first complete ascent, "if there be any virtue, if there be any praise," the author values it chiefly as it may give weight to this plea.

It is now little more than seventeen years ago that a prospector penetrated from the south into the neighborhood of this mountain, guessed its height with remarkable accuracy at twenty thousand feet, and, ignorant of any name that it already bore, placed upon it the name of the Republican candidate for President of the United States at the approaching election—William McKinley . . .

. . . The author would add, perhaps quite unnecessarily, yet lest any should mistake, a final personal note. He is no professed explorer or climber or "scientist," but a missionary, and of these matters an amateur only. The vivid recollection of a back bent down with burdens and lungs at the limit of their function makes him hesitate to describe this enterprise as recreation. It was the most laborious undertaking with which he was ever connected; yet it was done for the pleasure of doing it, and the pleasure far outweighed the pain. But he is concerned much more with men than mountains, and would say, since "out of the fullness of the heart the mouth speaketh," that his especial and growing concern, these ten years past, is with the native people of Alaska, a gentle and kindly race, now threatened with a wanton and senseless extermination, and sadly in need of generous champions if that threat is to be averted.

And so, dear friends, we take you back a century to the dawn of a new era for Alaska. A new national park, the first successful attempt to climb Denali, the people who loved the land, the pioneers who blazed the trails, the railroad that connected it all, and the incredible Curry Hotel in the remote Alaska Territory. We give you: *In the Shadow of Denali.*

Kim and Tracie

# Prologue

1917

Henry Brennan—the insufferable man—should've been dead.
But he wasn't.

Frank Irving cursed his luck. His partner was still very much alive.

It was all the fault of that too-good, overzealous guide.

It wouldn't be so bad if Frank hadn't been the one to hire John Ivanoff. But he had.

How was he to know the man was a native Alaskan who'd climbed around Mount McKinley so many times he had private nicknames for certain parts? He'd thought John sounded so normal, and *Ivanoff* was Russian.

He'd certainly seemed perfect on paper. Solid reputation as a guide—which Henry required—but no actual full-ascent experience, so he could be blamed for any fatal accident—which Frank required.

"Gentlemen, we need to take advantage of this good weather," the guide called from outside the tent. "Be ready to leave in ten minutes."

Fighting the urge to lose his breakfast, a sign of the altitude sickness he and Henry both shared, Frank began to shove everything into his pack. John Ivanoff was nothing but a tyrant.

Who knew the man would end up being such a conscientious guide, especially after he agreed to shorten the preparation schedule from six months to eight weeks? Such a man should be easy to buy, especially because John dreamed of opening his own mountaineering guided tour business. But no! He was another of those churchy Bible-thumpers like Henry. It made Frank twitch.

The side walls of the tent shifted with another gust of frigid mountain wind. Frank and Henry had made a fortune the past twenty years selling these very same tents to all the gold-rush-fever idiots who stopped in their Seattle store before heading to Alaska. It had been Frank's idea to make a killing off of all the crazies who thought dashing off to the frozen north to dig for gold would be their pot at the end of the rainbow. But he hadn't planned to stay in a tent himself. Ever. Especially not at the top of a mountain. And definitely not for this many weeks.

But desperate times called for desperate measures. And he was desperate.

Desperate to call the profits his own.

Not just half. *All.*

That's why he'd cooked up this harebrained plan to climb Mount McKinley. He was tired of sharing with his partner. And they'd signed an agreement when they started the company. So if he eliminated Henry . . .

It'd all be his.

So here he was. On the side of this stupid mountain. They'd trained for months on lesser mountains and talked of all the equipment they would try out and then advertise to sell.

Henry had been thrilled. The do-gooder. Always an outdoorsman, he didn't want to give up his own exploring for a job in the office at the factory.

So the opportunity was born. New national park. Big, treacherous mountain.

It was remote. And bound to be a place where a tragic mishap could occur and nothing could be done about it.

It all seemed so easy.

But then John Ivanoff happened. The man was everywhere, constantly watching. And—unfortunately—prepared for any possible scenario.

It should not have taken this long to find a way to get rid of Henry, but Frank couldn't do it when the native haulers were with them—too many witnesses—and he definitely couldn't finagle it with all the sled dogs around. They'd find the body for sure. So he'd waited.

As the helpers, sleds, and dogs stayed behind, the paths got steeper and the air got thinner. And his patience thinned right along with it. But he'd come this far. He might as well finish the climb. Perhaps it would even be good for business to make it to the top and then have tragedy befall them. He'd have the acclaim of the press for his success *and* the sympathy of the public for his loss.

Frank swept the tent flap aside, stepped into the frigid wind, and grimaced.

John coiled a rope, a sappy smile on his face. "We have to cross Cassidy Lane today. It's dangerous, but one of my favorite places on Denali."

The native name for Mount McKinley rolled off John's tongue with ease and some sort of weird reverence. Frank found it annoying. Since the President of the United States had signed something called the Mount McKinley Park Bill, that's what the mountain should be called. Not that Frank cared two nickels about the name. But, as Henry pointed out, it meant he and Frank could claim to be the first climbers to reach the peak *in* Mount McKinley National Park. Some team back in 1913 had a documented ascent, but that was before the new national park bill had been signed into effect. Not that it mattered. Frank only cared about the opportunity this afforded to be rid of his partner. He was tired of this wretched mountain.

"Cassidy Lane?" Henry poked his head out of the second tent he'd shared with the guide, since Frank hated to share and was adamant that he wanted privacy. "Named for your daughter?" He emerged with his pack, a knitted cap in hand and a fur hat dangling over one arm.

"Sure is." John kept winding the rope like it was as natural to him as breathing. "It's a dangerous, narrow path along a cliff. I almost fell off it once."

Frank's heart rate perked up. This was promising. "How long ago?"

"Many years." John's face sobered. "The weather changed on us instantly. What had been a calm, bright day like this one suddenly turned fierce."

Another gust of wind almost lifted Frank off his feet. This was calm?

"I didn't think I was going to make it." John reached the end of the rope, the loops perfectly matched. "But I kept thinking of my Cassidy, recalling every memory from the time she was born up to then, until I made it home."

Henry put down his pack, then pulled on the black knitted cap over his graying hair. Just the night before he'd told Frank they needed to experiment with different materials to find or create something that would be better at holding in body heat. Especially at these temperatures. He'd even tried to convince Frank that one tent would be better than two—less to carry, and they could share body heat. But Frank would have none of it. It was just one more reason he hated his partner. The man always came up with the most marvelous ideas and of course was given all the credit.

"When I told Cassidy—much later, of course—she made light of it and said that if I ever got here again, I would just have to take another trip down Cassidy Lane and I'd be sure to make it home."

"Instead of Memory Lane? How delightful." Henry slapped the guide's shoulder, the same sentimental smile on his face as the one John had worn a minute ago.

Frank wanted to lose the contents of his stomach right then and there. This time, however, it had nothing to do with altitude sickness. Fatherhood made saps of even the strongest men. Henry had been all but worthless since his brats had come along. Rushing home to be with his family instead of shouldering his fair share. Talking to customers about his son or one of the girls. How many did they have? Two? Three? Didn't matter. Because Henry's repellent brood wouldn't inherit any part of The Brennan/Irving Company. The business contract Henry and Frank signed when they first opened stipulated that should one partner die, the other partner inherited full control.

Which was why this plan worked.

He'd make a show of supporting the grieving family—with everything but actual money. Martha Brennan was a comely enough woman. She'd remarry, move away, and The Brennan/Irving Company would become The Irving Company.

No more sharing profits. No more running each and every idea by Henry. No more of the honesty-at-all-times practice. No more faking he actually liked these people.

Stupid Henry. Didn't he know how much money they could make now that they'd established a reputation for selling the best ropes, tents, and climbing attire in the Pacific Northwest? Now was the time to *cut* quality and boost profits.

Henry gave John another hearty pat on the back, then donned the fur hat and tied it. "What say you, expert guide? We still a go for the summit today?"

John nodded, glancing upward. "Yes, but as you can see, the clouds are draping him today. Once we reach the top, you'll have a beautiful view of the clouds below."

It bugged Frank that John called the mountain "he" and "him" all the time, but to be fair, everything about John Ivanoff, Henry Brennan, and this blasted mountain made Frank furious.

"Any danger of storms?"

"There's always that danger here. I don't see any immediate threat, but remember, storms roll in fast." John threw the heavy rope over his shoulder. "If you two are ready to go, I think we should head up. I've already done my tests on the ropes and ice climbs for today."

"We're already at 18,500 feet." Frank huffed for breath. "There's less than two thousand feet to reach the summit."

John nodded. "Two thousand feet that will take us at least six hours."

"Both ways?" Frank felt all the energy leave him. Would it never end?

Chuckling, John shook his head. "Well, we could always let gravity work with us on the trip down—if you'd like to go faster."

Henry pulled on his pack with what appeared little effort. "Well, I say let's go. I'm anxious to finish this climb, and I must say that sleeping in a warm bed in front of a roaring fire sounds awfully good after four long weeks trudging and climbing in the ice and snow. I'd like to have full feeling back in my hands and feet." He shook his head and patted his partner's back. "But that's why we're doing it, right? To experience the thrill for our customers?"

Reminding himself to play along, Frank tried to sound excited and supportive. "Lots and lots of customers. Yes. That's the plan. If the government would just get the road built into this area, we could bring more customers than we could ever imagine. All with John as our guide. We just won't tell the customers about not feeling their fingers and toes." He laughed too loud for his own ears.

"Of course." John's smile looked a little uneasy.

"Lead on, then." Frank ducked his head and adjusted his thick gloves over a thinner pair. No use giving away that John's dream of being their business partner for guided tours was as doomed as Henry's of a warm bed.

Henry carried a long walking stick—one carved with their names and the date—that they planned to drive into the snow at the top later that day. His eagerness shone in his eyes as he nodded to John. "I'm ready. Let's go!"

By two in the afternoon, their weary troop reached the southern peak of Mount McKinley. Even as the wind tried to knock him off his feet and the air was too thin for a decent breath, Frank couldn't help feeling a little euphoric. "We did it, boys . . . We're the first ones . . . to climb Mount . . . McKinley in the new . . . Mount McKinley National Park." His sentences were punctured by the many breaths he had to take.

Henry handed John the wooden pole. "The honor . . . should go . . . to you."

No it shouldn't!

But the guide grinned and plunged the marker into the snow. "Success!"

17

Hardly, but there was always hope. A hearty gale from the west brought his attention up. The clouds moved in at a rapid clip and were tinged an ominous gray.

"We need to get down, and quickly," John yelled and waved a hand at the clouds. "That doesn't bode well."

They hurried to take a few pictures. Henry and John wanted to have a visual record of the trip, and Henry thought it would make for great advertising. Of course he was right, but it only made Frank's hatred grow. And all he really cared about was getting rid of the man and getting off the wretched mountain.

With the pictures taken, Henry went to repack the camera.

"Here, let me . . . put it in mine," Frank said. "You need . . . to get your pack on . . . and your hands are shaking." No sense losing the camera and photographs if he had any success eliminating his problem.

"Thanks." Henry nodded. "A man never had a better partner." He slipped his backpack on again and moved to John's side as snow began to fall. "Do we have . . . time to get to safety?"

"Yes, if we . . . move fast. But stay sure of . . . your footing. Going down is often . . . more dangerous and . . . time-consuming. Be prepared for the gusts of wind . . . that may try to knock you off your feet, and blowing snow . . . can disorient you, so hold tight to the rope between us." John looked back to the clouds above. "We should try to get to camp. If that's not possible, we'll make a shelter on the way and ride out the storm." The building clouds blocked out the sun that only minutes ago had been quite intense. John handed a rope to Henry. "Secure it around you. This doesn't look good at all."

"I have a bad feeling . . ." Henry's words were lost in a swirl of wind and snow.

Frank took as deep a breath as he could at twenty thousand feet. Fear lurked behind John's eyes, which didn't bode well for the plan. Only one person was supposed to die up here. Not him, not even John.

Just Henry.

## 1

JULY 8, 1923—SIX YEARS LATER
CURRY, ALASKA—MILE 248 ON THE ALASKA RAILROAD

Cassidy Faith Ivanoff walked up the stairs from the basement of the Curry Hotel with a massive tray in her hands. The staff was all abuzz. The railroad was finally about to be completed, and there were hushed whispers about the President of the United States coming to stay in their hotel as well. Imagine that. The President himself! Here, in Alaska. As far as she knew, no other President had ever visited the territory. It would bring Alaska to the attention of the rest of the country.

With the completion of the railroad connecting Seward to Fairbanks, the Curry Hotel was the ideal mid-journey stopping point. It had been built by the railroad not only for guests and tourists, but also for workers. Rumor had it a large town was sure to develop around the beautiful hotel. But right now there were only a few buildings from when the community had been called Deadhorse—a water tower, a roundhouse, and a power plant to generate electricity.

But Cassidy could imagine the growth and it excited her. The months had flown by since she'd first been hired as the cook's assistant at the spacious and luxurious hotel. Born and raised in

Alaska, Cassidy and her father had been quite familiar with the area. Dad signed on to lead guests on guided tours, while Cassidy's passion for cooking made her a natural for the kitchen.

Unfortunately, cooking wasn't always the focus of her duties. In fact, she spent what felt like half of her time climbing up and down the stairs between the basement kitchen, provision rooms, and the main-level kitchen. Why they ever built the provisions rooms downstairs was beyond her. Must've been a man who designed it. Who never had to work in a big hotel like this.

"Cassidy, when you finish with the pickled onions, I need you to start on the crab salad." Margaret Johnson's voice prevailed across the room.

"Yes, Mrs. Johnson." The woman amazed Cassidy day in and day out. A hard woman, she was the hotel's head cook and Cassidy's boss. Rumor had it that she'd beaten out some big chef from San Francisco for the job. The manager insisted on calling Mrs. Johnson "Chef," but she still labeled herself as the cook. She ran the kitchen from 5:00 a.m. until 9:00 p.m. when the night cook took over. But he couldn't tie his shoes without her approval. Even off duty, she ran that kitchen. Day or night. And everyone knew it.

Cassidy smiled as she set the tray down and filled the elegant serving dishes with the pungent hors d'oeuvres.

No-nonsense and a little rough around the edges, Mrs. Johnson kept Cassidy on her toes. And Cassidy loved it. There had been few women in her life, but those who had been part of her upbringing were in many ways just like Mrs. Johnson. Blunt and to the point, without beating around the bush. It allowed for no doubt as to what was expected. But it tended to make Cassidy feel a little . . . lonely.

Setting the tray off to the side to be chilled, Cassidy reached for the crab legs and peeked at the woman barking orders to the kitchen hands. True, everyone else feared—even dreaded—the head cook, but beneath that gruff exterior, there was a glimmer of something deep and soothing. Cassidy already had a soft spot in her heart for her.

Never having a memory of her mother, Cassidy found she often craved the company of older women, and she liked and respected Margaret Johnson. Maybe over time . . . they could be friends.

"Quit your day-dreaming, Cassidy Faith. We have hundreds of mouths to feed a fancy dinner to and I won't allow you to mess up the schedule."

And maybe not.

The two girls washing dishes giggled at the sink. Everyone knew that if Cook used your middle name, she was more than serious.

"Sorry, Mrs. Johnson." She couldn't keep from smiling to herself—she could always try, right? She donned her protective gloves, broke the shell of the first crab leg before her, and started pulling out the thick pink-and-white meat. Sweet and rich, it was one of Cassidy's favorites. She had lived off the land and sea of Alaska her entire twenty-three years.

Her father, John, was half-Athabaskan and had met and fallen in love with an Irish missionary's daughter. When the missionary couple heard of seventeen-year-old Eliza's plans to marry this native man, they were appalled at the "mixing of races" and demanded Eliza turn her back on John. But Eliza defied her parents and married him anyway.

Only a year passed before she died right after childbirth, and her parents left Alaska and told John it was God's punishment. They wouldn't even see Cassidy or acknowledge her existence.

Cassidy grew up knowing that she had been named after a family surname on her maternal grandparents' side, but she hated that she would never know them or know where her name came from. How could anyone turn their back on family? It baffled her to no end. Even after all these years. Strangely she felt as if it were all her fault—that she'd done something wrong without having had any say in the matter whatsoever. Dad assured her that this wasn't the case, that pain had driven her grandparents to make the choice they'd made. Still, it haunted Cassidy. She'd tried for years to imagine how she might go about contacting her grandparents and healing the division between them and her father, but there never seemed to be even a hint of what might work. She had no idea of where her grandparents had gone or even if they were still alive.

The shells piled up as she made swift work of the crab. The thoughts and memories kept her mind spinning and her hands busy.

Her middle name, Faith, was the last gift she'd been given by her mother. Over the years Dad had told Cassidy how Eliza Ivanoff prayed over her baby, blessed her with her name, and took her last breath. He'd challenged Cassidy to live up to her name on more than one occasion.

Just recently, in fact. A few months ago, when they'd left their home of Tanana—the only place she'd ever called home—to come work in Curry, Dad said it would be a grand step of faith. And so it was.

Cassidy would never have guessed the blessings that would come by taking that step. But she was indeed blessed.

She loved it here.

The Curry Hotel was more magnificent than any building Cassidy had ever seen. From the rich red carpets, the dark woods, and the deep leather chairs in the lobby, all the way to the gleaming kitchen with its Duparquet range and shiny aluminum and copper pots. There were even electric lights and hot water. Such things were never seen in most of Alaska, and yet they were here in Curry. The Alaska Railroad had outdone itself. And the enormous number of visitors proved its success.

She hadn't understood at the time that her Dad needed something different. After the successful summit of Mount McKinley in 1917, he'd changed. Maybe because he'd always wanted to open a guide service and that wouldn't be happening anytime soon—especially since the park still wasn't easily accessible—and maybe because having lost one of his climbers weighed him down. He'd probably never get over the loss, even though he'd told Cassidy that the man loved the Lord and was certain to be in heaven.

Their faith in God was also the Ivanoffs' foundation for living, and her father preferred to work with people who were of like mind. She'd only been seventeen when her father made that climb, but she knew that he blamed himself for the death of the climber. He took responsibility for getting the men up the mountain and returning them safely back down. Losing one of his clients had devastated her strong father, and she wasn't at all certain he would ever fully recover. It had stolen a good deal of his joy and brought plans for his own business to a rather abrupt halt. So he'd been working for the railroad all these years as an expert on the land and game. He'd supplied the workers with food and had been useful to the company in plotting out the best route. Highly esteemed by all who knew him, John Ivanoff was the best man she'd ever known. But even with that and the railroad's success, Cassidy knew her dad maintained a sense of failure.

"When you're done with that box, there's a second one waiting," Mrs. Johnson reminded her of the present task.

"Yes, Mrs. Johnson." Cassidy heard the agitation in the older woman's voice. Mrs. Johnson always worried about the clock and whether everything would be done in a timely manner. So far they had never missed serving a meal on time or in the finest presentation, but still the woman worried, so Cassidy did her best to speed up her actions. She wanted to please Mrs. Johnson for many reasons, not the least of which was her desire to earn the woman's respect and friendship. Even with all of her efforts, however, the task proved difficult. Mrs. Johnson wasn't one for frivolities, which apparently included friendships. The woman had little to do with anyone during the working hours—except of course to command her staff into perfect order. Then, when the workday concluded, Mrs. Johnson went off to her quarters to be alone. She seldom was seen at all in her off-hours. But Cassidy wasn't going to be deterred. She had faith that if she pursued the friendship with Mrs. Johnson, it would eventually come about.

Cassidy's hands worked through more than a hundred crab legs from the first box and started in on the next. The scent of Mrs. Johnson's famous Parker House rolls filled the kitchen and made Cassidy smile. She and Dad had many challenges to face in their duties, but taking their place among the Curry Hotel staff seemed right. Yes, this had been a good step of faith for them both. And the excitement and challenge of the Curry Hotel made her happier than she could've dreamed. It made her father happy that they could work in a capacity that allowed him to keep an eye on her. The Alaska Territory was still more than seventy-five percent male, and she liked the protectiveness of her father. It also didn't hurt that she found comfort in being able to keep a closer eye on him as well.

As the resident recreational guide, John Ivanoff led hiking and fishing tours for the guests. He taught them all about Alaska's incredible wild flowers, berries, and plants, and helped them reel in large trophy fish to take pictures of and show their families back home. Then there were the truly adventurous groups that would travel by boat across the river and hike for miles up the ridge to gain the spectacular view of the High One and the surrounding mountains. He'd been kept very busy, and Cassidy was thankful that he was soon to have a full-time assistant to help.

"Thomas!" Mrs. Johnson's shrill tone made everyone jump, and all work clattered to an abrupt halt.

Cassidy laid a hand on her chest. That certainly jolted her out of day-dreaming. As she looked around the room, she spotted the seventeen-year-old kitchen boy, a wobbling stack of pots behind him. His face was ashen as he quaked in his boots. Oh bother, what had he done this time to rile the cook? A resounding crash behind the boy gave everyone the answer. He closed his eyes in resignation.

Several of the kitchen maids giggled.

"Kindly remember, Thomas, that you cannot haphazardly stack the large pots. There is a system, and everything must be in its place." Mrs. Johnson's tone was at least a tad softer than her initial screech.

More giggles.

"And there will be no laughter at Thomas's plight." Their boss rounded on the young women, hands on her hips. "Or I will have you scrub the floor by hand."

Straight faces and nods answered as they rushed back to their duties.

The bustle of the kitchen began again, but Thomas stood anchored to the floor, his cap in his hand.

"Cassidy, please assist Thomas in the proper placement of the kitchenware."

"Yes, Mrs. Johnson." Cassidy smiled at the young man as the older woman walked away. "Let's get this sorted, shall we? I must hurry and get back to the crab salad."

He nodded. And his stomach rumbled loud enough for Cassidy to hear.

She tried to cover for his embarrassment. "If you look closely, each shelf is labeled with the size of the pot that sits there. Only two in each stack. But once you learn it, it's not hard. They really just go in order of size from the smallest to the largest of big stockpots. All the other pots hang from the ceiling over there, but you probably can see that for yourself. Just don't forget to line these handles up. She can't stand for any of them to be crooked on the shelves. She always says it's for ease of picking them up."

Grabbing the huge cauldrons from the floor, Thomas sighed. "I'm sorry I was in too big of a hurry to notice." Another big sigh as he fumbled with a large pot that probably outweighed him. "Seems I can't do anything right. If I'm too slow, I get hollered at, and if I try to speed up, things aren't done properly and I *still* get hollered at."

"You're learning, Thomas. And that's what matters. Mrs. Johnson may be tough, but she's fair. Pay attention and do your best. Besides, she knows you're still growing and all of us were clumsy in those stages." Cassidy stepped back to let him settle the items in their places. "And you know what? Next time you feel you're being 'hollered' at, why don't you just remember that they're doing it to teach you the correct way."

"You're always so positive." Thomas smiled down at her as he placed the last pot in its place. He stood back, looked at his work, and then reached forward, straightening the handles. "Thank you for always being so nice to me, and for your help."

"Oh, we were all your age at one time and have had to learn new jobs. The hotel only opened in March, so we'll keep learning together." Cassidy turned and wiped down her apron. Then she threw over her shoulder, "And I like being positive—makes the world a bit sunnier, don't you agree?"

"But it's so embarrassing to fall down and drop things. I admit it's been nice to finally grow taller 'cause I was always the shortest in my class. But my brain doesn't seem to know the difference, and my feet keep getting in the way." He followed her back through the kitchen.

"Everyone has to go through growing pangs. Give it time. You're doing just fine." She grabbed a roll off the cooling rack. "Here, eat this quick. It should help you through the next hour." Looking at Thomas broke her heart. He seemed so down. "You know what? I have an idea."

"Will it help me not be such an oaf around here?" He downed the roll in two bites.

Poor Thomas. She nodded. "Like I said, we all go through that stage. But I was an exceptionally clumsy child. I tripped over everything—even nothing at all—and fell down constantly. My dad always had a funny saying for me after he'd picked me up and brushed me off. It made me smile and maybe it will help you." She looked down at the pile of crab meat and the crab legs left to shell.

"What'd he say?"

Cassidy bit her lip. Maybe it was a bit silly for this boy who was almost a man. "Well . . . I'm a bit embarrassed to say it."

"Go on."

"It'll have to be our little secret." She leaned closer and winked.

He cracked a half smile and the twinkle in his eyes was back. "I promise."

"Well, you see, I loved to give hugs. Always have, really. And not just people. I hugged our dogs, the pigs, chickens—I even tried to hug a squirrel once. That one didn't go over too well with the squirrel, I'm sorry to say."

He snickered and covered his mouth. "Sorry, I was just picturing it."

She gave him a smile and gathered the celery and onions she needed for the salad. "Anyway, after I would fall down, my dad would say, 'I guess the floor needed a hug.'" Cassidy couldn't help but laugh at the memory now. "I can't tell you how many times I hugged the floor . . . or the stairs . . . or a rock, a log, or the grass."

He laughed out loud.

Mrs. Johnson cleared her throat across the kitchen.

Thomas straightened. "I best get back to work. Thanks again, Miss Ivanoff. I'll never look at falling down the same way again." His smile was as big as his face.

"You're welcome. Now off you go. I'm sure you have quite a list to accomplish, as do I." She handed him another roll.

Thomas tucked the roll in his apron pocket and walked out of the kitchen.

Mrs. Johnson joined Cassidy. "I suppose he did a decent job. At least the handles are straight."

"He really wants to please you." Cassidy pulled her gloves back out of her apron. "He's such a good young man."

Her boss shook her head. "I appreciate you encouraging him, but it seems he makes double the work for everyone."

"He's young and learning to handle himself." Cassidy hoped Mrs. Johnson wasn't thinking of having him fired. "I'm sure he'll improve."

Mrs. Johnson looked less than convinced. "Perhaps with any luck at all. Now. If we could just keep him from catastrophe for a whole day . . ."

Cassidy patted her arm and smiled. "But then we wouldn't know what to do with ourselves. He keeps us alert, doesn't he?"

The head cook huffed. "But what I wouldn't give for just one *dull* day around here."

A hush fell over the kitchen and Cassidy turned around.

"I'm sorry, Chef Johnson, but that won't be happening today."
The hotel manager's eyes glowed with mirth. And since he rarely
visited the kitchen—normally just sent a messenger—his presence meant big news.

Mrs. Johnson sauntered forward with her hands clasped in
front. "Well, you could have at least let me dream it for a moment, Mr. Bradley."

He raised an eyebrow and kept smiling at their head cook.
Not many people could get away with teasing the woman. "I
shall remember that for future notice." He cleared his throat.
"We have a fancy group with the *Brooklyn Daily Eagle* coming
up for a formal dedication of the Mount McKinley National
Park. It is a large group of about seventy, and we have been
asked to help host and provide food for the ceremony. A number
of staff will be asked to go along as well to assist and serve."

Mrs. Johnson didn't even flinch at the news. "We are up to
the task, Mr. Bradley. Just let me know when."

He grinned and turned partially back to the stairs. "Just as
I knew you would be. And as to the *when*—it's tomorrow."

# 2

A large cloud of steam escaped from the engine as Allan Brennan boarded the train. Finally. He'd made it to the Alaska Territory.

Claiming a seat by the window, Allan nodded at the conductor.

"Ticket?" the man asked as a dozen or so men poured into the car. Their boisterous voices all but drowned out the older man's voice. He punched the ticket and handed it back to Allan before moving on down the aisle.

With his bag stowed, Allan settled in to enjoy the scenery. The journey by Alaska Steamship from Seattle to Seward had been rough as far as the seas were concerned, but the beauty had been far beyond what he could ever imagine. All the tales his father told him were true.

Alaska truly was God's glorious display. There was nothing he'd ever seen that could compare. The men around him must have been used to the sight as more than one of them pulled their cap down over their eyes and settled in to sleep.

The weariness of travel was upon him, but Allan never could sleep sitting up. Besides, there were too many memories and thoughts of the future barreling through his mind to allow sleep to claim him. No matter how tired his body.

As the train gained speed, the swaying and rocking steadied into a constant rhythm. Leaning his head back, he wished his father could be with him. He'd spent his whole life following Henry Brennan around. Hiking, climbing, fishing, hunting. It didn't matter; if it was outdoors, they'd done it together.

Until it was time for college.

Then his father insisted he get a good education. But Allan wanted nothing more than to work by his father's side in the family company.

*"The time for that will come, son. There will be plenty of work for you to do once you've finished college."*

And with that insistence, Allan headed for the university. No sooner had he finished his schooling than the United States joined the war in Europe. His father and his business partner, Frank, were planning a grand expedition to scale Mount McKinley and Allan had planned to go with them, but the government needed men to fight in Europe and so he went to war instead. If only he could turn back the clock.

The last time he'd seen his father was a farewell at the train depot in Seattle as Allan headed off to become Captain Brennan and serve his country.

"I'm very proud of you, son," his father had said. "You will be in my prayers constantly. Just remember that even in this turn of events, God has a plan. And don't worry about climbing McKinley. The mountain will still be there when the war is over."

But his father wouldn't. Allan learned only a few months later that his father successfully summited Mount McKinley but had not survived the descent. The letter from his mother had found Allan at the front.

In the middle of a horrific battle, he learned he no longer had a father. And the thought threatened to crush him. He'd tried to harden himself to the news as grief clawed its way up his throat and almost overpowered him, but the war raged on around him and reminded him all too often of his loss. The more men he lost on the battlefield, the more he worked to bury his own sorrow. Life would never be the same again.

Returning home to Seattle and his father's company after the war didn't help. Henry Brennan was everywhere—which soothed and hurt all at the same time. Even though Frank Irving was a longtime family friend, he'd changed since Henry's death and angrily placed the blame on their expedition guide.

Allan inherited half of his father's share of the business as the only son, while the rest went to his father's partner. But it didn't change the fact that he had no desire to work in the factory. It was just too much after the loss of his father and the devastating effects of the war. So putting the entire company in Frank's capable hands in the meantime, he left his mother, Seattle, his sisters and their husbands, and headed off to learn more about mountain climbing. The only real connection he felt he had left with his father was Mount McKinley in Alaska.

And now he was on his way. After all these years.

The train slowed.

"Anchorage!" the conductor announced as he passed through the car. "Next stop, Anchorage!"

Some of the men moved toward the exit even while the train was still moving. The sound of metal on metal could be heard as the brakes brought the train to a stop. Allan cast a quick glance out the window. It didn't look like much of a town.

Several men disembarked with large duffel bags, no doubt workers for the railroad. Some of the remaining appeared to be sleeping, while a few at the end of the aisle were engaged in a heated argument. Just when Allan thought things might get out of hand, one of the men burst into laughter and slapped another on the back. The others joined in the merriment and things settled back down.

Two men entered Allan's car. The first was a young lad with nothing but a flour sack stuffed with what must be his belongings. He slipped into a seat beside one of the sleeping passengers. The second, an older gentleman, nodded to the seat across from Allan.

"This seat taken?"

"No. You're welcome to it." Allan offered a smile.

"Name's John." The newcomer removed his black fedora and held out his hand.

He shook it. "Allan. Nice to meet you."

"All aboard," the conductor called from outside the window. He'd no sooner given the call than the train lurched forward and chugged slowly out of the station.

Stowing his hat above him, John ran a hand through his hair. "I love train travel." The man sat and looked out the window. "These puffer-belly steam locomotives sure are amazing, aren't they?"

"Indeed they are." Allan hadn't thought too much on the subject, but agreed anyway. "Do you live in Anchorage?"

"No, no. I was just there on some business for the railroad. How about you?"

"It's my first time in Alaska."

"Oh? Well, let me congratulate you on your choice to visit God's country! I hope you love it. My homeland is a little bit of heaven—even if it is much removed from the rest of the world."

Allan chuckled. "Thank you. It definitely is far removed—I didn't realize *how* far until this journey. I've heard stories all my life, but haven't made it until now." He felt his smile diminish. "The war held me up for a bit and then . . ." This poor stranger didn't deserve his melancholy memories. "It doesn't matter. I'm glad to be here."

"So what brings you up here?"

"A number of things." Allan paused, uncertain how much he wanted to say. "I'd heard so much about it that I wanted to see Alaska for myself. I also took a job. That's why I want to know everything I can." The conversation focused all on him made him uncomfortable. Time to change the subject. "What do you know about Mount McKinley?"

"Oh, more than we have time for on this train ride." John leaned forward, his eagerness apparent. "In fact, up until the age of twelve, I lived just north of the High One—er . . . Mount McKinley. Then when my father died, we moved to Tanana. I've lived there until recently." John smiled. "What would you like to know about the mountain?"

"Is it really as massive and dangerous as the stories I've heard?"

"Yes, indeed. It's over twenty thousand feet and a treacherous beast to climb. The weather is unpredictable, and an earthquake a few years back changed the landscape of the mountain and its glaciers. Oh, but what a view."

Allan leaned forward too. "Does this mean you've climbed it?" A thrill started in his toes and raced up his spine. There were only a handful of men who had climbed the king of the Alaska Range.

"I have." The man's face fell and he looked out the window and leaned back. "But that's a story for another day."

Maybe the man never made it to the summit. Precious few had. "So you must know a lot about the other mountains in the Alaska Range as well?"

He nodded but kept his gaze toward the window. Several moments passed with only the *clackety-clack* of the train to fill the space around them. "They are the most beautiful sight in all the world. Sultana—Denali's . . . McKinley's Wife, stands just to the west and south of him. Beautiful and even more danger-ous, she's incredibly steep—much more so than the High One."

"Why do you call it Denali and the High One?"

John's dark eyes twinkled. "Because that's his name. I'm part native Alaskan—Ahtna-Athabaskan, to be precise. The native peoples of this great land named the mountains centuries ago. Denali means the High One. Sultana—or Mount Foraker, as you may know it—means the Wife."

Allan pulled a notepad and pencil out of his coat pocket. This would be good to take note of. "So who decided to call it McKinley?"

John chuckled. "That's a sore subject up here. It's only been in the last couple decades, and many Alaskans aren't too keen on it. Let's just say a gold prospector did and leave it at that."

The story intrigued him, but he respected the man's reserve. He seemed so knowledgeable and yet something seemed to hold him back. There was so much to learn. Maybe the gentleman thought it best to not overwhelm him. But Allan pushed on with his questions. He simply couldn't resist. "What about bear and moose? I've heard they're abundant and that gold prospectors had a lot of trouble with them."

John looked at him with his smile back in place. "There's a lot of them, yes—also caribou, dall sheep, and wolves—but some of the prospectors' stories are a bit exaggerated. Besides, those prospectors invaded the natural habitat of the creatures, wouldn't you say?"

Allan thought about that for a moment and nodded. "You're right. In fact, isn't that why the President made it a national park to begin with—to protect the wild game?"

"Yes, he did. But they didn't have a superintendent to man-age it until two years ago."

"How do you protect a national park with no one up here?"

"Exactly. There was a lot of poaching going on. But thankfully, they brought on Harry Karstens as superintendent. It's a huge job, but he's up for the challenge."

Allan leaned forward again. He knew that name. "Wait. The same Harry Karstens that was part of the first complete ascent of Mount McKinley? I read the book put out by his partner, Hudson Stuck."

"One and the same."

Guess there couldn't be a better choice than a man who knew and understood the mountain so well. "Does he have any help in his role as superintendent?"

"Not really. At least from what I hear, he's the only one paid for the job. And it's a big one."

"I can only imagine. There're still no roads in or out?"

"No. But the railroad does provide the access that will be needed for roads to be built farther into the park."

Writing down the facts he wanted to remember, Allan let the conversation die down. To think he was so close to where his father had last walked. Maybe there was some other explanation for what happened to Dad. He could only hope. His father's body had never been recovered, so maybe there was a clue on the mountain somewhere. But what chance did he have at climbing it? He'd been hired to do a job. He'd best focus on that first. One day, he would make it up the mountain. One day.

His mind filled with questions and he realized he had the perfect opportunity in front of him. "John, do you mind if I ask you more questions? If I'm going to be working up here, I'd like to learn everything I possibly can."

"I'm happy to help. It's always nice to pass the time with good conversation."

"I've read incredible stories about the gold rush up here. Is there really gold for everyone?"

John chuckled. "If only that were true. Well, I take that back. I would venture to say there's enough gold for the world up here, but it sure would take a lot of men, a lot of work, and hundreds of years to bring it out."

As the train passed through thick trees and brush, Allan realized how true that statement had been. There wasn't much "civilization" in Alaska yet and from what he could tell, there wouldn't be for quite a while. "So what about the stories that talk of huge berries, and salmon that can be pulled out of the streams with your bare hands?"

"Those are true. You just have to know where to find them." John crossed his legs and rested his hand on one knee. "My favorite are the salmonberries."

For some reason that didn't sound appetizing. "There's a berry that tastes like fish?"

"Heavens, no!" John's laughter filled the car, causing several of the men to momentarily glance their way. "They're just *called* salmonberries. Look like giant raspberries and can be orange, white, or pink."

The rest of the afternoon passed in good conversation and Allan filling his notepad with scribbled notes. It was easy to forget his exhaustion while conversing with John. The man was a consummate storyteller and walking encyclopaedia.

Eventually, the train began a steady deceleration.

John stretched. "Well, we should be getting close to Curry. That's our stop. If you're continuing on, you'll spend the night there."

"Curry is my final stop as well." Allan reached a hand forward. "It was a pleasure, John. Thank you for your abundant insight. I'm sure my new boss will appreciate the crash course you gave me."

"It was *my* pleasure. You are most welcome. I hope we will

see much more of one another." John clasped Allan's hand and shook it.

The train puffed and squealed as it pulled into Curry. Chaos ensued as soon as the train came to a stop. Allan grabbed his belongings and his hat and followed John out of the car.

They stepped onto the platform, and in the crowd a young lady with dark hair smiled and waved. Her eyes seemed to twinkle. "Dad!"

A massive two-story structure dominated his view. A couple of bay windows framed the lower level on either side of the canopy denoting the Curry Hotel Depot. The broad wooden platform stretched from one end of the hotel to the other and beyond. And all this. In the middle of nowhere.

"Dad!" The waving young beauty drew closer.

John chuckled and turned to him. "That's my daughter. It's nice to have a welcoming party, isn't it? Let me know if you need anything. Just ask anyone at the hotel for John Ivanoff and they'll find me." He walked away and toward his daughter.

Everything seemed to stop. Allan felt his pulse pounding in his ears. Ivanoff? John Ivanoff?

The noise of the platform died away.

Looking from side to side, Allan tried to shake the feeling. But the world blurred around him instead. Several moments passed before he could see straight. Then his hearing returned. The engine behind him gave a huge huff. People were talking. Laughing. Milling about.

Off in the distance, the dark-haired lady held on to John's elbow as they walked into the hotel.

But how could this be?

Had he really just spent the day with the man responsible for his father's death?

3

Mr. Bradley claimed Cassidy's father as soon as they walked in the door.

"John, good to see you!" The men shook hands. "Your new trainee should have been on that train as well. Did you meet him?" Mr. Bradley rarely took time to wait for a response, much less breathe. Always too much to do. Too much to say. "The summer schedule is getting overly full, so you'll need to get him in shape as quick as possible." He turned to walk away. "Go find him. His name's Brennan. Allan Brennan." And with that, he headed for the main desk in the lobby, talking all the way. "Mrs. McGovern, I am in need of the books for today."

"He always needs something." Mrs. McGovern elbowed Cassidy.

Cassidy laughed. "He never stops, does he? Sometimes I don't even hear the words—they just seem to all meld together. Isn't that right, Dad?" Turning toward her father, she gasped. "Dad! You're pale as a sheet." Grabbing his arms, she steered him toward a leather chair by the fireplace. "What is it? Are you sick?"

He shook his head and sat. "Brennan. I had no idea." The words whispered on an exhale.

"What? That his last name was Brennan? I'm so confused."

She lowered herself to look into his eyes. "Please tell me what's wrong."

"I'm fine."

"You don't seem fine."

Her father shook his head again and looked at her with a stiff smile. The light in his eyes when he greeted her off the train was gone. "Nothing to worry about." He stood up. "But I do need a favor. Would you mind finding the young man I was with on the train? You probably noticed us shaking hands when you were waving to me. He'll need to get settled and then I'll meet with him in an hour in the baggage room." His face was stern. "Can you do that?"

"Of course. I'm afraid I wasn't listening to Mr. Bradley's announcement all that close. What is the man's name?"

"Brennan," he whispered. "Allan Brennan."

Something wasn't right. Her dad had looked forward to the hiring of an assistant for weeks, so his sudden turn couldn't be in regard to that. And no matter what he said, she *was* worried. Something bothered him.

"Did you eat today?" She knew her father was given to over-looking that simple need when he was pressed with work.

Again he shook his head, but this time his voice was less strained. "I forgot."

Relief washed over her. "Well, you need to go to the kitchen right now and have Mrs. Johnson give you something to eat. Tell her you've had a spell."

Patting her hand, he nodded. "I'll take care of it in a few minutes."

Watching her father walk to the railroad agent's office, Cassidy puzzled over it.

He turned and looked at her. "Hurry! I'm fine and I promise I'll get something to eat."

Stuffing her hands into the pockets of her apron, she went in search of Mr. Allan Brennan.

Outside on the platform, it wasn't hard to find him. He stood in the same place. Case beside him, hat in his hands. What was that all about?

Cassidy walked the last few steps to him and cleared her throat. His blond hair picked up the sunlight. "Mr. Brennan, I presume?" As he looked up at her, she couldn't help but notice the pain etched across his face and in his green eyes. Pain and something else. Was it anger? Surely not. No doubt it was just the confusion of his new setting.

She reached out to him. "Are you all right?" Goodness, first Dad and now his new assistant.

Her touch appeared to break through his state. "I apologize." He straightened his shoulders and looked directly into her eyes. "Yes, I'm Allan Brennan. But how did you know my name?"

Cassidy laughed. "Mr. Bradley—the hotel manager—just told me." She stuck out her hand in greeting. "You'll find up here in Curry that we all know everyone pretty quickly. I'm Cassidy Ivanoff. You'll be working with my father."

He took her hand and shook it. But the longer he shook it, the firmer his grip became. "So your father is John Ivanoff?"

"Yes."

"He'll be training me?"

"Yes."

"And you're his daughter?" He stopped shaking her hand but continued to hold it.

"Yes, we've established that." She smiled and looked down at their hands. "Would you mind if I have my hand back?" Even though he acted a bit odd, Cassidy felt sympathy for him. She'd never get over the pain she'd seen in his eyes.

He released her hand. "Pardon me, Miss Ivanoff. I believe all the travel has gotten to me. I'm not at all myself." His tone took on a more formal sound.

"All's forgiven. Exhaustion and busyness take their toll on all of us. Even my father forgot to eat today. Why don't you get your things? I'm to help get you settled. You have a meeting with my father in . . ." She glanced down at the watch attached to her apron. "Fifty minutes in the baggage room."

He picked up his large case. "This is all I have. Lead the way."

As they entered the lobby, Cassidy pointed to the left. "The dining room and main-level kitchen are over there. And to the right are the agent's office, the baggage room, and several other rooms. Up the stairs are guest rooms, as well as straight ahead beyond the stairs. Downstairs is the section gang bunkroom, provisions rooms, downstairs kitchen, storage, and the laundry facilities." She walked to the main desk in the lobby to the left of the grand staircase. "The manager's office is behind here, and Mrs. McGovern is the head housekeeper. We'll check in with her about your accommodations."

Cassidy stepped back as the housekeeper gave swift instructions to Allan. While she waited, she studied him, wondering where he was from, why he was in Curry, and what troubled him so much.

"Cassidy." Mrs. McGovern's voice always sounded pinched when she was in a hurry. "Your father said you would show Mr. Brennan around."

Cassidy nodded. "Yes, ma'am. I have a few minutes, but then I'll need to get back to the kitchen." Turning to Allan, she smiled. "Follow me, please. If you haven't noticed, we're quite efficient around here. The Curry Hotel is a busy place."

Allan followed her out the front door and to the north of the hotel. "I can see that." His tone was rather gruff.

Cassidy couldn't help but feel she'd done something to annoy the man. They walked in silence for a few seconds.

"I met your father on the train. He seems very knowledgeable."

Forgetting Allan's mood, Cassidy couldn't help laughing. If only this man really knew. Her father had more knowledge in his pinky finger than most men could hope for in a lifetime. "He is at that. He knows every plant, tree, shrub, hill, mountain, and beast in the interior of Alaska. If you want to know anything about hiking, climbing, or even what plants *not* to eat—he's the expert."

"Is he a tough man to work for?"

"Heavens, no." Cassidy stepped around a hole. "He's a wonderful man. Kind and patient. But I will say that he'll expect absolute perfection because Alaska demands it. This part of the world is most unforgiving."

They reached the staff housing and Cassidy checked her watch again. "Gracious. I must be going. We have a delegation coming through tomorrow to dedicate the national park. Don't forget about your meeting with my father. He's a stickler for being on time."

Removing his hat again, Allan half smiled. The anger seemed to leave his voice. "Thank you. I'll make sure I'm there." He extended his hand.

Cassidy placed her hand in his, fully expecting to end their tour on a shake. Instead, Allan held her hand again and gazed into her eyes. His eyebrows furrowed. For a moment, the intensity unnerved her. Pulling her hand away, a little flutter started in her stomach. "I must be . . . I have to go." She hated the way she stumbled over her words, but kept moving. No need to further her embarrassment. She honestly didn't know what had gotten into her.

The man was handsome, but so were many of the fellas who

came through Curry. It certainly didn't give her a reason to swoon as soon as he smiled. Foolishness. That's what it was. Besides, she just met the man. Granted, he looked pretty depressed when she first saw him, and the smile did amazing things to his strong face. . . .

Gracious, she wasn't a ridiculous female. She refused to be like the other girls. Always trying to shorten their hems, wear more makeup, and try cigarettes. No. Not her. Cassidy Faith Ivanoff vowed to never try to impress a man.

If God had someone for her, He'd have to bring him all the way to Curry and love her exactly the way she was.

So what if God had brought Allan Brennan here to Curry? That didn't mean that He brought him here for *her*. She'd never be the *bee's knees* all dolled up in *glad rags* to go out on the town like all the young kitchen maids. It wasn't like any of them even had a town to "go out" on. There wasn't anything in Curry or even Talkeetna for that matter. But oh, to be young. They looked at the future with such bright and starry eyes.

Which made her feel ancient at only twenty-three. No. She didn't feel ancient. Well, maybe a little. But it wasn't like she didn't love her life. She loved the hotel. Loved her job. Loved to cook. Loved to meet all the people who came through their neck of the woods.

But for the first time, maybe she *did* want someone other than her father to love *her*.

•••••

Allan sat waiting for John Ivanoff to appear, wondering the entire time how he should handle the situation. He had enjoyed speaking to the man on the train, but then he hadn't known who John was. Hard to imagine that he could act as though nothing had changed between them when everything had.

"Glad to see you're punctual, Mr. Brennan, but I could have surmised as much after meeting you on the train." John gave a half smile and motioned to the man behind him. "This is Mr. Bradley, the manager of this wonderful establishment, and our boss."

"Pleased to finally meet you, sir." Allan shook hands with the manager, then turned back to John. "Your daughter told me that punctuality was important to you—it's always been important to me as well." Allan thought the man looked weary—almost like he had the weight of the world on his shoulders. Perhaps something had happened, some bad bit of news had come his way. Was that why Mr. Bradley was here?

"You won't be heading out on any guided tours tomorrow." The manager crossed the small room and looked out the window. "We have people coming to officially dedicate the park. We'll have to take supplies to the park entrance—it's just a short distance by train from here. A party of sorts has been planned with a barbecue. Your job is to be the muscle for the event, and to assist Mr. Karstens in every way possible."

John nodded.

"Yes, sir." Allan wrestled with his feelings. He could see John was upset about something, but Allan wanted answers.

Mr. Bradley left the room and closed the door.

Silence stretched as John shuffled some papers on the desk.

Allan had come all this way from Seattle to learn the truth about what happened on that fateful day back in 1917. Still, he wasn't cruel. He didn't want to make things worse for John. The man might never give him the answers if Allan offended him first thing. He might even get himself fired, and then he'd never know. But why didn't John bring it up? Maybe he didn't recognize Allan's last name. Had John forgotten his father—Henry Brennan—so quickly?

John took a seat behind the small desk. "Then there's going to be the event on the fifteenth of July with President Harding. That group will be coming in on the fourteenth, and I'm still uncertain as to whether there will be time for anything more than the actual event. We will need to be prepared for almost anything."

Allan nodded. "I understand." But he didn't.

"I know from our conversation on the train that you have a keen mind and a desire to learn. I also know from the information you supplied Mr. Bradley before he decided to hire you that you already know a great deal about vegetation and wildlife. That's definitely to your benefit."

"I've spent much of my life outdoors and have made it my habit to learn." Why wouldn't John acknowledge the obvious conversation that needed to be addressed? Was Mr. Bradley coming back?

"Well, while it will be to your benefit, Alaska is unlike any place else you've probably been. The isolation alone makes it almost impossible to easily recover from mistakes."

Like the mistake that cost Allan's father his life? It was all Allan could do to keep from voicing the question aloud. Now just didn't seem the right time to get into the matter. Especially if their boss was set to return.

John didn't appear to notice his discomfort, however, and continued talking. "The isolation is one strike against you. The unpredictability of the elements is strike two. I've lived here all my life. I've learned from the best and most knowledgeable about the weather signs and such, but the truth is everything can change up in the twinkling of an eye. Whether it's the weather or a grizzly bear charging you from out of nowhere—you can't let your guard down for even a moment. Do you understand?"

Allan nodded, his mind racing with accusations. But somebody let their guard down and his father died.

"A man can seem to have touched all the bases and still fail." Was this his way of apologizing for what happened? Did John even remember his father and what happened six years ago?

"So does this proverbial baseball game have a strike three?" Allan fought to keep his voice steady.

John looked at him strangely for a moment, then nodded. "Strike three is around every bush—every tree—every river. A man's own arrogant self-assurance is the worst enemy of all. I've seen men come here so certain they knew what they were getting themselves into—so boastful and full of themselves. They were unwilling to listen to instruction or to receive correction. They thought they knew it all."

Allan stiffened. He couldn't help but wonder if John was implying this was the case with his father and Frank. He gripped the arms of the chair. "And what happened?"

John looked up. "Strike three. They were out. The game was over."

•••••

Thomas Smith hauled the last bit of scraps out to the animal feed shack. Mrs. Johnson had been barking ongoing commands since Mr. Bradley told her about the fancy people coming through tomorrow. Thomas felt like he couldn't keep up. But he had to keep trying.

If he could just hang on to this job long enough and prove to Mr. Bradley that he was a hard worker, maybe he could be trained for another position. Maybe one day, he could make something out of himself working for the Curry Hotel.

Most seventeen-year-old orphans never had a chance like this. So he'd best not mess it up. Taking a deep breath, he emptied the huge tub of its scraps and went to the pump to clean it out. Cook would never allow him to bring it back dirty. And he wanted her to be happy with him. His future depended on it.

Granted, he didn't have a lot of book learning. But he could read and write and do simple arithmetic. The missionaries at the orphanage had seen to that. Maybe he could learn more if he needed to. He'd always been told that God would give him knowledge if he asked. Thomas wondered if God would give him better balance and less clumsiness if he asked.

"If You could"—he glanced heavenward—"I'd appreciate it."

A rudimentary education in the Christian faith along with his book learning were things he was thankful for. The missionaries felt it was their duty to save the souls of the native children at the orphanage, and although Thomas was white, he was often told that without accepting Jesus as Savior, his soul would be doomed. It sounded like a terrible thing to be doomed, so Thomas had quickly agreed to repent from his sins—although he wasn't exactly sure at the time what those sins were, since he was just a very little boy. But over the years, he'd repented to God every time he missed the mark. He'd learned that much. And he knew that Jesus was his only hope.

That became all too clear when the missionaries kicked him out, along with several other boys, when they'd reached their teen years. Overcrowding at the orphanage made it necessary, even though they provided free labor to the missionaries. Still, the missionaries had taught him to pray and believe in God, and sometimes that was all that got Thomas through the day. He didn't have earthly parents who loved him, but he knew there was a heavenly Father who did.

Now if he could just keep from dropping or spilling anything tonight, he could breathe a sigh of relief.

As he walked back to the hotel, Thomas thought of Cassidy's help earlier. She was so nice to him. Even when he messed up. And there was something about her eyes. They were always . . . shining. Like she was—what was the word Mrs. Johnson used?—*delighted* about something.

He could imagine making it through each day if he could just hear her laugh or see her smile.

The bustle of the kitchen greeted him as he walked back in and put the tub under the worktable where it was supposed to go. Making sure it was stable and the handles were straight, he took a moment to catch his breath. As he looked up, he spotted Cassidy coming up the stairs with a large tray.

"Lily, we need to make sure the hollandaise is done in precise timing, so please have the egg yolks and butter ready for me in five minutes." Even when giving an order as the cook's assistant, her voice singsonged through the air.

The kitchen maid nodded—"Yes, Miss Ivanoff"—and scurried off.

Thomas took that opportunity to move forward. "Let me take that tray for you, Miss Ivanoff."

"Why, thank you, Thomas!" She relinquished her hold on it and pushed her hair back into place. "It was getting quite heavy."

"Where do you need it?"

"Over there at my workstation by the stove. That hollandaise won't make itself." The most glorious smile lit her face as she beamed directly at him.

It took the words right from his mouth. All he could do was nod.

"Thomas!" Mrs. Johnson's voice made him jump. "I need you to refill the flour bins and fetch some more cream from the creamery."

"Yes, ma'am." With a look back at Cassidy, Thomas was sad

to see she was already back to work. But what he wouldn't give to see her smile again.

He raced to the creamery and hefted one of the huge crocks. Even if he was clumsy, at least he was strong. The younger kitchen boys couldn't lift these.

In record time, he made it back to the kitchen and earned an eyebrow lift and nod from Mrs. Johnson, which was no small feat. Feeling sure of himself, he grabbed the two large flour bins and ran down the stairs to the provisions rooms. He filled both to the brim and headed back to the stairs, taking them two at a time.

When he reached the main kitchen, Mrs. Johnson had a hint of a smile on her face. "Good job, Thomas, right when I needed—"

Before he realized what was happening, he tripped over his own foot. Determined not to drop anything, he held fast to the metal bins.

But the flour had other ideas. The fine white powder flew up as he tumbled down.

Landing with a thud and *poof* of white dust, Thomas found himself on his back holding two metal bins with a shower of white descending over the whole kitchen.

# 4

John walked toward the manager's office, hoping for a few minutes with Mr. Bradley. It had been a long day and tomorrow would be even longer. Seeing young Brennan had turned his world upside down. For years, he'd been able to push aside the horrible loss of Henry Brennan, but the appearance of Allan brought it all front and center.

Their meeting had taken a great strain on John. It was apparent the young man was agitated—even angry. And who could blame him? No doubt there were unanswered questions, and the only man he'd had to talk to was Frank Irving—a man John knew to be nothing but trouble. John thought to put the matter out there for discussion, but Allan didn't seem willing. At least not yet. Sooner or later, they'd *have* to discuss it. As to how he would deal with it . . . John didn't have a clue. Maybe Bradley could give him some guidance. This situation affected him as well, since they were both employees, and John had never lied to the man.

Voices echoed out of the office. Apparently his planned conversation wouldn't be happening right now.

"The hollandaise was completely ruined, the meringue inedible, and the fried fish had to be refried to get the raw flour off. Our poor dinner patrons had to wait an extra three minutes for the next course! Three minutes, Mr. Bradley. As you know, that is completely unacceptable."

John entered the office and saw their manager appearing grim. Mrs. Johnson stood on the other side of the room with her hands on her hips, Cassidy to her right with her hands folded in front, and Thomas to the right of her, his head down. "Mr. Bradley, I'm just asking for a reprieve. I'm no longer vexed about the flour incident—although it will probably take days to clean that dust out of everything—but with the city paper people coming through, I need perfection to—"

Thomas sniffed but kept his head bowed.

The head cook lowered her arms to her side and sighed. "I just could use a few days without a mishap. The kitchen is no place for trial and error, so either he goes or I do."

Bradley looked over at Cassidy. "Miss Ivanoff, are you able to provide the help our chef needs in the absence of Thomas?"

Cassidy nodded at the manager. "While I can't fill Thomas's shoes or lift the heavy items he hauls for us each day, I am willing to help in any way I can." She cleared her throat. "But Thomas *is* very valuable to us, sir, and is a good worker."

The gangly orphan boy lifted his head a little at that.

"Thomas . . ." Mr. Bradley came around his desk. "I know—we all know—that you are working very hard here for us. But I also understand that Mrs. Johnson has a valid plea. It's not completely fair to burden the assistant cook with extra work either."

The young man nodded.

"Your timing couldn't be more inconvenient, Chef Johnson, but—"

John moved forward. "I'm sorry to intrude, Mr. Bradley, but perhaps I could be of assistance."

Bradley extended an arm to him. "Certainly, John. What ideas do you have?"

"Well, I'm not quite sure I understand all that has happened"—he'd definitely have to ask Cassidy about the flour incident later—"but I do know that Mr. Brennan just arrived, and while he will no doubt be a big help the next couple days with the dedication of the park, we could also use extra hands on our trip. There's quite a lot of equipment to be hauled and set up. Perhaps young Thomas could assist *me* for a few days?"

Relief washed over the young man's face. He closed his eyes, as if waiting for the judge to rule.

Mr. Bradley nodded. "Mm-hmm. I like the idea." He walked back around his desk. "Yes. I think that will be a good solution." He looked up at his head cook. "Is that satisfactory, Chef Johnson?"

Mrs. Johnson gave a curt nod. "Yes, Mr. Bradley. Thank you."

The boss looked at Cassidy again. John watched several expressions go across her face as the manager spoke to her. "Do you have anything else to say, Miss Ivanoff?"

"Only that"—she turned and smiled at the woman beside her—"I believe Mrs. Johnson and I agree in saying that Thomas hasn't done anything on purpose to upset the kitchen; neither has he done anything with malicious intent. He's just had a few . . . accidents. But we appreciate his work."

Always the peacemaker and looking out for those less fortunate. His Cassidy. She had a heart of gold.

Mrs. Johnson stiffened. "I don't need anyone to speak on my behalf. Thomas is loved by all the staff, but a kitchen isn't run on sentiment. I need proficiency and order."

"But you will allow him to come back to work for you?" Mr. Bradley asked with a raised brow.

The older lady harrumphed. "I'm not unreasonable. After a few days, yes, I'm sure we will all be right as rain."

"Good, then, it's settled. Don't let me keep you from your

duties in the kitchen." Mr. Bradley sat in his chair. "I'd like a few moments to speak with Thomas and Mr. Ivanoff."

John caught Cassidy's eye and winked at his daughter before she followed Mrs. Johnson out. That girl had her hands full with the harsh woman, but if anyone could handle Mrs. Johnson, it was Cassidy.

Mr. Bradley waved John closer. "John, thank you for stepping in." He got up and walked over to Thomas. "I'm sure Thomas will work hard for you the next few days. He's a good listener. Just make sure he keeps his feet under him at all times." The boss patted the young man's shoulder and walked out to the front desk.

Long arms and legs didn't hide the hunch in the boy's shoulders. What had he gotten himself into? First, he'd have to keep Thomas busy, but he'd also have to keep him out of trouble as well. And if he'd learned anything from his daughter's stories, it was that his work had been cut out for him. "It's all right, son. I won't bite."

"Yes, sir." He toed the floor with his boot.

"You do know that I'm Cassidy's father, right?"

The boy looked up. Just as tall as John himself, the boy—no, the young man—finally looked him straight in the eye. "No, sir. I didn't."

"Well, she's told me a lot about you. And it's all good."

"Thank you, sir. Miss Ivanoff has been very good to me since Mr. Bradley hired me on."

"Glad to hear it." He gripped the young man's shoulder. "Now, why don't we discuss how you can help me tomorrow?"

"Yes, sir." The boy relaxed.

"The original plan was for this large delegation to go to the entrance of the park via the railroad and then travel twelve miles on horseback to the Savage River camp for the ceremony. But we heard last night by telegram that because of a late-arriving train, they will not be able to travel that far. They've changed their plans, and Superintendent Karstens is working frantically to move all the equipment back from the Savage River. Now the event will take place at the park entrance right off the railroad. That's why they've asked for our assistance. We're not only taking up food and additional items that are needed, but we'll be helping to set up the chairs, tables, and anything else. Do you understand?"

"Yes, sir."

John walked over to the window and peered to the north. "This will be a huge boon to the national park, this territory, and the railroad, Thomas. Did you know that last year only thirty-four people visited the national park? The year before that, it was only seven." He turned and pulled out his pocket watch. "And now we will have the largest group ever to come through to dedicate the park, followed by the President to complete the railroad. These are exciting times."

"Yes, sir. I'm ready to help, sir."

John stuck his right hand into his vest pocket. "That's good to hear. But let's go over a few things, all right?"

Thomas nodded.

"First, don't hesitate to ask me questions if you don't understand what I've instructed you to do. Second, Mr. Brennan will also be in charge of you, so listen to him well." John watched for wariness in the boy. "Third, let's slow everything down. Take a bit more time to do things. The terrain will be much rougher, and you'll need to take your steps carefully. Work hard, and together with prayer, we will get through this."

"Yes, sir." There was a light in the young man's eyes that hadn't been there before. He stood a little taller and straightened his shoulders. "I'm a man of prayer too."

John smiled. "I'm glad to hear it, Thomas."

"I'm not real good at praying with a lot of fancy words, but I pray a lot."

"Fancy words aren't necessary. If they were, God wouldn't listen to most of us."

Thomas seemed to consider this a moment. "When would you like me to report to you in the morning?"

"Let's get started at five."

"Yes, sir." Thomas smiled. "I'll do my very best, sir."

"I'm sure you will."

He turned and headed toward the door but tripped and dropped his hat. As he went to pick it up, he fell on his face. After a brief moan, the boy stood again and found his voice. "I'm sorry, sir. It won't happen again, sir." Redness crept up his neck and face.

"It's quite all right, Thomas. Like I said, just take your time." He had to work to keep from chuckling out loud. No wonder poor Mrs. Johnson was beside herself with exasperation. "Say, you know what I used to tell my daughter when she was constantly tripping over her own feet?"

"Yes, sir, I know." The young man gave a lopsided grin. "I guess the floor just needed a hug."

•••••

As the train pulled into the McKinley National Park station early the next morning, Allan was surprised at how little had been built here. Wasn't this the glorious and grand entrance to the national park he'd longed to see for six years?

But instead, he was greeted by a few small shacks, and what appeared to be some hastily erected tents. The park headquarters was no more than a shanty, and the only structure of any size was a log roadhouse. Curry had been tiny compared to the great cities of the United States, but the Curry Hotel hadn't been lacking in anything. Even in the middle of nowhere. But here? It seemed a bit of a letdown to Allan's high hopes. He wondered if his father had felt much the same when he came through. None of these buildings were even here at that time. Neither was the railroad.

The group from the *Brooklyn Daily Eagle* might be a tad disappointed. But Allan kept his thoughts to himself. They couldn't even see the mountain from here—why didn't they have the ceremony at another location? There had been some spectacular views from the train. But maybe that's why originally they were going to the Savage River to have the ceremony. He looked back to the west. He knew off in the distance stood a most magnificent sight—Mount McKinley. And he was missing it.

John carried several large baskets, followed by Thomas, who hauled chairs.

Thomas gave him a wide grin. "Did you see McKinley? Isn't it huge?" He didn't stop to get Allan's answer.

And Allan could only nod. The mountain was incredible. The massiveness of it—its sheer presence was intimidating. He'd climbed mountains in the States and yet nothing could even compare.

"I need you to help Thomas get these chairs assembled," John said as he passed Allan with another load. "The mountain isn't going anywhere. You'll get to see it again."

The words hit Allan hard. His father had said the same thing. In fact, it was one of the last things he'd said to Allan.

John continued. "The delegation should be here by eleven, and I don't need to remind you that we need to make a good impression."

Allan could only nod. He hadn't expected this to be so hard.

Why hadn't he just gotten everything off his chest yesterday when he'd had the chance? Now he'd had too much time to mull it over, and all that had accomplished was to make him angry. He needed this job. But would he be able to keep it after he confronted John?

Through the hours of the morning they worked, and the heat became more intense.

Watches were checked as anticipation grew. The group had been known to dedicate several national parks in the great nation of the United States, so to have them come to Alaska was indeed an honor.

Out of the corner of his eye, Allan saw Cassidy Ivanoff speaking with Mr. Karstens and her father. It appeared the two men had great respect for each other, but why wouldn't they? They were two of the few men to ever successfully climb to the summit of the mountain for which this great park had been named.

A slight breeze kicked up a whirl of dirt and Cassidy reached up to secure her hat, her dark hair coiled in a knot at the base of it. While he'd only known her a day, something tugged at Allan when he looked at her. But he couldn't put a name to it. The Ivanoffs were a fascination and fear for him all rolled into one. Perhaps he only felt that tug because she was the daughter of the man who'd left his father to die on Denali. Allan felt bile rise in his throat and forced it back down. If he didn't confront John soon, he'd explode.

*"John Ivanoff should be jailed for murder. The man left your father to die on that mountain. He didn't even care enough to search for him."* Frank's words haunted him.

What if Frank's story was true and John was completely responsible for his father's death? What if it *wasn't* true? Over the years, Frank's story had changed and he'd gotten more livid to the point of refusing to speak of it. And if the storm that hit them was as bad as he implied, how did he even know what happened? Could his father have still been alive when the others left him?

That thought was even more horrifying. Containing his emotions became the hardest battle of all. Allan felt like he was in a fog, not able to discern reality from nightmare.

The only bright spot in this horrid dream was Cassidy. Her sunny, positive disposition had a brilliant effect on everyone around her. Even though he didn't want it to. Could she really be the daughter of a murderer?

Allan shook his head. John didn't actually murder his father. But from what he understood, the man did leave his father to die on that mountain. And what role did Frank truly play in all this? As soon as the thoughts entered his mind, his gaze was pulled back to the Alaska Range and beyond that, its tallest peak. Would he ever know the truth?

"Allan!" John waved. "Come join us, I want you to meet the Seventymile Kid before the delegates detrain."

He had little choice but to put his thoughts aside and do what John bid. Approaching the trio, Allan admitted a sense of awe in meeting Harry Karstens. The man was a legend. He'd participated in the Yukon gold rush, making big money carrying supplies up the ice staircase carved out for those going north to seek their fortunes. He'd earned the nickname "Seventymile Kid" after spending time on the Seventymile River searching for gold. But more impressive, Karstens had been part of the very first successful ascent of McKinley.

"It's an honor to meet you." Allan extended his hand.

John interjected. "I apologize. If you'll excuse us, Cassidy and I have something to attend to."

"Of course, we can talk later." Karstens tipped his hat. "Cassidy, it's always a pleasure."

Once they were gone, the clean-shaven Karstens grasped Allan's hand in a firm grip. "I'm more than pleased to meet you. I knew your father. Good man."

The comment took Allan by surprise. "You did?"

"Indeed. Met him on more than one occasion, in fact. First ran into him at the store in Seattle. Then we met in Anchorage a couple times. We shared a lot of common interests." Karstens' expression sobered. "I was very sorry to hear about his death."

Allan swallowed hard. "Father loved it here. We wanted to one day make the climb together—after I returned from the war."

"It's a grueling climb and definitely not for the faint of heart, but you would have enjoyed it together. Your father loved a challenge." Karstens shook his head. "When our team made that first ascent, we had more than our share of trouble."

"I'd love to hear about it sometime. Frank never told me any details of the actual climb, and while I did read about your expedition with Hudson Stuck, I'd love to hear about it from you."

"I'd forgotten about Frank." A frown etched the man's face. "I can't say I had the same experience with him that I did with your father." He cleared his throat. "So . . . John tells me you're up here to assist him. It'll test your mettle to be sure, but if you stick it out, I think you'll never want to leave."

"I'm already quite besotted, sir." Allan looked in the direction of the great mountain. "In fact, I hope to follow in my father's footsteps and climb Denali one day. So I'll need all the advice and stories you have time to share."

Karstens slapped him on the back and his mood seemed to lighten. "I'll do what I can. You don't smoke a pipe, do you?" His eyes twinkled.

The question took Allan by surprise. He cocked his head slightly. "A pipe?"

The park superintendent chuckled. "My carelessness with

a pipe started a fire that destroyed a good portion of our supplies. Burned our baking powder and sugar, and let me tell you what—when you're up there at fifteen thousand feet, it's not like you can just go buy some more."

The train let out a whistle as it approached, stealing everyone's focus.

"Well, it looks like the important folks are here." He gave Allan another pat on the back. "We'll talk some more later."

As the train puffed its way up the line to the station, everyone gathered at the platform to greet their prestigious guests. Allan tried to put aside Karstens' comment about Frank, but it was hard. What had he meant in saying that he didn't have the same experience with Frank that he'd had with Allan's father? Karstens wasn't keen on the man—that much was clear.

The delegates began to emerge and the real work began. Greetings went round and round as the people stretched their legs, commented on the beauty of the mountains, and spoke of the events of the day.

After refreshments were served by Cassidy and her staff, a rotund gentleman worked to hush the crowd. "Thank you, yes, thank you, ladies and gentlemen." He held up his hands until all was quiet. "I'd like to introduce our speaker for the dedication of the park today, Mr. William Hester, Jr.—the son of our esteemed president of the *Eagle*."

The applause was exuberant as Mr. Hester took the primitive stage. His words were eloquent, and Allan found himself greatly moved that this group of people would care so much to come all this way. He hoped they could look beyond the rustic conditions to the beauty around them. He watched the people listen and offer polite encouragement.

One particular reporter with a camera seemed focused on Cassidy. She appeared completely unaware of the man taking pictures; instead her attention was focused on Mr. Hester. As Allan studied her, he understood why the photo fellow was so enraptured. Cassidy had such stunning features. Dark hair and dark eyes, the lines of her face were elegant . . . noble even. His shock upon first arrival had obviously rendered his senses useless.

All too soon, applause brought his attention back, and Allan realized he'd missed the entire speech as Mr. Hester cleared his voice and spoke louder. "I'd like to conclude by stating that on this date, the ninth of July, in the year of our Lord, 1923, I declare that Mount McKinley National Park be formally dedicated to its rightful owners, the people of the United States."

Everyone stood and offered hearty applause.

Mr. Karstens, attired in his superintendent's uniform, addressed the crowd next. "Thank you all for coming. We'd now like to invite you to a mountain sheep barbecue to conclude our ceremony today."

Allan applauded with the rest of the group and then felt a tug on his elbow. Turning, he realized it was John. "I'm sorry, sir. I didn't realize you needed me."

"Nothing to apologize about. I just wanted to let you know that after the meal, the delegation will be boarding the train and heading to Fairbanks. After we help Karstens and the rest of the staff to disassemble the tents, he's allowing us to use a few horses and head into the park for a bit. This time of year, it will be light on into the night. It would be good for you and Thomas to see all of this for future reference."

"Yes, sir."

John walked toward the press delegates and then shook hands with many of them. Allan watched with mixed emotions. The man before him seemed nothing like the man Frank had described to him all these years.

His thoughts warred with each other. Last night, Allan hadn't gotten a lick of sleep because of it. Morning came all too early, but he put a façade in place, determined to do his best for the day. But behind it, a seething anger wanted to build over the death of his father. And yet John wasn't a man Allan wanted to hate. Quite the contrary.

Frank had declared John to be inept and callous. But nothing could be further from the truth. In fact, those qualities seemed more likely to fit Frank than John. All of his adult life, Allan had been wary of Frank, yet he chalked it up to some sort of displaced frustration that Frank survived when his father hadn't. Still, the ruthlessness about Frank always left a sour taste. Another reason why he couldn't stand to be at the factory working with the man.

In contrast, John seemed more like his father . . . Henry.

But even so, how could he ever respect and learn from the man who'd taken everything from his family? It seemed like just another of God's cruel jokes.

# 5

Frank Irving's secretary, Lucy, opened his office door. "Excuse me. This just came by messenger." She left it on his desk and scurried out.

*Brennan* was embossed on the outside. Good grief, what did that woman want now?

Opening the note with his gold letter opener, Frank hoped it was news that Allan Brennan had met some terrible demise.

The few lines of script jumped off the page. "No!" He crumpled the note in his hands.

Lucy rushed back in. "Did you call for something, sir?"

"No, and get out!" Frank leapt to his feet and locked the door behind his retreating secretary.

He stomped back to his desk and picked up the phone. "Get me my lawyer. Now."

The line rang back. "Cyrus, we need to talk."

"Frank, I have to be in court in an hour."

"Well, you better get here in the next two minutes, then."

*Click.* At least the man knew where his bread was buttered.

Pacing his office, he counted to 207 before Cyrus walked in, his shiny shoes squeaking on the floor. "Well, what is it this time? I've already told you I can't you help you with—"

"I've just had word that Allan is in Alaska."

"What?" Cyrus stopped preening in front of the mirror. "Why?"

"Probably because he wants to climb the stupid mountain where his father died."

Cyrus sat in a chair and crossed his arms. "So why is it so urgent that I'm here?"

"If you would have done your job properly ten years ago, I wouldn't be in this mess, so don't take that tone with me."

His lawyer leaned forward. "Pardon me, Frank. But I couldn't control your partner any more than you could. The document was legal and out of my hands."

"But you could have at least warned me before I risked my life climbing a twenty-thousand-foot mountain."

A heavy sigh left the man's lips. He squeezed them together. Several seconds passed before he spoke again. "I'm going to remind you one *last time*, Frank. *You* asked for the documents to be prepared. I prepared them. *You* signed them. Before Henry ever saw them or consulted his own attorney—and, might I add, *against* my advice. Henry had his own lawyer look at the papers before he signed them. Had Henry not written an addendum to his will—perfectly legal, I might add—*yes*, you would have gained control of everything. But he did. I truly hate repeating myself, but it seems you aren't willing to let it through your thick skull that I had *nothing* to do with the legal addendum to his will that he had drawn up, and I didn't have any power whatsoever to change anything that was in signed and legal documents. You argued with the judge and lost. You'd already gained half of Henry's holdings, so you now own seventy-five percent of the company. Please let it go."

Frank turned on him. "You fool. This isn't something to just 'let go.' The agreement was for the surviving partner to receive *all* the holdings of the company!"

"Ah, but that's where you're not above the law, Frank. In your case, if you had been the one to die, yes, everything would have reverted back to Henry. Because you have no children. But as you well know, Henry left half of his holdings to his son, Allan, while the other half did indeed come back to you."

"But that's not good enough." He couldn't admit that it had been bad choices on his part. He had invested and was losing. A lot.

Cyrus stood. "Thank you for wasting my time today so that I could explain once again why you didn't inherit *everything*. Next time you call me, it'd better be important." He walked to the door, but Frank slapped his hand on it and kept him from opening it.

"Don't tell me what to do. You work for *me*! Remember? I know where every penny you've made came from and I can bring you down." His anger boiled inside him. "Do not cross me." Frank stood back and straightened his jacket. "I need to discuss how much time I have to bring more capital in to cover the investments I've made. And what legal measures I have to prolong that time."

Eyes narrowed and arms crossed, Cyrus stayed put. "I'll be glad to help you with that, Frank. As long as you don't bring up the Brennan mess again."

"Fine." He slicked his hair back. "I just needed to vent and lost my temper."

"Good." Cyrus walked back to the chair. "And, of course, I'll be charging my regular fees."

Frank seethed. Everyone wanted his money. "Of course." He pasted on his business smile. But as soon as he got his hands on the rest of the company, he'd change even more things around here. Greedy lawyers and annoying secretaries could easily be replaced.

•••••

Cassidy walked out of the roadhouse wearing her favorite pair of riding pants and the soft, brown leather boots her father had given her for her birthday last year. Every once in a while it sure was nice to not be in a dress and apron. Slinging her bag with her other clothes and water canteen over her shoulder, she looked forward to a bit of time away from the hustle and bustle of the hotel. Quiet. Mountains. And lots of fresh air. Just like what they used to have all the time. Before they joined the staff at the Curry. And exactly what she needed after the hectic busyness of the past few weeks, and especially the last few days.

Her father seemed changed since his return from Anchorage. She'd tried to talk to him about it last night, but he only told her it would work itself out. Then there was Allan. Friendly one minute and sullen the next. Almost as if the man fought some unseen war and the Curry Hotel was the battlefield. But why? She'd been praying for him and knew her father needed the help, but Allan Brennan was a conundrum.

As she made her way to the horses, Cassidy shook her head of the worrisome thoughts, let her hair out of its tight updo, and braided it. Much better. And much more conducive to trail riding in the park. Maybe they'd see some caribou. But hopefully not any grizzlies. She plumb didn't have the energy to deal with that today.

Her father rode up next to her. "I'm glad Fitzgerald cleared you to go with us today. You looked like you needed it."

"I look that bad, huh?" Cassidy winked at her father. "As the agent for the railroad, Mr. Fitzgerald knew it was best to listen to Mrs. Johnson's advice. After all, she usually gets what she wants. And after Mr. Bradley's surprise announcement yesterday about this event, I must admit it has been grueling. But I love what I do."

"I know, dear." He looked off into the distance. "And I'm glad for it."

"What about you?" Cassidy eyed him seriously. "You know I'm worried about you."

"I'm fine. There's a matter that needs my attention, but doesn't need to worry you. I promise it will be resolved and everything will be fine."

"I wish you'd confide in me." She touched his arm. "We've always talked through our troubles in the past."

Her father patted her hand. "And we will continue to do so, but this is something I have to do alone. At least for now."

She pasted on a smile. Stubborn man. "So Thomas and Allan will be joining us today?"

Her father looked solemn and nodded.

"What kind of expedition do you have planned?" Over the years, his work for the railroad had taken him many places along the line from Seward to Fairbanks. He'd been known as the resident expert since the president of the railroad hired him to take him out surveying before the national park was in place. Dad always loved this kind of thing. But perhaps he hadn't been feeling well. What if he'd seen a doctor in Anchorage and received bad news? After all, he'd just commented on having to do this alone. If it was something physical, he would naturally feel that way.

They rode in quiet silence for a few seconds. "I just need to show Allan what it's really like out here, what the railroad's plans are for eventual expeditions into the park from the hotel and from McKinley Park. And Thomas . . . well, he has a lot to learn about everything. But I can tell he loves the outdoors. He might make a very handy assistant one day."

"Isn't Allan your assistant right now?"

"Yes. But he was hired on to apprentice under me so that eventually there would be another full-time guide. We'll both need adequate assistants if we are to fulfill all the plans the board has for us."

Their horses meandered to the stream where Dad had

instructed the others to meet them. Dismounting, he picked up the gear that awaited them and settled some on Cassidy's horse, and the other supplies to his own.

She breathed in deep. Oh, how she loved the mountain air. And from here, there was nothing to intrude on the fresh scent. No trains, laundry, ovens, or even smelly kitchen boys. Glorious. Just glorious.

Closing her eyes, Cassidy let it all wash over her. It was here in the shadow of Denali that she felt God's presence so strongly. She could almost hear Him speak in the rustling trees and the rippling streams. His power in the majesty and glory of the panoramic beauty spread out before her.

"Thank You, Lord." She barely breathed aloud. She wanted nothing more than to spend the day in praise and worship. But hoofbeats behind her broke her reverie and she opened her eyes. No need for Allan to think she was a silly female who daydreamed all the time.

"All right. Looks like we have everyone." Her father moved to her left as Allan and Thomas rode up. "We're going to head west over some rough terrain, so take your time. The horses— as long as they aren't pushed—will secure their footing. I'd like both of you men to take note of your surroundings at all times, including the plant life and animals you see. I'll answer any questions you have."

"What about Miss Cassidy, sir?" Thomas's voice squeaked a bit on the end.

Her father patted the young man's shoulder. "Thank you for worrying about my daughter, but she knows almost as much as I do about Alaska. She can handle herself."

"Well, I don't know about knowing almost as much as you, but I did have a good teacher." Even with her banter, she couldn't seem to persuade her father to truly smile.

"Does everyone know how to use the rifle attached to your saddle?" Dad asked, then continued, "Prayerfully, we won't need them, but just in case we come across some aggressive wildlife, it's best to be prepared."

Manipulating the lever action of the Winchester, Allan checked to see if the weapon was loaded. Cassidy knew his response would meet with her father's approval. From the time she was little, Dad had always said the first thing to do when handling a firearm was to check to see whether or not it was loaded.

Thomas shook his head. "I've never fired any gun, Mr. Ivanoff."

"Thanks for your honesty, Thomas. I'll be sure to teach you the proper handling of weapons. Stick close to me and you'll be fine."

"I'm good to go." Allan sheathed his rifle.

"All right, then. Cassidy, you go ahead and take the lead on this first section. Thomas, you follow her, then Allan, and I will bring up the rear. Keep your eyes open."

Cassidy didn't need any more encouragement. With the wind at her back, she prodded her horse over the stream and into a steady walk. Thomas was full of questions for her father, so she listened to the men's voices behind her and enjoyed the beauty of the day and the mountains before her.

"Are you a fisherman, Thomas?" Dad's question filled the air.

Cassidy didn't bother to hear the young man's answer. They had emerged from a thicket of spruce into the open moraine, where a lush green carpet of vegetation was brightened considerably by the first fuchsia blossoms of fireweed. Not far away, an Arctic fox skittered for cover while several young caribou danced across the field under the watchful eye of the High One. The view took her breath. It must have done the same for the others because everyone went silent.

They rode on in awe. Cassidy remembered other trips she'd made with her father. Over the years they'd camped in places just like this, enduring all seasons in order for her to learn everything she could about surviving off the land. It was on those trips Dad shared stories about their Athabaskan ancestors and some of the lore they had handed down from generation to generation. It was in a setting just like this that Cassidy learned that falling in love for the first time didn't necessarily require another person.

When she looked down at her watch, an hour had passed. Dad and the others were in an intense conversation about the various species of trees and vegetation. Thomas didn't know what any of the plant life was called, but Allan proved he'd studied before coming to Alaska. As they neared another, larger stream, Cassidy pulled her horse to a stop and turned to glance at the men.

"Are we ready for a rest?"

"I think so." Dad looked at the others and nodded.

The guys all dismounted at the stream.

"I need to stretch." Allan reached high. "I haven't been on a horse for a while."

Thomas wandered off a ways. "Mr. Ivanoff, what is this?"

Cassidy's feet hadn't even touched the ground when she turned. Gasping, she realized what Thomas was reaching for and jumped. "Thomas! Don't touch it!" She took off racing toward him, her father not far behind.

Their young charge yanked his hands back and held them aloft as if someone were holding a gun up to him. "I'm sorry!"

Cassidy smiled as she reached him and sucked in big gulps of air. "Don't apologize. It's all right. But did you touch it?"

"I . . . I don't know."

"Let's go rinse it off in the stream just to be safe." She grabbed

Thomas by the shoulder and dragged the poor lad over to the water. "That's pushki—cow parsnip. And while it can be eaten once it's peeled and has lovely flowers, if you touch the hairy stem, it emits a chemical in the sap that will burn you in the sunlight and will itch like the dickens. You'll be miserable for days. And we don't want that, now, do we?"

He shook his head.

"Why don't you wash up real good in the stream and we'll take a break."

Dad and Allan had followed them to the stream, and both men nodded in agreement.

"I'd actually like to speak with you privately, sir, if you don't mind." Allan clasped his hands behind his back.

Her father nodded, but his face was serious indeed. "I had a feeling you would." He extended an arm. "Why don't we head upstream?" He turned toward her. "Cassidy, would you save me some of that wonderful lemonade?" He stepped closer and lowered his voice. "And keep Thomas out of trouble."

"Of course, Dad." She plastered a big smile on her face, hoping to convince him that she didn't suspect a thing. Which, of course, was far from the truth.

As she brought items out of the saddlebags, she wondered what Allan Brennan could possibly have to speak to her father about. In private, no less.

Allan Brennan. Brennan. Hmm. Dad had been upset after hearing the last name *Brennan*. What could have troubled him so?

Laying out the leftover tea cakes and cream, it all came back to her. The man who died on her father's expedition up Mount McKinley had been named Henry. Henry *Brennan*. She covered her mouth and tried to think. What should she do? She remembered her father telling her that Henry's business partner blamed him for Brennan's death. In fact, he vowed to ruin John. Was that why Allan had come? Was the job merely a ruse to get close to his enemy? To think she thought him handsome—gracious, what had come over her? The questions poured out one on top of the other like a waterfall. Would Allan try to hurt her father? No. He didn't seem to be bent on revenge. But she didn't really know him, did she? And that look. When he was standing on the platform. Was that why he was here? How could she have been so taken in?

"Thomas, I need you to keep an eye on the horses. I'll be right back."

"Yes, ma'am."

Grabbing the jug of lemonade for an excuse to intrude in case she needed one, Cassidy raced off to find her father.

Hopefully before it was too late.

# 6

"Why didn't you tell me who you were on the train?" Allan couldn't hold it in any longer.

John sat on a large boulder at the edge of the stream. "I didn't know who *you* were. As far as I remember, we didn't exchange surnames."

It wasn't until they'd shaken hands in front of the hotel that Allan had first heard John's last name. He was right. There was no reason for either one of them to know who the other was.

"I'm sure you want to know more about the 1917 expedition up Denali." John gazed at the water.

"And the death of my father, yes." He didn't mean to sound so angry, but his patience was gone, his voice tight and thick. Every negative thing Frank ever told him about the expedition came back to haunt him now. Pleasantries would get them no-where—Allan simply had to know. Today.

John seemed in no hurry to speak, but he at least had the decency to offer an uncomfortable expression as he shifted his weight.

"Well?"

"Your father was one of the most intriguing men I've ever met. We became good friends over the weeks of our journey. Unlike his partner, Frank, Henry and I loved everything about the expedition—being outdoors, climbing . . ." He turned his head completely away.

"What?"

"We had some incredible theological conversations as well. Your father really knew his stuff. He helped me to overcome some anger and resentment toward my wife's parents that I'd long since buried."

"I'm sure he did." Allan grimaced. His faith had waned after the death of his father, leaving in its wake resentment toward God. God, who could have kept his father alive, but didn't. Allan knew his father would have reprimanded him for his attitude—had he been alive. But he was dead and that was why they were here having this conversation in the first place.

"John, I need to know what happened to my father. And I need to know now. I don't want to discuss politics or religion or any other nonsense." He knew he sounded like a child having a tantrum.

The man ducked his head, gave a heavy sigh, and then looked him square in the eye. "Son, I can tell you're hurting, but your father had a deep faith. He hardly thought it nonsense."

"Perhaps he was a fool for his beliefs." Allan didn't know where that had come from. He'd never thought of his father in that way.

As if reading his mind, John countered, "Your father was a better man than most I've known, and I don't appreciate you disrespecting him in such a way."

"How dare you!" Disrespect? And this man claimed to know his father after a few measly weeks? "What about the disrespect you are showing by not being honest with me?"

John stood. "I don't mean any disrespect, son."

"Stop calling me son! My father was the only one with that right." He hadn't meant to sound so harsh, but now that things had taken that turn, he was hard-pressed to contain his agitation. "I need answers, John."

"I know . . . Allan." He sighed long and hard. "Because I needed them too. I think I still do. The day your father died was one of the worst of my life. Made even more so because of the circumstances."

Allan couldn't take it any longer. "What exactly *were* those circumstances? Because Frank told me it was all your fault. Was it? Are you to blame for my father's death?"

"Now, you wait just a minute, Mr. Brennan!" Cassidy's voice came from behind him.

He turned and narrowed his eyes, watching her stomp through the thick tundra grass.

"I am so sorry that you lost your father"—she set a jug of something down on a rock and planted her hands on her hips—"but I can't believe you would stoop to blaming *my* father! Your father knew the risk he took when he hired Dad to take him up the mountain. Dad would have made those dangers very clear."

"Cassidy, please." John straightened, his stance wide and imposing. "If you're going to stay, I need you to be quiet and listen." His voice was firm.

She huffed and crossed her arms.

Allan calmed a bit. Something about Cassidy's indignation shamed him. Where had all this ugliness and anger come from? Would that make his father proud? He removed his hat and ran a hand through his hair. "I just want to know the truth." He stopped short of apologizing for his tirade.

"I wish I knew, Allan. I wish I knew." John walked closer and stood only a yard away, staring at the mountain. "The trip up was fairly good. We had a few problems here and there, but otherwise it was uneventful. The weather held—surprisingly so. We summited the southern peak around 2:00 p.m. that day. Your father was so proud and all smiles. After we placed the marker in the snow, I noticed the weather was turning rapidly." He rubbed a hand down his face. "So we started our descent immediately. There was a rope between all of us so we couldn't lose each other in the blinding snow. I *watched* him secure it around his waist. By now there was no need to double-check his work." Several moments passed as he clenched and unclenched his jaw. "The wind picked up—light at first and then it became fierce and turned into a whiteout. As the seasoned climber I went first, to make certain the footing would be sure. Frank followed and then Henry."

"Why was my father last?"

"Because he was more experienced than Frank. Simple as that. Frank didn't seem to care; he just wanted down. I think he knew how out of place he was compared to your father and me."

Allan nodded. "Go on."

"We didn't stop moving. Just worked our way down in the storm. The stronger the wind grew, the more I gave serious thought to stopping and putting up shelter, but I felt confident we could make our high camp. We pressed on with very little visibility, and I felt a great sense of relief when we reached the camp. That is, until I discovered Henry was no longer behind Frank. And the rope was intact."

Allan felt a chill go through him. "So what are you saying?"

"I don't *know* what happened to him. The only way for the rope to be intact was if Henry untied it himself."

"Why would he untie the rope? Wouldn't he have told Frank if he did that?"

"The storm was too much—you couldn't hear anything above the wind's roar. And you couldn't see anything—not even your hand in front of your face."

"So you just left him there?" Allan's anger mixed with his sorrow.

A silent tear traced a path down the older man's face. "No. I would never abandon a man." He came closer and laid a hand on Allan's shoulder. Allan wanted to move away but found he couldn't. It was as if an invisible force held him in place.

"We had to wait the storm out at the camp, but I told Frank I wasn't going on without Henry. He balked at the idea, but I think it was because he was coming down with something. He had a terrible fever once the storm was past. So I left him in a tent and went in search of your father."

Allan closed his eyes. "You went back for him?" Frank never mentioned that.

"I searched for two days, Allan. Up and down the same path we had taken. The only conclusion I could come to is that he lost his breath and couldn't keep up, so he must have untied the rope to take a break rather than get dragged and fall. It's not unusual when a man is oxygen deprived and disoriented for him to make poor decisions. We were all suffering a bit of altitude sickness, but your father seemed the best out of all of us. He'd been completely rational and able to maneuver on top of the summit. Still the storm could have caused him to panic. Once he was detached from us, he could have gotten lost, fallen into a crevasse, or any number of things. I searched for hours on end, but at the conclusion of two days, I knew it was pointless. Frank was worse and I had an obligation to get him safely down before I lost another man on the mountain."

Allan's eyes snapped open. "Frank has always blamed you for what happened."

"No more than I blame myself. I was responsible for that expedition. I was the one with experience. I was the one who signed on to take them. It was . . . *my* fault."

The man was more than willing to accept his part in what happened, but what *had* happened? Allan felt no closer to the answer than when they'd begun the conversation. Worse still, there was no sense of satisfaction in John's declaration and acceptance of responsibility.

Anger radiated throughout him, even more than before. All these years . . . he'd believed everything Frank told him. But maybe that's why Frank blamed John—because he couldn't bear his own guilt over not knowing what happened to his partner.

Cassidy gave Allan a look he couldn't decipher and went to her father. "Dad, I'm so sorry. I didn't know you went back to try to find him. Is that how you lost those toes? When you went searching?"

John looked down at his daughter. "It was easier for me to keep it to myself. I didn't handle the loss of Henry very well, and you were only seventeen. You didn't need any more burdens to carry. And a little frostbite for me was nothing compared to the loss of a friend."

Allan couldn't bear the conversation between father and daughter. No one else should be hurting! He was the one who lost his father. "If you'll excuse me. I need a few moments."

Walking away from the Ivanoffs, he tried to make sense of all he'd just heard. What happened? If John saved Frank's life by getting him down the mountain, then why did Frank blame John for Henry's death? Was Frank even lucid at that point? Or was that how Frank coped with the loss of his lifelong friend?

The emotions roiling inside him were more than he could manage.

Why did Dad untie his rope?

•••••

Tuesday's staff meeting in the downstairs kitchen was packed. Cassidy squeezed through a group of the maids to be near Mrs. Johnson.

"How was the dedication service yesterday?" the older lady whispered to her as others continued to gather.

The staff had gotten back to the hotel at such a late hour there hadn't been time to talk about the service and then this morning there had been so much to catch up on, Cassidy hadn't had a chance to fill Mrs. Johnson in on the details.

"The dedication was lovely." Cassidy smiled. "We weren't as close to Mount McKinley as I would have liked, but it was very nice regardless."

"I'm glad it went well. And your trek into the park?"

"It could've been better."

"Oh, really?" She straightened as Mr. Bradley entered the room and softened her voice. "Well, you can tell me about it later. Today will be busy. We have chocolate mousse on the menu as well as lemon soufflé. I'll put you in charge of the mousse."

Mr. Bradley cleared his throat and silence descended on the room. "The reason this morning's staff meeting includes everyone is because we need to reiterate how important it is that the President of the United States will visit our hotel. The Curry Hotel is the prize jewel of the Alaska Railroad, and what better way to welcome our country's leader than to show him the very best Alaska has to offer."

Murmurs and whispered words grew through the room.

"I know you are all excited about the President's visit, but let me continue please."

Everyone hushed.

"Thank you. We've had word that the presidential party has reached Alaska via *The Henderson*." Their manager held a telegram aloft and glanced at it. "In a few days, they should reach Seward. And from there, they will take the Presidential Special—a collection of elegantly appointed cars designed by our railroad for this auspicious occasion—all the way to

Fairbanks. The ceremony for the completion of the railroad will be in Nenana." He lowered the paper and pulled out his pocket watch. "Now, considering today is the tenth of July, we have roughly four and a half days to prepare for the President's group of approximately seventy people."

A few gasps erupted.

"Mrs. Johnson, I'd like to see your plans for the menus by three o'clock this afternoon."

"Yes, Mr. Bradley. Miss Ivanoff and I will be in your office as scheduled." Margaret Johnson never seemed to fear a challenge.

Cassidy felt her palms beginning to sweat. Was she up for the challenge as well?

"Mrs. McGovern, I will need a detailed schedule of the laundry and the tallies for all pieces that come through our facility. The President wishes to have an update, since we service not only the railroad and this facility, but the hospitals as well. He mentioned something about a congressional delegation, so make sure you have every detail. You will also need to have room designations." He looked down again. "Let's meet at three thirty."

"Yes, sir." There was that pinched tone again from the head housekeeper.

"Mr. Ivanoff and Mr. Brennan . . ." Mr. Bradley turned to the men on the side. "There will not be time for a lengthy expedition, but they have requested a short nature walk from our best guide to show them the splendors of Alaska."

"Yes, sir. We will plan for such an event." Cassidy's dad nodded.

"Good, good. Bring your plans tomorrow." The manager looked down at his papers again. "I believe that is all for now, but let me say again that there will be absolutely no tolerance of shenanigans in the coming days. This visit needs to be perfect. Our reputation is on the line."

"Yes, Mr. Bradley." The voices of the staff echoed in the room.

And off he went. Up the stairs and on to some other important task, Cassidy was sure.

Wiping her hands on her apron, she turned to Mrs. Johnson.
"Do you think . . ." Maybe this wasn't such a good idea. She
chewed on her lip. She needed to vent some frustration, and the
very best way was trying something new. Besides, she'd wanted
to ask for weeks now.

"Well? Do I think what?" The cook raised her eyebrows.

She'd never know if she didn't try. "Do you think I could
help with the soufflés tonight?"

Her boss sighed. "Hmmm . . . I know you've been wanting to
learn, but there's an awful lot to accomplish today. And soufflés
can be very tricky, since they have to be served immediately."
Mrs. Johnson squinted. "We will be having the same two desserts on Friday. Let's wait until then. Do you think you can get
the mousses done before luncheon so they can chill? Then you'd
have time to practice."

"Yes, ma'am." More sweat covered her palms, but she wiped
it away on her apron again.

"All right, if you think you can get everything else done, you
can help with them. And after our meeting with Mr. Bradley
today, you can watch how I make them step by step."

"I know I can do it. Even if I don't take a lunch break on
Friday, it will be worth it."

Mrs. Johnson laughed. "I do love your enthusiasm, Cassidy.
If only everyone could see the world through your eyes."

• • • • •

If only more people really *could* see through Cassidy's eyes.
John's daughter had a way of cheering everyone up—of offering help where she could. And he desperately needed help right
now, but this kind of help wasn't going to come from Cassidy.

*Lord, tell me what to say.*

John waited for the other staff to leave the room. Allan stood beside him, apparently waiting for instruction. The rest of their journey into the park yesterday had been—from Allan's part—silent. Thomas asked lots of questions, John and Cassidy gave information, but the tension had been fierce as Allan refused to speak any more about the expedition.

Cassidy hugged John as they returned, and even though she didn't say it, he knew she was struggling with anger toward Allan. Fiercely loyal, Cassidy would try to protect him from attack.

But in this case, he deserved it.

When the last person retreated up the stairs, John turned to his apprentice. "I can only imagine that this is very difficult for you, Allan. I know how much it has affected me personally. But I do feel you are a good man. Your father was a very good man, so I'm sure he raised you to follow in his footsteps."

Allan's jaw tensed but he said nothing.

"The best I can do is apologize again for the tragedy of losing your father. And to say to you that I take full responsibility. I was the guide. It was my job to bring them up and down that mountain safely." John held out his hand. "I pray that one day you will be able to forgive me."

Allan stared back at him and then looked down at the offered hand. "I appreciate that, John. As you know, this was quite a shock for me, and I am asking for your patience in this matter as I work through the facts."

"If you feel that you can't work with me, I'll find you another position."

Allan appeared surprised by this. "No, that's not necessary." The younger man reached out and took John's hand. "In the short time since my arrival in Alaska, I have already come to respect you." He sighed. "And I owe you an apology as well. It was wrong of me to accuse you in such a way."

"It was understandable, son. I don't blame you for it. As to your respect, I will seek to earn it every day." John released his hand. "But this will be a demanding summer for you, I'm afraid. There is a lot to learn, and we need to trust one another."

Allan nodded. "I came here to learn everything I can, to follow in my father's footsteps, and to finish what he started. I will work hard."

"And you'll be able to do as I instruct? You were very angry yesterday. And with good reason, but I need to know that you'll answer to me and heed my instruction." John hated pressing the issue, but it had to be voiced. There wouldn't be room for grudges. They needed trust. And a lot of it. "Will you be able to trust me?"

For a moment Allan said nothing, but then he gave a curt nod. "I will do whatever is required of me. You have my word."

• • • • •

Cassidy sat outside enjoying a few idle hours. Despite their complicated schedule, the work was well in hand. Mr. Bradley had agreed to let Thomas continue helping Cassidy's father and Allan, much to Mrs. Johnson's relief. Cassidy had to admit that Thomas's absence had made things in the kitchen run much smoother. Poor Thomas.

She flipped through a magazine that had been left behind by one of the guests and soaked in the sun's warmth after a few chilly days of rain. The magazine featured advertisements for cosmetics and modern time-saving appliances—efforts to entice old-fashioned women to throw off their shackles of nineteenth-century thinking, Cassidy mused. Inside the back was an ad for "The Eden—The Supreme Achievement in Electric Washing

Machines." A smiling woman stood beside her new washing machine, looking for all the world as if this were the only place in the world she wanted to be. Further perusal revealed ads for various other appliances, foods, and clothing.

A giggle escaped her as Cassidy read about the latest in undergarments, designed to free women from the damaging effects of corsets. The new formless styles required wrapping one's chest to make it as flat as possible. Camisoles and step-ins were the rage, the latter being a one-piece article of clothing that took the place of bloomers and chemises. Silk was the fashionable material of the day for everything from undergarments to outer wear. Macy's advertisement showed dresses with hems that nearly touched the floor, all in the straight, formless style that the modern woman was supposedly delighted to wear.

"What's so funny?"

Cassidy snapped the magazine shut at the sound of Allan's voice. She felt her cheeks grow hot. What was he doing here? "Nothing really." She pushed the magazine aside. "I was just amused by some of the advertisements." At least that much was true without explaining exactly what had caught her attention.

Allan glanced down at the magazine. "So are you going to bob your hair?"

Cassidy's gaze went to the cover and the model whose hair was clipped to a length just above her collar. She shook her head. "Not me. I can't imagine how much work that would be. It's a lot easier to brush mine out and braid it without worrying about putting in pin curls or slicking it up with whatever it is they use to plaster it into place."

"I'm glad. I'd hate to see you cut it."

She didn't like being the focus of his attention, especially after yesterday. He'd been so angry. Of course, if her father had died on the mountain and she didn't have answers, she'd probably be angry too. But it made her wary of Allan, since she didn't know him.

The silence stretched.

"You lived in Seattle before coming here, didn't you?" Best to offer an olive branch if possible.

"I did." He took the chair beside her. "Why do you ask?"

"No reason in particular. I just remember Dad saying something about that."

Allan frowned. "I see."

Cassidy heard the tone of his voice change. "So you still blame my father for your father's death?"

The question surprised her almost as much as it obviously surprised Allan. What had gotten into her? She hadn't meant to be confrontational—in fact, she thought she'd been trying to be neutral—but it was too late to take back the words now.

"No. But I don't know what I think." He looked out across the lawn. "It's hard to figure out what one should think or feel when the information given is in conflict."

"My father is a good man. I'm not just saying that because I'm his daughter. You can ask anyone who has known him for any length of time. He was devastated when your father was lost. He thinks he hid it well, and in truth he probably did better than most men, but I could see how much it ate at him."

She paused only a moment to let the words sink in. "I once overheard him discuss that climb with Superintendent Karstens. Dad told him that he kept going over and over all the details of the climb, trying to figure out if he'd somehow been neglectful or blind to the dangers. Mr. Karstens told him he could second-guess himself until the end of his days and it wouldn't change anything. Dad said he'd give just about anything if he could go back in time and do things different. Mr. Karstens asked him what he'd do differently and Dad said, 'Whatever it would take to bring Henry Brennan out alive.'"

For several long minutes neither one said a word. Cassidy hoped Allan would believe her father's sincerity. Her father would have traded places with Brennan, even knowing it would have left her orphaned. That was just how Dad was—how he would always be. The needs of others were more important than his own.

"My father's business partner, Frank Irving, said your father was cavalier in his attitude about the risks and that the weather had been threatening before they even made the summit climb."

Cassidy felt a surge of anger. "My father would never put people in danger. It would serve no purpose. And if he were as cavalier as your Mr. Irving suggests, why would he risk his own life? Perhaps Mr. Irving is the one who was negligent. After all, as I recall, he was on the rope between your father and mine. If it was such an easy thing to keep track of your father in the storm, then why didn't Mr. Irving realize he was gone?"

"You think I haven't asked myself those questions?" Allan fixed her with a look that betrayed his frustration. "I have looked for answers ever since learning of what happened. I owe it to my father to learn the truth and I can't rest until I do."

"And what if you never get those answers?" Cassidy forced herself to hold his gaze. "What if there aren't any?"

He shook his head. "I don't know."

"Is it truly so important to blame someone for what happened? It won't bring your father back."

"No, but it might make someone account for what happened."

"How?" She shook her head. "People come up here and get hurt or die all the time. Your father knew the risk of climbing the mountain before he went. He knew that my father couldn't guarantee his safety—that he had no control over the weather or ice fields or any other part of the mountain. He accepted that—so why can't you?" She got to her feet, afraid that if she didn't leave, she might say something she'd regret. "I hope you find peace of mind. I truly do. But it's been my experience that such peace only comes through God."

A turmoil of emotions rocked her insides as she walked away. Why did it matter so much that he came to terms with this? Was it just because her father was the object of his doubt? Or was it something entirely different?

She cared about Allan—just as she did everyone who worked at the Curry Hotel, but perhaps she cared too much. She found herself thinking about him—looking for him at various times. At first she thought it was simply out of concern for her father, but now . . . now she wasn't at all certain that was all there was to it.

Shaking her head, Cassidy did her best to put the matter behind her. There was no way for her to make matters right between Allan and her father—they were going to have to settle this between them. So why did she feel so cold?

A wave of loneliness washed over her. Dad was dealing with this incredible loss all over again and was shutting her out. And then there was Allan.

She barely knew the man. But that look in his eyes when they'd met told her that he understood pain and heartache. Maybe even a touch of loneliness. Like her.

There seemed to be a connection. But what if she had just imagined it? Had longed for it? She shook her head. Losing her heart to Allan, a man who would accuse her father like that, would do nothing but complicate the matter further.

# 7

John laid his copious notes on Bradley's desk. "Here are all the details for the nature walk we plan to take the presidential party on Saturday evening."

Another day had flown past with details, planning, meetings, and of course the constant guests to attend to in the hotel.

The manager studied the page. "This looks outstanding, John. Thank you." He scribbled something on the paper. "How is Brennan working out?"

"Fine, sir. He's a hard worker."

"Did you know that he's part owner of an outdoor equipment company?"

"Yes, sir. I did." Would there come a time when Allan would share with the manager about John's failings? Of course it wasn't like Bradley didn't know about the death of Allan's father.

"A very enterprising young man. He even mentioned the possibility of speaking to the railroad about selling some of his gear here in Curry."

John nodded, a knot forming in his throat. "If you don't need anything else, I'd better get moving. We are taking a group fishing this afternoon."

"Well, I hope they catch the big one."

"Thank you." John headed out the side door of the office. The biggest problem he seemed to have right now was not the full schedule, not the training of his apprentice, and not even the fact that Thomas had a tendency to bumble up even the simplest of tasks.

Right now, he battled himself.

With Allan's appearance in Curry, the confrontation up at the park, and their conversation in the basement yesterday—John couldn't get past the one glaring issue.

He couldn't forgive himself.

The circumstances around the death of Henry Brennan haunted him. He thought he'd put the situation behind him. But all of Allan's questions brought it back to the forefront of his mind.

Had there been anything else he could have done to save Henry?

And now, Henry's son was here. Flesh and blood. Seeking answers.

While John knew what Allan sought could only be found in God, he still felt responsible. Even more than that.

He felt guilty.

For failing Henry.

And for failing Henry's family.

Taking the stairs down to the basement, John prayed for wisdom. Cassidy had noticed he wasn't himself and had questioned him. No sense in worrying anyone else with his problems.

*Boom!*

The stairs shook. John rounded the corner into the section gang dining room. "Hello! Everyone all right?"

"Mr. Ivanoff—help! Over here!" Thomas's voice came from the laundry on the other side of the basement.

A cloud of white smoke billowed out of the door.

John raced over. "What's happened?"

"One of the pipes burst. I had just brought a load down from the train and fell. I thought it was my own clumsiness, but when I looked up, the ladies were on the floor."

It hit him. This wasn't smoke. It was steam. John looked at the south wall where Thomas pointed. Mrs. McGovern and two maids lay crumpled in the corner. Hissing came from the burst pipe.

"Thomas, you've got to get help. Everyone you can."

•••••

Allan collided with Thomas as the young man raced up the stairs. "Whoa, what's your hurry?"

"Mr. Ivanoff said to get everyone I could to help. A pipe burst in the laundry."

Allan nodded. "I'll go down. You grab everyone you find."

"Yes, sir."

He'd felt a jolt as he'd stood on the train platform. But since the train was leaving, he didn't give much thought to it.

The whole laundry was steam powered. That meant if a pipe burst, then boiling hot steam was flooding that area. The initial pressure would be abated, but the pumps would keep sending it until they could shut it off.

At the base of the stairs, Allan slipped. The floor was already wet from the water vapor and mist from the cooled steam, and the humid air almost choked him. As he reached the laundry, sweat poured down his face.

He found John carrying Mrs. McGovern out of the room. "Any more?"

"There's at least two more maids huddled in the southwest corner."

Taking a closer look at Mrs. McGovern, he noticed that her

face was very red. Had she been burned by the steam? Allan didn't have time to think about the condition of the others. He plunged into the simmering room and went down to his hands and knees. He'd be more apt to find them that way.

Steam filled the room in a great white fog. Allan reached out and found hands grabbing for him.

"It's so hot! Help us, please!"

Allan latched on to an arm and pulled. A young maid's head hit his shoulder.

"Please help Marie. She's not talking anymore."

He carried the maid out and passed John on the way. "There's another maid unconscious in that corner. Her name's Marie."

The steam filled the basement of the hotel quickly. Allan set down the young girl as thunderous footsteps were heard on the stairs. "The floor's slippery. Be careful!" He only hoped they'd heed his warning.

He followed more men back into the laundry as John carried the other maid out.

John shoved her into Thomas's arms. "Get her out of here." He ripped off his jacket and vest and threw them down the hallway.

The suffocating heat had to be taking its effect on his boss. But Allan followed his lead and ran once more back to the laundry. Several men were turning the giant valve to shut off the steam supply. John stood in front of the busted pipe with towels to keep the steam at bay. Allan grabbed more towels and went to help. The heat was almost unbearable. But if John could sacrifice himself to help the men, then so could he.

It took several minutes, but the room began to clear. Every man was soaked from head to toe. Two maintenance workers came in with large wrenches and clamps.

Mr. Bradley slipped as he came around the corner, and he

grabbed on to the doorjamb. "Oh, thank goodness, you got it stopped!" The manager looked around the room at each man. "Thank you all."

The men all nodded, each gasping for air. "It took too many of us to get that wheel turned. Too hot and too slick," one of the men said. "That needs to be fixed. Coulda been a disaster."

"Do we know what happened?" Mr. Bradley asked.

"No, not exactly," the same man replied. "Must have been a weakness in the pipe. We'll get it repaired right away."

"It's a tragedy to be sure. Do we know how badly the women were hurt?"

"Not yet," John replied. "We just managed to get the last one to safety."

Allan breathed heavily, his hands on his hips. "It was John and Thomas who rescued the women, sir."

Mr. Bradley went over and shook John's hand.

Allan left the room and walked slowly to the dining room. Chaos ensued as everyone started cleaning up. Water was everywhere.

But his thoughts kept going back to John. He'd risked his own life over and over again to save someone else. Even blocking the boiling steam so the other men could shut it off. How many men would put themselves in harm's way like that?

But then an even more troubling question seared his heart—if Allan hadn't had an example to follow, would *he* have done the same?

·····

The individual crystal dishes filled with luscious chocolate mousse sat in the large icebox chilling. Cassidy couldn't be prouder. They were her best yet.

"They turned out lovely. The texture is simply divine." Mrs.

Johnson licked her lips. A sure sign of her satisfaction and pleasure.

Cassidy bounced on the balls of her feet. She kept her hands clasped in front of her to keep from hugging the older woman for the praise. "Thank you, Mrs. Johnson."

"I pity the men and women who've never tasted a mousse like this."

Wow. Three compliments in a row. She wasn't sure she was *that* deserving.

"All right. Well, we seem to be ahead of schedule." The head cook checked her watch and then wiped her hands on her apron. "Let's try a single batch of soufflé for the staff to enjoy. And if it turns out properly, we can do them together for the dinner guests."

What a challenge! Mrs. Johnson's lemon soufflés were famous. Cassidy had longed to make them since she'd arrived. And how incredible would it be to serve them to the wealthy crowd at dinner?

They gathered the ingredients together and set it all out on Cassidy's station. The older woman gave the eggs to Cassidy. "Separate them."

"Yes, ma'am." This was a job she could do in her sleep. Well, almost. Cassidy giggled to herself.

"What on earth has struck you as funny this time?"

"Nothing. Sorry." She worked very hard to look serious but feared she looked more like a fish.

Mrs. Johnson smiled and shook her head. "No one could ever accuse you of being melancholy, that's for sure." She grabbed a whisk and a clean bowl, and went right back to business. "Wipe the bowl down with a drop of vinegar. Only a drop, mind you."

"Yes, ma'am."

"It's time to whip the egg whites. Now one of the most important things is to make sure you do *not* overbeat them. They need to hold a stiff peak but not be dry."

The recipe really wasn't that difficult. Whipping the yolks with sugar and lemon zest, gradually adding hot cream, and cooking until it was pudding-like. Then folding the fluffy egg whites with lemon into the mixture. In no time, Cassidy felt she'd have it down to a perfectly timed routine.

As she gently set the tray in the oven, she said a little prayer.

Mrs. Johnson wiped her hands on a towel and headed toward her desk in the opposite corner. "Let me know when they're done. I need to check the list for the night cook and then must speak to Mr. Bradley. I shouldn't be long."

"Yes, Cook." Cassidy stared at the oven with her hand on her watch. Mrs. Johnson said it was a precise amount of time. But what if she messed it up in some way?

Several minutes passed as Cassidy cleaned up her worktable, glancing at her watch every ten or fifteen seconds. Time would never pass at this rate. The rest of the staff moved in steady rhythm, preparing their parts of the sumptuous feast for tonight. But she couldn't stand it any longer. Maybe if she just peeked in the oven it would set her mind at ease.

Mrs. Johnson spoke with two of the kitchen maids and headed toward the dining room. Now was Cassidy's chance. She pulled on the handle of the massive door and gently opened it a few inches.

Well, they didn't look like they were supposed to. In fact, they were all a touch lopsided. She closed the door. Maybe they rose up one side and then the other?

Trying to hide her disappointment, Cassidy checked her watch. Three and a half more minutes to go. She stomped her foot. The job of assistant cook hadn't just been handed to her. She'd worked really hard for this position and had studied and cooked and cooked and studied some more. Why, of all the kitchen workers, she could make the best hollandaise. Mrs. Johnson even said so, and that's why the job was always hers. Everything from demitasse to the perfect poached egg, chocolate mousse to roast lamb, Cassidy could cook it.

She just needed confidence in herself. The soufflés would be fine. She knew what she was doing.

One more glance at her watch told her it was time. Opening the oven door with towels in hand to grab the soufflés, she hoped for success.

But when she set them down, disappointment crept up her spine. They were all still crooked.

One by one, the individual soufflés deflated into their cups like turtles into their shells.

She wouldn't cry. She refused.

A couple of the kitchen maids walked by. One frowned and *tsk*ed at her. "Those don't look like the chef's."

The other whispered. "It's because it's Friday the thirteenth, don'tcha know? Nothing can go right today. Just look at the mess down in the basement."

Mrs. Johnson chose that moment to reappear, and Cassidy wanted to hide under the table. Instead, she placed her hands on her hips and studied her creations. Like a good student would do. Learn from her mistakes.

Without a word, the head cook grabbed a spoon. Dipping it into a cup, she filled her spoon with a bite. She blew on the hot morsel before popping it into her mouth. "Delicious, Cassidy."

She frowned. "But they collapsed."

"Yes, they did. But at least they taste like they are supposed to. Now we need to figure out what went wrong. And it had nothing to do with Friday the thirteenth. Such foolishness." The older woman scowled at the young help, and handed Cassidy another spoon. "Try it yourself."

Not wasting a moment, Cassidy did just that. And while the pleasing flavor and texture made her feel a sense of accomplishment, that didn't make up for the fact that they didn't look like they were supposed to.

"Before they collapsed, I noticed they were a little uneven."

"Yes, ma'am."

"So I'm guessing you forgot to run your finger around the edge of each cup to ensure they were clean of batter?"

"Um . . ." Had she? "I probably did forget."

"And did you use upward strokes with the butter when you prepared the dishes before sprinkling them with sugar?"

"Hmm, maybe not upward strokes."

"Did you perchance open the oven while they were baking?"

She winced. "Yes, I did."

"I had a feeling." Mrs. Johnson almost smiled. "I did that my first time too. Opening the oven will make them collapse almost every time. And while all soufflés will still go down after a few minutes, you want them done, not soupy, and nice and high for the presentation. That's why they are served immediately."

Cassidy nodded. She'd wanted to impress her boss, and now she'd made classic mistakes. All because she was in too big of a hurry—not wanting to be patient.

"There's a lot to learn, Cassidy. But you need to remind yourself that you are the assistant cook here! That's a hefty position." The woman waved for the staff to come over. "Now, while everyone tastes your delicious first efforts, you can work on the second."

A little bit of shock rolled through her limbs. "Truly, you want me to make them again?"

"As my father always used to say, when you fall off the horse, you must get right back on." The woman grabbed another spoonful. "And Cassidy?"

"Yes, ma'am?"

"Yum."

# 8

The temperature at nine in the evening still held the heat of the day as Allan walked along the train tracks. So many thoughts battled for attention—maybe the bright sunlight could help to burn them all away. The long daylight hours of summer in Alaska still baffled him. Hands in his pockets, he meandered along.

Off in the distance, Cassidy sat on a log. He hadn't meant to follow her outside, but he did. Would she want to talk to him?

His footsteps on the gravel caught her attention.

"Hi."

"Hello." She gave him a small smile. "What brings you out here?"

He shrugged. "Just needed a stroll, I guess." Hesitation brought him up short. Might as well be honest. "Actually, I saw you come out here."

"Oh?" Was that reluctance behind her eyes?

He pointed to the log. "May I?"

"Certainly."

Allan sat and kicked some rocks with his shoe. "I need to apologize to you."

Her shoulders lifted and she straightened. Gone was the smile.

"I was unfair to your father. And I'm sorry."

She looked back to the west. "While I appreciate your apology to me, I'm wondering if you've apologized to him as well—since he's the one you were unfair to." There was no malice in her tone. In fact, he heard—and almost felt—kindness and compassion in her voice.

"I have. He's been very patient and understanding."

She looked at him then and folded her hands in her lap. "I wasn't very considerate of your feelings either. All I heard was the pain in your voice and the accusations. I only wanted to protect my father. I'm sorry for jumping in where I shouldn't have."

He nodded. "It's perfectly understandable on your part, Cassidy." Turning toward her, he removed his hat. "Just as I am seeking to understand my father's death and want to defend him and his actions, I know you are doing the same. And I respect that."

With a nod, she turned her face back to the west—the sunlight making her dark hair shine. "So you're no longer angry?"

Tough question. He sighed. "I'm trying to work on my anger over my dad's death. I know it's wrong. But no, I'm not angry at your father. He's a good man." He leaned closer to her, trying to catch her eye. "And I'd really like for us to be friends."

"Oh, Dad already thinks very highly of you. You're friends." She turned her head and gazed at him.

He smiled. "I meant"—he waved his hand between them—"that I'd really like for you and me—Cassidy and Allan—to be friends."

She tilted her head to one side and studied him, then shook her head and gave him a brilliant smile. "I already thought we were, so of course we can be friends."

"Well, I did wonder, because I had made you pretty mad—and rightfully so."

"I have moments of anger, Allan. Even with friends. And we *are* friends."

"Wonderful." If only his anger was just moments . . . one of these days, he'd have to tackle it. But he couldn't bear the thought of not having Cassidy as his friend. Best to change the subject. "Now, I was wondering if you could help me with some of the wild flowers around here."

She stood and he followed. Easy conversation flowed between them as they walked up and down the train tracks. Allan hadn't felt comfort like this in a long time. If only he could rewrite the past, he might have a chance for a happy future.

• • • • •

Thomas carried the last load of heavy equipment into the lobby. His arms ached from all the hauling.

"Put it over there by the fireplace," Mr. Bradley directed and pointed while writing on a paper with his other hand.

In all his seventeen years, Thomas had never seen anything quite so grand as all the preparations for the President of the United States. Of course, he'd never seen electric lights or running water until coming to work at the Curry Hotel a few weeks ago. The orphanage he grew up in didn't have either. In fact, most people in remote parts of Alaska didn't.

It was a thrill to get to use an indoor water closet rather than racing out in the cold to use a drafty privy. But he guessed the President wouldn't know about such things.

The maids set up a table with a fancy tablecloth as Thomas began unloading the crates.

The manager walked up behind him and laid a hand on his shoulder. "You're doing a good job, son."

"Thank you, sir." Thomas reminded himself of John's wise words every day, to take a bit more time so he wouldn't drop anything or trip. "But do ya mind me asking what all this is for?"

"Why, it's a radio!" Mr. Bradley tucked his thumbs into his vest.

Thomas stood next to him and looked back at the jumble of pieces. "What's a radio?"

He chuckled. "Son, I think you'll have to experience it to understand. Radios make it possible for us to hear music, concerts, speeches, news, and all kinds of things from many miles away. In fact, they are installing an up-to-date long-wave receiver in Seward as we speak. We've been told that with the increase in power, they've been able to hear broadcasting from Long Island, New York, all the way in New Zealand. And that's nine thousand miles away."

"Well, ain't that ducky." He had no idea what it meant, but it obviously was a big deal to the manager. Especially to rush to get it installed, since they were expecting the presidential train at any moment.

Mr. Bradley laughed. "Yes, Thomas, it is. It will make it easier for us to stay connected up here. And we wanted the President's group to see that here at the Curry, we are up to the very best standards on everything."

Two men joined them and went to work on all the pieces. Wood and wires and round mesh-covered things. It was an odd puzzle to put together.

Thomas stood transfixed. Even though he had no idea what a radio did, the idea of it fascinated him.

The next moment, hissing emanated from the boxes.

"The static will get worse at certain times of day because of the long hours of sun in the summer." One of the men spoke to the manager. "We'll find a station to test today, but you'll have to look for others once the receiver is fully functional."

With a turn of the knob, everything changed. All of a sudden, the lobby was filled with voices. Speaking at quite a clip, the voices weren't anything Thomas could understand.

"Sir, what is that?" He stepped forward, mesmerized by the machine in front of him.

The one turning the knob stuck his ear up to the side of it. "I believe that's Russian."

Unable to find anything else but the hissing, the man turned it off. "Well, at least we know it works."

"Yes," Mr. Bradley nodded. "But it's probably not best to be playing Russian radio for the President when he arrives."

The man packed up his bag of tools as red crept up his neck and ears. "I apologize. I can't control the reception. But in a few days, you should be able to hear more variety." He placed his hat on his head and rushed out the front door of the hotel, followed by the other man.

Mr. Bradley paced in front of the fire. "Well, I guess we will just have to keep trying it."

A long whistle sounded in the distance, followed by two short ones, and then another long.

A smile broke across Mr. Bradley's face. "Thomas, it's time to meet the President."

Staff members flooded the lobby from belowstairs, abovestairs, the dining room, and kitchen. Everywhere Thomas looked, someone was straightening a tie, brushing off an apron, or fixing their hair.

The maids and kitchen staff lined up in the lobby at brisk attention while the agent and his men, Mr. Bradley, Mrs. Mc-Govern, Mr. Ivanoff, and Mr. Brennan all went outside.

"Thomas!" Mr. Bradley waved at him. "Come with me, just in case we need your help."

"Me, sir?" His voice squeaked.

"Hurry up."

Cassidy caught his elbow as he headed for the door. "Straighten your hair, Thomas, and put your cap on." She wiggled his tie tighter around his neck. "Stay still." She gave him a quick smile. "Now go."

He wiped down his apron just to be safe. Straightening his shoulders, he headed out the door and onto the platform.

The train had puffed to a stop, and several men checked around the platform and train.

Thomas watched all the other staff. Ramrod straight. Shoulders back. Everyone waited in anticipation.

A door finally opened and people began to disembark. Several more men looked around the platform and went into the hotel. When they came back out, one of the men went straight to a car in the back, one that looked just a bit spiffier than the others. He opened the door and a few elegant people emerged.

Flash lamps from several photographers popped and sizzled as Thomas realized they were capturing this moment in history. And he was a part of it.

And then . . . there he was. An older gentleman with piercing eyes, silver hair, and bushy black eyebrows. The President of the United States of America. Standing in front of him.

Mr. Bradley extended a hand. "Mr. President, it's an honor to have you here in Curry, Alaska. I'm Alexander Bradley, the manager of the hotel."

"Why, yes, Mr. Bradley. How good to meet you. And who is this tall young man?"

The President was smiling at him. Mr. Bradley nudged him with an elbow. Thomas wasn't sure what to do, so he stuck out his hand. "I'm Thomas Smith, sir."

A flash lamp went off near his face and he had to close his eyes against the brilliance. When he opened his eyes, the party had moved down the platform.

He couldn't help but smile. What a gift Mr. Bradley had given him. He'd have this story to tell for the rest of his life. He, Thomas Smith, orphan—had just met the President and shaken his hand.

•••••

The dining room was decked out in its finest. A smile split Cassidy's lips. How exciting to be part of something so important as feeding the President and First Lady. She did a final check over all the serving dishes to ensure nothing had spilt on any of the edges. They were ready.

George, the head waiter, approached her, his white embroidered towel hanging over his left arm, the crispness of his black jacket in stark contrast. "I would like to go over the details of the menu with you."

"Of course." Cassidy pointed to a dish. "We will start with the grapefruit cocktail, olives, salted peanuts, and fresh salmonberries with cream. Then we will move to the cream of tomato. It will come out in the white-and-gold soup tureen." She watched for his nod of approval. "The next course will be boiled king salmon à la Seward, crab in shell, and the tasting spoon of smoked salmon. Following that, roast turkey with sage dressing, sweet potatoes, garden peas, and then a light salad." She went round to the other side to gather serving dishes and spoons. "Dessert will be baked Alaska and will be followed by Roquefort cheese and crackers and demitasse."

"Wonderful. Thank you, Miss Ivanoff." George turned and walked toward the other black-and-white-suited waiters.

She checked her watch. Their guests would arrive at any moment. Scurrying back into the kitchen, she checked on the sponge cakes for the base of their dessert. Everything was as it should be. As she glanced around, she realized the noise level was much lower than normal. Everyone moved quickly and without a word. Spoons scraped on bowls, an occasional pot clanged, but the importance of their guests seemed to have glued everyone's lips shut. The thought made her want to giggle, but she thought better of it. Best not to provoke Mrs. Johnson yet again.

Mrs. Johnson marched through the kitchen, arms behind her back. She glanced at Cassidy. "I take it we are ready?"

"Yes, ma'am."

No sooner were the words out of her mouth than the booming voice of Mr. Bradley welcomed their guests into the dining room.

Time moved at a doubled pace after that. Each serving platter had to be perfect, the food the exact temperature, and each course precisely timed. When the roast turkey went out of the kitchen, Cassidy was already hard at work on the meringue for the baked Alaska.

Exhausted after beating the shiny peaks, she wiped her brow before assembling the individual desserts.

Mrs. Johnson headed her way. "Seems I have my hands free for a few moments. Let me help with that."

"That would be lovely. Thank you." Cassidy scurried to the icebox for the pre-molded rounds of ice cream. They worked together as if one were the right hand and the other the left. Cassidy had observed Mrs. Johnson for so long now, she could almost guess what she would do next. The baked Alaska took shape as they stacked ice cream on the cakes, and then smothered them in meringue. With this done, the trays went into the hot oven to bake the meringue around the luscious dessert.

While Mrs. Johnson crossed the room to instruct one of the maids, Cassidy carefully watched the clock. The meringue would brown in less than four minutes at the high temperature and she wanted to make certain it didn't burn. The time flew by.

"Beautiful!" Mrs. Johnson said as Cassidy pulled the tray from the oven. "A dessert fitting of the President, don't you agree?"

"Most assuredly, yes!" Cassidy grinned and began plating the desserts onto their serving platters.

"Wow." Thomas walked over to the table where the mountains of baked Alaska sat. "What is it?" A stream of waiters entered and snatched up the trays.

Cassidy wasn't certain why Thomas was in the kitchen and could only hope that Mrs. Johnson wouldn't become riled. But to her surprise the head cook handed him a small bowl. "Baked Alaska. Try it." So the woman had a soft spot for the young man after all, didn't she? "It's cake and ice cream baked with a meringue around it."

His eyes grew wide. "I can eat this?"

"You sure can. But be quick about it, you'll be needed to help clear the tables." Mrs. Johnson pulled the last tray from the oven. "And the rest of you may have one as well. You've all earned it."

The kitchen staff all flocked to the table where Mrs. Johnson handed out dessert. It didn't take long for everyone to have a mouthful of the creamy dish.

Cassidy gave Thomas a nudge. "What do you think?"

"It's . . . amazing. You're amazing . . . I mean . . . well, you made this, right?"

She laughed. "I did."

He nodded. "You did a real good job." He continued to look at her as if he might say something else.

Mr. Bradley rushed in, and plates and spoons clattered to the table as everyone stood at attention. "Mrs. Johnson, I'd like you and Miss Ivanoff to accompany me into the dining room."

"Yes, sir." At least the older woman had the clarity of mind to respond. "Is something wrong?"

Cassidy blinked and looked around the room. All eyes were on her.

Mr. Bradley just motioned to them. "Come on, hurry."

"Let's go, dear." Mrs. Johnson grabbed her arm and Cassidy forced herself to swallow the ice cream in her mouth. She looked down at her apron and quickly swiped her mouth with her hand. It wouldn't do to meet the President with food on her lips.

Quiet conversation filled the room as all the dinner guests smiled and ate and drank from little coffee cups. In the center of it all sat a distinguished man and smiling lady.

Mr. Bradley held out an arm. "Mr. President, might I introduce to you our head chef, Margaret Johnson, and her assistant, Cassidy Ivanoff."

The gentleman stood and bowed to them. Goodness, no one had ever bowed to Cassidy before. Was this how the well-to-do greeted one another?

"I can't tell you what a privilege it is to meet you ladies. This meal has been one of the finest I've ever had, and I asked your manager here to allow me to say it to you in person."

"Why . . . thank you, Mr. President." Mrs. Johnson curtsied.

Cassidy just stood there. She didn't even know how to curtsy. Was she supposed to? She bent her knees a little and nodded.

The President came closer and smiled at her. "I take it your father is the knowledgeable guide who is to take us all on a hike later this evening."

"Yes, sir. Thank you, sir. It should be a beautiful night for it. There are still hours of daylight left."

"Is there anything in particular that the delegation and I shouldn't miss?"

"The fireweed, sir." Cassidy cleared her throat. "It's my favorite and is spectacular up the ridge."

Several of the women murmured to one another.

Mrs. Harding came a little closer and put her hand on her husband's arm. "Did I hear that we would have fireweed honey in the morning at breakfast?"

"Yes, ma'am. You did." Mrs. Johnson patted Cassidy's shoulder. "In fact, it's harvested right here by our own Miss Ivanoff."

"How lovely. I can't wait to try it." The First Lady put a hand to her waist. "But I'm in need of a strenuous walk after that feast. Or I won't be able to eat for days."

The President moved forward again. "Thank you, ladies, for your time. The meal was delicious."

As the prestigious couple turned and walked toward other guests, Cassidy and Mrs. Johnson both exhaled at the same time. It elicited an "almost" chuckle out of Mrs. Johnson. "That wasn't so bad now, was it?"

Cassidy shook her head. But she didn't think she'd ever forget how nervous she felt. Mrs. Johnson didn't look completely unmoved by the experience. The woman had a way about her that always seemed indifferent and reserved, but Cassidy could see by the gleam in the older woman's eyes that she was pleased.

*Crash!*

The sound of broken crystal and china hitting the floor filled the room. Cassidy closed her eyes, afraid to look, but knew she must. Peeking through one open eyelid, she looked toward the noise. Sure enough. Thomas was sprawled on the floor, an empty tray beside him. An unbroken china cup still rattled as it rocked on the floor. Looking back to Mrs. Johnson, Cassidy could see the expression of mortification on the older woman's face. Thomas was sure to be fired.

Cassidy raced over to his side, hoping to diffuse the situation before Mr. Bradley or Mrs. Johnson had a chance to blow up at the poor kid. Photographers readied their flash lamps.

But Mrs. Florence Harding beat her to him. The First Lady reached down a hand and helped Thomas up. "I'm so sorry, young man. I stepped directly into your path, didn't I?"

"No . . . no . . . no . . . ma'am. Not at all." His head shook back and forth at a rapid pace and cast a glance in the direction of the manager. He straightened his shoulders. "I'm sorry, ma'am. I was at fault."

"Nonsense. And don't try to coddle me just because I'm the First Lady. I take full responsibility." The woman was a genius. She had the whole room hanging on every word. Even Mr. Bradley was smiling, and no one would dare contradict her, even though they all knew it hadn't been her fault.

She reached a hand up and laid it on Thomas's shoulder. "You know, it reminds me of when I ran the *Marion Star* years ago. I had all those newsboys trained to move so quick"—she snapped her fingers—"that I often got in the way and tripped them up when they'd pick up their papers because I wasn't moving fast enough. Again, please accept my apology." The woman beamed a smile at Thomas while a photographer took another shot.

"You're . . . you're . . ." Thomas couldn't seem to stop stuttering, but Mrs. Harding only smiled and gave him another pat on the shoulder.

"You are a very capable young man, and if I had a son, I would want him to be just like you." After one more pat she elegantly walked away.

If Cassidy had been on regular speaking terms with Mrs.

Harding, she would've thanked her profusely later and then asked to learn her skills. The woman could smooth over a disturbance like no one Cassidy had ever seen.

It must take a lot of practice being a politician's wife.

The thing that mattered right now? Thomas was out of trouble. At least for the next few minutes.

9

Allan walked through the crowd checking to make sure everyone who needed a walking stick had one. Some of the women's footwear was questionable, but he'd already discovered with one woman's scathing glance that it wasn't a topic up for discussion if he wanted to live to see another day.

Biting his tongue, he handed out walking sticks instead.

John was up at the front being quizzed by the President. Hopefully he was having more luck than Allan had with the women. While it was wonderful their country's leader showed such an interest in this territory, Allan almost wished that this land could remain more of a secret. He'd only been here a week and he wanted to stay forever. No wonder his father loved this place.

Thoughts of his father brought his gaze back to John. For years, he'd blamed the man for his father's death. But the truth wasn't so easily found. Their conversations from the train—before they knew who the other was—haunted him day and night. His boss was consistent. Understanding. Even trustworthy. And the more he learned from John, the more he questioned the details from Frank. And the more he thought about the stories Frank told, the more he realized they didn't pan out. There were discrepancies. All over the place. Not just in the McKinley expedition.

His father once told him that gut instincts were good to heed. He thought of it as divine guidance—the Holy Ghost. Allan never gave it much credence. In fact, he thought his own gut instincts weren't all that accurate. It often seemed his feelings about people were complicated by the events that surrounded them. Father would have said to judge the fruit of the individual—the overall outcome of the person's life and treatment of others. Allan, however, tended to jump to conclusions. Momentary lapses of judgment became reasons to distrust and a single poor choice marked a man as incompetent.

One thing had always been clear—Frank never loved the outdoors like the Brennan men. Granted, he was very business-minded and successful, but he'd rather stay in his office and have meetings than go exploring himself. That in and of itself didn't make the man unworthy of trust, but Allan had to admit there were times when Frank grated on him. Frank was quick with a harsh admonishment for underlings. Allan had seen him fire a man for nothing more than misplacing an invoice. And if he were honest with himself, Allan knew he'd just as soon not work with Frank at all.

But how could Allan turn his back on his father's lifelong friend? Didn't he owe him . . . something?

With Frank and the rest of his family back in Seattle, Allan found it easy to focus on Alaska. He'd written to let them know that he'd arrived safely and what he was doing. His mother would be more than proud that he was following his father's footsteps. What he left unmentioned was his growing confusion over John Ivanoff and the accident that had claimed his father's life. He'd come here hoping for answers, but it seemed he'd only managed to unearth more questions.

"Allan" —John's voice broke through his reverie—"I believe we are ready."

He glanced up at the salt-and-pepper-haired man. "Yes, sir, we are."

John led the way down a path that he and Allan had trampled down in the days prior. At this time of year the tundra grass was thigh-high, so to make it easier for the guests, they'd widened the path from a one-person walkway to about a four-person width. John had also been quite observant to remove any obstacles from the path. Could a man so conscientious as that have been less so when dealing with a climbing expedition? One that pivoted on life and death in the best of circumstances? Of course that had been years ago. Allan had heard that John was forty-five years old, so that would have made him just thirty-nine when he'd led the expedition in 1917. A man's character was surely set into place by that age, so it seemed unlikely he would have changed all that much. Not only that, but Allan had heard others talk about John. People who'd known him for many years. They all thought highly of him.

"Oh my. Just look at the flowers!" Mrs. Harding exclaimed.

Her statement started the ladies' comments on the brilliant colors, while the men asked about the area's wild animals. Their first planned stopping point was about a third of a mile down the path, but they'd gained about five hundred feet in elevation and already some of the ladies were struggling.

Looking down on a brilliant field of wild flowers, John stopped to explain which ones were which. Allan couldn't help smiling. John understood the abilities and inabilities of his clients. He was accommodating them without bringing it to their attention.

One of the ladies came forward with a flower. "What is this lovely blue one?"

"This is arctic lupine, one of my favorites to look at, but be careful, lupine is extremely poisonous." He took a small sketchbook out of his pocket. "Now, if you compare it to this one"—he pointed to a page—"this is the Nootka lupine, and it is my favorite of the lupine. I've seen them in the Chugach Mountains south of here and in the Aleutian Islands. Fields and fields of them. Their shape is fuller and almost like a Christmas tree, wouldn't you say?"

"Oh, yes. Beautiful." The lady set the flower in a basket she carried over her arm and went to inspect others.

John pointed to another group of flowers. "See the yellow ones in this grouping? Those are Alaska poppies. And those purple ones are purple mountain saxifrage."

Mrs. Harding carried two similar dark pink flowers. "Mr. Ivanoff, what can you tell me about these two? I thought they were the same, but now I don't believe so."

He smiled at the First Lady.

Allan studied the flowers. They indeed looked awfully similar, so he moved closer to listen.

His boss lifted the first one. "This one is called Eskimo potato."

The group around him laughed. One of the men hollered out, "Now, why would they call a pink flower a potato?"

"That's a good question. The natives have been known to eat the root of this plant for centuries—thus the potato name." John picked up the other flower. "While this one is called a wild sweet pea. If you look at the leaves of both, see how much they look alike? But the sweet pea has larger flowers and the roots are thought to be poisonous on this one." John handed them both back to the President's wife. "Legend says that many lives have been lost confusing the two. That was very astute of you to see the difference, Mrs. Harding."

"Are you an Eskimo?" One of the men interjected. He fixed John with an intense gaze.

"I'm part Athabaskan. That's one of the native peoples in this part of Alaska. There are many groups—tribes, if you would.

Those normally thought of as Eskimo are actually Inuit, Inupiat, and Yuit."

One woman stepped closer. "Do they really live in igloos—those houses made of ice?"

John smiled. "An igloo isn't just a house of ice. It can reference any house. But yes, there are those who out of necessity build houses of ice blocks. I've made similar shelters myself."

This created a sensation of murmurs amongst the tourists, while also stirring additional questions.

"Is it true that Eskimos don't feel the cold?" This question came from the same man who'd asked if John was an Eskimo. He eyed John as if he were some kind of strange specimen just discovered.

"People are people no matter the color of their skin or origin of their birth, and they acclimate the same," John replied. His expression was congenial and his tone suggested endless patience. "We who are native to Alaska get cold just like everyone else. It might be just at a considerably different temperature than you because of the climate we live in."

Mrs. Harding seemed to take pity on their guide. "I'd really like to see some fireweed now—if we may."

"Hear, hear," voiced the President.

"Then let's continue on." John smiled. "There's a beautiful view of it ahead."

Allan brought up the rear and watched a few of the women bobble in their crazy shoes, but said nothing. He knew the next stop would be a grand place to view the fireweed, and that is where they planned to turn around and head back. The President looked weary.

Hadn't he heard in the news that they'd been on a countrywide trip by train before they headed to Alaska? No wonder the man was tired.

As they reached the next point, *oohs* and *aahs* were heard throughout the group. Not only were the mountains of the Alaska Range visible over the ridgeline across the river, but an unending field of vibrant pink fireweed could be seen on the other side of the ridge where they stood.

John spoke in a loud voice. "As you can see, the flowers open from the bottom of the plant and over time will bloom all the way to the top. The legend of the fireweed is that when all of the blooms reach the top, winter will be on its way in six weeks. And I can tell you that for all of my life, the fireweed has been correct in its prediction." The group laughed.

The President gathered his entourage closer with a wave of his arms. "I've asked John to tell us a little more about Curry and his Athabaskan heritage while we take a rest."

The ladies sat on many low-lying rocks, while the men situated themselves on the ground.

Allan passed around the water canteens and then set his walking stick in front of him and rested both arms on it.

The history of the native people in this vast land was fascinating, but John only shared about them for a couple of minutes. He moved quickly into talk of Denali—now Mount McKinley—and how the new national park could change the face of Alaska and its tourism. From there, he praised the Alaska Railroad. "As you will see tomorrow, the railroad is finished. From Seward to Fairbanks, this land is now opened up for the world to see God's handiwork. It's a land rich in wild game, fish, and even gold." He pointed to the Curry Hotel below them. "And our government had the ingenuity to build at this incredible location, right here on the river and on the railroad, in the middle of the rail line, so that we could share this with the world. Although, I don't know about you, but I'm glad they changed the name from Deadhorse to Curry."

Chuckles resounded from the group.

"And I'm sure it doesn't take much of an imagination to know where the first name came from."

After some more chatter and questions, a man next to the President raised his hand. "I don't know about the rest of you, but I'd like to climb a little higher to get a better view of that twenty-thousand-footer."

Others nodded and murmured agreement.

"Mr. President, wouldn't it be a good idea to build a shelter people could hike to so they could see this spectacular view?"

"Indeed it would." He sat on a boulder.

John moved forward. "Whoever would like to climb a little higher is welcome to join us, but make sure you have sturdy shoes. There's not a direct path."

A few men stayed with a number of the ladies while the President and the rest of the group followed John up the side of the steep hill. Allan brought up the rear, assisting where he could.

"Aahhhh!" One of the younger men cried out and fell to the ground. He rolled to a sitting position and took hold of his ankle. "I stepped in a hole. I think I might have broken my ankle."

John was at his side almost immediately and assessed the injury. He ran his hands along the man's ankle. Allan noted the man was wearing shoes rather than the recommended boots. Had he the proper footgear, he probably wouldn't be in this kind of trouble now.

"I'm no doctor, but I'd say it's a sprain." John sighed. "However, we need to get you down the path quickly before the swelling gets too bad and we can't get that shoe off." He looked to Allan and waved him closer, speaking in a quieter tone. "I need you to finish the walk and get everyone back safely."

Allan nodded.

"I'll need another man to help me get Mr. . . . ."

"Brown." The injured man cringed as John lifted him to stand on his good foot.

"To help me get Mr. Brown down to the hotel."

An older but fit gentleman raised his hand. "I'll be glad to help."

Allan moved forward to the President as they watched John and the other man work their way back down the path. It all happened so fast.

"Mr. Brennan, lead on."

He nodded and moved forward, his thoughts all over the place. Why didn't John just ask *him* to take the injured man down? Allan was, after all, the junior man. He couldn't lead an expedition, much less one of this magnitude. With the President, for goodness' sake!

Several minutes passed in silence as they trudged up the hill. What struck him the most was John's servant attitude. It didn't make a difference to the man about whether it was the President or some man of no rank whatsoever. He went to him immediately to take care of him. Now, what did that truly say about this man that Allan called boss?

"Tell me more about this great mountain and Mr. Ivanoff." The President interrupted his thoughts.

Allan turned to see the President and First Lady smiling expectantly. Looking out at what he could see of the top of Mount McKinley, Allan stopped. "I'm afraid I must admit that I'm merely an apprentice. John is the expert, and I'm an inadequate replacement for him."

"But he must believe in you and trust you if he's asked you to carry on with us."

Allan considered all that he knew. "Mount McKinley is called Denali or The Great One by the native people here. That's the original name. It's over twenty thousand feet high and is highly glaciated granite."

The President laid a hand on Allan's shoulder as he took another big step and turned. "It's quite the view. Have you ever climbed it?"

"No. John has, but you'd have to speak to him." Allan hoped his tone didn't sound too dismissive.

"I can only imagine that would be an arduous journey and would take quite a man to accomplish such a feat."

"Yes. My father climbed it, and he was quite a man. He made the trip with John." Allan hadn't meant to mention his father and immediately regretted it.

"He must have told you wondrous stories."

"I'm sure he would have, but he died up there." Allan looked again at the mountain. "The stories I've heard have all come from other sources." He looked back at the President. "If you get the chance, you should talk to the park's superintendent, Harry Karstens. He was one of the very first to summit the mountain."

The older man frowned. "I am sorry about your father. What happened, if you don't mind my asking?"

Allan shook his head. "I don't mind, but I have no answers. My father's business partner was also along on the trip and he told me a terrible storm came up just after they reached the summit. My father was lost in the storm. They never found him."

"That must have been very hard for you. I'm sure it was hard on John and your father's partner as well. John doesn't strike me as the kind of man who would easily leave a comrade behind."

Allan didn't know what to say. The President's words seemed to pierce his heart. No. John didn't seem like the kind of man to leave someone behind.

"Well"—President Harding exhaled loudly—"I believe it's

about time to head back to the hotel. Tomorrow will be a busy day and I'd like to check on Mr. Brown."

Allan stood for several moments thinking about the President's words.

Maybe it was time he put aside the anger that had been born out of Frank's rage and allow that perhaps John was truly the good man he appeared to be. The kind of man who wouldn't have left his father on the mountain had there been any other choice. He'd already told Cassidy that he wasn't angry. But had he meant it? Or had he just longed for her friendship? He hated how his emotions seemed to rock back and forth like a ship at high seas. What kind of man was he?

The kind to sacrifice himself to rescue people from a disaster? The kind to put one injured man's needs ahead of his own desires?

Those were things that described John. But not Allan. The thought struck him hard. He wanted to be that kind of man. The kind of man who was like his . . . father.

And his father had believed and trusted in John.

It was time he believed and trusted in John as well.

•••••

Even with all the profits of The Irving/Brennan Company, the money was running out. And Frank didn't like that one bit. He needed more of it—not less. Especially to keep funding his new investments that weren't doing so well right now. But they would.

They had to.

He'd always been brilliant at the business side of things. So why were his choices and his investments failing? He didn't like feeling . . . desperate.

He swirled the last bit of golden bourbon in his glass, then lifted it to his lips and gulped. Prohibition didn't help matters any. He had to pay exorbitant prices to get the good stuff. Pity he couldn't get in on that scheme. There were millions to be made in bootlegging, but so far his queries into such matters had been met only with suspicion.

Walking over to the window, he cursed Henry Brennan.

For decades they'd been friends. Even though Henry was always the good one, the friendly one, the popular one—he'd never excluded Frank and his melancholy, pessimistic ways. But then they went into business together. All of Henry's ideas ended up successful. It got to the point where Frank's ideas were barely heard—except by Henry. When the company became even more successful, the board always looked to Henry, not Frank—as if the outdoorsman was the brains, even though he was *never* in the office.

Still, Frank stuck it out. He showed up day after day and became quite a savvy businessman. Before long, he learned how to skim profits off the top, and money became the ultimate prize.

Who cared that Henry had a wonderful marriage, the idyllic family life, and everyone thought he was the driving force behind the company? That all would change. With enough money, Frank figured he could buy his position of prestige.

Then Frank's wife left him, with a contemptuous letter spewing her hatred toward him, his lack of love for anyone or anything but money, and his fault at not being able to give them children.

The anger and hurt of that time pushed him over the edge— beyond a line he'd thought of crossing, but never thought possible.

So he'd plotted and planned and found a way to rid himself of Henry. If he couldn't have the idyllic life, then neither should his partner. Besides, Frank needed the money.

The plan worked, but not completely. Somehow he'd missed the loophole that Henry could write an addendum to his will and add that Allan would inherit half of his father's share. But three-quarters of the company wasn't enough for Frank.

It was time for something more drastic. The Brennan family was nothing but a drain on *his* company. The stupid son-in-law worked for him, Allan took his quarter share, and who knows what else he'd lost to them over the years.

No more.

There had to be a way to get rid of Allan. After that, it would be easy enough to get rid of Henry's son-in-law and any other Brennan connection.

Frank walked back to his desk and sat down. Drumming his fingers on the mahogany top, he thought of a different plan. Murder wasn't necessarily needed. What if . . . a family member was found to be the one embezzling? And they were all in cahoots?

He smacked the desk with the palm of his hand and smiled. Yes. That would work. He could start with blaming Henry's son-in-law, Louis. And then through the investigation, he could frame them all for scheming against him—stating they were unhappy that Frank received so much of the company when Henry died. There were already two sets of books, and it would be easy enough to create a third that would indict Louis.

Now it would all play into Frank's hand. He would prove that Louis had been stealing profits to line his own pockets. It was their fault. They weren't happy with the will, so the sad little Brennan family had cheated poor Frank all these years.

Ah yes. Poor Frank.

To avoid a scandal that would bring shame upon his name, Allan would agree to sign over the whole company to Frank. He would have no other choice. Frank would be sympathetic but firm. Once Frank pointed out that if charged, Louis would go to prison for a very long time, Allan would agree to most anything. He wouldn't want to see his sister and her children left destitute and shamed.

Frank steepled his fingers together and leaned back in his chair. He could rescue his teetering investments and make even more money.

He would have it all, and this time nothing would go wrong.

C assidy breathed in the crisp morning air. The Curry Hotel
sat in the valley created by the Susitna River between two
small ridge lines outside of the Alaska Range. The ridge across
the river and to the west was about twenty-five hundred feet,
and the ridge behind the hotel was somewhere around three
thousand feet. She loved the safe and sheltered way it made
her feel, encircled by these crests and hills. As if surrounded
by family. It was . . . cozy.

But the thing she didn't like was the obstruction of the view
of the full Alaska Range. If she wanted to see it, she had to
climb. Most mornings she had neither the time nor the energy.
But today had been different. She'd been wide awake at 4:00
a.m. and couldn't do a thing about it.

So she donned long pants and boots and headed up the steep-
est trail on Deadhorse Hill with her satchel and rifle slung over
her back. It was the harder way to go, but it was a good deal
shorter. And today, she wanted to get there as soon as possible.
The summer daylight was nice this early in the morning, but
she knew it would end up being a scorcher later, when she'd
be working in the kitchen.

The events of the past couple weeks flew through her mind.
It wasn't every day they dedicated a national park and posed

for pictures in the paper, or had a visit from the President. On the fifteenth of July, after the President and all his people left, life went on at the Curry. Even though they were all completely worn out, they still had plenty of guests to take care of—the train didn't stop running just because the President came to Alaska. But oh, what fun they'd had listening to Mr. Bradley read the telegrams from his friends in Nenana.

Apparently, the President had missed the golden spike the first time he swung, and then he decided to just tap it in, since he had to hammer in the iron one that would stay in its place. But even this close to the actual location, the stories had already been changed and rearranged to fit the storyteller. And the heat had been so bad that day that several people passed out. Of course, the people of Nenana heard through the grapevine that many of the visitors had worn extra layers of undergarments since an "Alaska expert" had told them how cold it would be.

Cassidy shook her head. People's fascination with the Alaska Territory was growing, and so, she assumed, would the stories. She was thankful for the press and the advertising—she really was. Alaska would develop and be known. But she already missed the quietness and solitude of the way it had been.

Before so many new people came to work at the Curry, there'd been much more solitude. Yet she'd never felt lonely. The difference now was . . . what? She'd tried to make friends among the staff, and although everyone treated her well and seemed to like and respect her, there weren't *real* friends to be had. Not friends she could discuss anything of depth with. They were all caught up in the shallow frivolities of the day.

Except maybe . . . Allan. They were friends now. She'd noticed that he took time to find her and speak with her at least a few minutes each day. He was very nice . . . but . . .

She shook her head. She liked Allan a bit too much, perhaps.

Still found herself looking for him and thinking about him. Was that normal?

Best to get her thoughts off the intriguing Mr. Allan Brennan. But she did long for a true friend. Someone to share her thoughts and dreams with. Someone to discuss faith and questions she had in her study of God's Word.

What an odd feeling to be constantly surrounded by people in the hustle and bustle of life and yet feel so very alone.

As she reached the top of the ridge, she made her way to her favorite rock. She plopped down and put the rifle beside her. She hugged the satchel close, not bothering to take it from her shoulder, and looked out at the mountains she knew so well. What would the future hold for her? Now that the railroad was done, the national park was in place, and people were coming. Even though the Curry was lavish and beautiful with amazing amenities, the rest of Alaska was still harsh and wild. It's not like she'd have the chance to meet a lot of men her age. At least not men who would meet her criteria. She wanted a good man like her father. A God-fearing man who paid more than lip service to his faith. Sometimes it seemed like those men didn't exist—that her father was the last of them. Pulling her knees to her chest, she wondered about the plans God had for her. Was it just to be a cook at the Curry Hotel?

Or would she get to have a family of her own one day?

Cassidy laughed out loud. That wasn't exactly modern-girl thinking. Most women her age were caught up in rights for women, since they could now vote, keeping up with the men, changing their hairstyles and their clothes to rebel against the labels of the fragile female. And heavens, the new young maids were always talking about liquor, cigarettes, and things between men and women they shouldn't know about.

Getting a job at the Curry had been educational to say the

least. Her sheltered little world quickly changed as everyone sought to educate her in the times. But after the shock wore off, she realized these things had been happening since the beginning of time. She was perfectly fine with keeping her dress hems at a modest length and didn't need to learn all the new lingo of the day. Nor did she care to try liquor or cigarettes, much less even speak of girls who wanted to be known as flappers.

So where did she fit? There weren't any cities around. And she certainly couldn't leave Alaska or her father to travel to the over-crowded and modern cities of the States—this was her home.

Pulling her Bible out of the satchel, Cassidy opened it to the book of Daniel. She'd been studying it with her dad for many months now—trying to decipher all the difficult passages in the later chapters. But her favorites were still the stories in the first six chapters.

Starting at the beginning, she read through chapter three without pause. As she looked up to the sky, she wondered if she'd be strong enough to make the same choices as Daniel and his friends, Shadrach, Meshach, and Abednego. Would she stand firm should the test arise?

A rustling sound from somewhere behind her made Cassidy reach for her rifle.

"Cassidy? Hello?"

The male voice jolted her from her spot. No one had ever disturbed her up here.

Thomas's head came over the ridge and she breathed a sigh of relief. "Thomas, I'm so glad it's you." She set the rifle back at her side.

He smiled at her and leaned over to catch his breath. "That's a hike up here. How often do you do it?"

"Now, you're not going to give my secret away, are you?" She placed her hands on her hips.

"Nah, I just saw you climbing up here when I was down at the creek, so I thought I'd follow you." He stood up straight. "Make sure you're all right and all."

She worked to keep the smile to herself. "I'm perfectly fine. Thank you."

"Oh, good." He sat on the grass. "Whatcha reading?"

"The Bible."

"Oh."

"Have you read the Bible?"

"Sure, Miss Cassidy. The orphanage was run by missionaries and we had to read the Bible. If you didn't read it, the preacher would smack you over the head with it. He swore he'd get God's Word into us one way or the other." He smiled at his joke.

She couldn't help it. The picture his words conjured up in her mind made her laugh. She struggled to gain her composure. "That's not very nice. I'm so sorry that man hit you with the Good Book."

"Well, it packed a wallop to be sure, and I guess it motivated us to read our assigned verses." Thomas smiled. "Hey, at least I got you to laugh."

"That you did, Thomas." She shook her head and opened her Bible back up to Daniel. "Did you have a favorite book in the Bible?"

Thomas shook his head. "No, I guess I liked the New Testament better than the Old. The Old Testament made God sound mean and overbearing. Like the preacher."

"Not all of the Old Testament is that way." Cassidy scooted over a bit and patted the rock. "Why don't you join me and I'll tell you what I've been reading. It's in the Old Testament and it's really quite amazing."

"Sure, why not?" He jumped up and made a beeline for the place beside her.

"I've been reading in the book of Daniel. Do you remember any of the stories about him?"

"He was the one in the lion's den, right?" When Cassidy nodded, Thomas took on a look of pride. "I guess that's all I know about him."

"Well, there's so much more. And by the time we get to the story of the lions' den, Daniel was an old man. But he was a very young man when the book begins. A little younger than you, in fact."

"Really?"

"Yes. And he was very handsome and smart. It even says, 'well favoured, and skillful in all wisdom,' but the problem was he was taken from his family—kidnapped—to a foreign land in order to serve a pagan king who didn't believe in the God of all creation." Cassidy realized maybe she needed to ask a really important question. "Do you believe in God, Thomas?"

"Of course I do."

"And you believe in Jesus?"

"Why, sure, He's God's son. He died on the cross for us. And that's why we have Easter."

"That's right." At least he had some basics. "Well, here he is—Daniel with three of his friends—all taken from their homes and forced to live in this foreign land. You see, they were taken because they were 'the best,' and the king wanted to collect them, kind of like trophies. Good-looking, wise young men. Anyway, in this land, they were to be trained for three years and would eat and drink the king's meat and wine. This wasn't slave food—this was the good stuff. But guess what Daniel did?"

"What?"

"It says that he chose not to 'defile himself' with the king's food—he wouldn't take it! This made the man in charge of them upset because it was his job to make these good-looking young men look even better and get even smarter. So Daniel asked the man—his name was Melzar—to allow them only to eat pulse and water for ten days and then to compare them to the rest so that he could prove to him they weren't going to starve or look worse. But they didn't want to disobey God."

"What is pulse?"

"Seeds and vegetables."

"That's not much to keep them going, is it?"

Cassidy thought about that for a moment. "I guess I never really thought about it that way, but you're right. Melzar agreed to do as Daniel asked and when the ten days were up, guess what happened?"

Thomas was intently focused on the story. "What?"

"Verse fifteen says, 'And at the end of ten days their countenances appeared fairer and fatter in flesh than all the children which did eat the portion of the king's meat.' So Daniel and his three friends looked better than all the others, and then verse twenty tells us that at the end of the three years of their training and supposed great fattening up from the king's good food, 'the king found them ten times better than all the magicians and astrologers that were in all his realm.' So they were smarter and wiser too, and they were only probably around eighteen or nineteen years old at this point."

"Huh." Thomas frowned. "How'd they do it?"

"*They* didn't do it. God did. And they simply obeyed."

"You like that story?" His brow crinkled even more.

"I do."

"Why?"

That was a question she'd never been asked. "Well, I guess because it makes me want to be like Daniel."

"You want to be kidnapped and taken away?"

"No, but it makes me wonder how I would fare if something

like that happened to me. My life has been easy, full of love and fun. I've never had any hard challenges come my way, and I want to be willing to stand firm when they do." Saying it out loud made her thoughts more real. Her life had been just about perfect. And definitely easy. Here, she'd been wallowing in thoughts of loneliness and longing for things the Good Lord hadn't blessed her with yet. It was shameful how selfish she'd been.

"Is that why you're so positive all the time?"

Another question that nudged her to think. Was it? Was it easy to be positive and encouraging and happy when things were good because that's pretty much all she'd known? "I don't really know, Thomas. I like to be an encourager, yes, but I want to be more than that."

"I think you're pretty perfect just the way you are, Cassidy."

"Oh, but I'm not." The more she examined her heart, the more she wanted to learn. A sudden and new craving for the Word overwhelmed her. "Thank you, Thomas. For helping me to see so clearly today."

"I didn't do nothing." A blush crept up his cheeks.

"Yes, you did." Cassidy stood up and straightened her shoulders. "No matter what, I want to dare to be a Daniel. And I don't think I've been doing a very good job. But that's going to change."

$$\bullet\bullet\bullet\bullet\bullet$$

The two days since Thomas had talked to Cassidy passed way too fast. And there hadn't been much chance to speak with her since. But he'd thought about her. A lot.

And what she'd said. About Daniel. Thomas couldn't get those thoughts out of his mind. He had a lot of questions. More than anything, he longed to make something of himself. Not always be labeled as an orphan. But how?

Could Cassidy's Bible have more answers in it? He never knew there was a story of a boy his age doing anything significant. Now he wanted to learn more.

He wanted to be a man. And an honorable one. One people respected. And one who didn't drop things or stumble over things. Daniel had been well respected by the king himself when he was only eighteen. Could Thomas learn that much in a year?

As he carried another tub of scraps out to the feed shed, Thomas spotted Mr. Ivanoff. He wanted to be like Cassidy's father. The older man knew so much about everything and loved to teach other people.

And boy was he patient. Every day Thomas had worked for him, Mr. Ivanoff never lost his patience—even when Thomas messed up. Unlike Mrs. Johnson, who made him feel like he was in the army every time she barked her commands or scolded him for another mistake.

He watched Mr. Ivanoff walk down to the roundhouse where they did maintenance on the railroad engines. Maybe he could catch him later today and ask him for help.

If anyone could teach him about how to be a man, it'd be John Ivanoff. And maybe he could teach him more about the Bible too.

•••••

Allan stared up at the ceiling for a long time. Sleep was slow in coming and unfortunately that gave him more than enough time to think. He thought about his trip to Alaska and all that he'd hoped to accomplish and realized that very little of it had been done.

He'd found John and had been able to ask about his father's death, but the answers had been less than helpful. He'd found his own love of Alaska and undeniable feelings for one of her daughters. Cassidy Ivanoff was unlike the women he'd known in Seattle. Even his sisters were far more concerned about their appearance or the quality of their furnishings. Many of the women who moved in his family's social circles didn't even know how to cook, much less enjoy it as much as he'd heard Cassidy did.

But always there was a barrier between them.

"I can't very well pursue her unless I resolve my anger with her father and Dad's death," he whispered to himself.

But Allan wasn't even sure that anger still existed. For so long he'd been mad at John and what had happened. Even worse, Allan had been mad at God. He still was. God had given him the very best of fathers and then, like a greedy child—had taken him back. No warning. No concern for the people who were left with the loss. God had even chosen the very poorest of timing. Allan hadn't been able to be there to comfort his mother when she learned of her husband's death.

"It wasn't fair." He shook his head. "You aren't fair. You demand too much."

It was the first time he'd talked to God in a very long time, and for a moment, despite his mix of emotions, Allan felt a connection that had long been absent. It was as he'd felt when he and his father had prayed together. The feeling passed much too quickly, however, and the anger and disappointment returned. Would he ever be able to put this behind him? Would he never find peace again?

# 11

The cloudy skies and drizzly rain reflected Allan's mood. The week since the President came through flew by with more training from John, plans for future expeditions, and preparation for nature walks and fishing trips. His brain felt at times like it would explode with all the information. But what was worse? The misery he felt. He'd asked for John's patience with him after the older man had sought forgiveness. And everything within him wanted to like and respect John. A lot.

Not only John, but his beautiful daughter as well.

A couple of times this past week, he'd spotted her hiking up Deadhorse Hill long before anyone but the night crew were awake, her long dark hair in a simple braid down her back. That familiar pull whenever he was near her tugged at him again. But he had no idea what to do with his feelings. He was not in a good place right now.

All his dreams about Alaska were coming true. He just hadn't expected to meet John. Or to like the man. He wanted to forgive him. He did. But how?

And then there was Cassidy. Loyal, dedicated, fun-loving, encouraging Cassidy. The more he was around her, the more he was drawn to her.

She probably didn't even have a clue the attention she

generated around the hotel. From wealthy guests all the way down to Thomas—the men adored her. And not just her attractive looks. But the way she made everyone feel loved and special. How did she do that? Allan didn't even like himself half the time.

Walking to the front desk, Allan tried to corral his thoughts back to the tasks of the day. Somehow he needed to shake off this gloomy attitude.

"Mr. Brennan, you have a letter." Mrs. McGovern waved it in the air.

"Thank you." Taking the envelope, he saw the return address was from Seattle. He checked his watch. Not enough time to go back to his room, but he could head downstairs to the section gang dining room and find a little privacy.

As he opened the envelope and read the first few lines, he wished he'd saved it for later.

*Allan,*

*Hopefully you know that I think of you as the son I never had. And so I must speak my mind. I am appalled to find out that you are apprenticing for the very man who killed your father. As your father's longtime friend and business partner, I must advise you against any further work with this man. He is not to be trusted. He should never be allowed to work again as a guide. How dare he masquerade as an expert? To the presidential delegation as well! I'm horrified.*

*What does your mother think? Have you told her? I can only imagine the heartache this will bring to her. It's time you gave up this foolishness and returned home. I can't stand by and watch you destroy your relationship with your family by befriending the very man who took it all away. In fact, I think you need to go to the legal authorities and find out if there's a way to press charges against*

*this man. Just the thought of him makes my blood boil.
It should do the same for you.*

> *I await your response,*
> *Frank*

While Allan knew that Frank blamed John and that he cared
for the Brennan family as if they were blood, he also knew that
hatred and anger couldn't be the answer here. Hadn't he just
decided it would be right to forgive John?

But Frank had been family for a long time. What if Allan
had been wrong to trust John? Was he a charlatan? Or was
Frank the one who was lying? Allan hated to admit it, but over
the years—with all Allan had witnessed—he didn't really trust
Frank.

How could he find out who was truly responsible for his
father's death?

• • • • •

The walk from the water tower to the hotel was short. Too
short. John needed more time to think, so he turned around
and started back. The reservations from the wealthy flowed in
on a daily basis, and with them came the requests to be taken
on "real Alaskan adventures"—the men wanted to fish and see
bear, and the women wanted to see the mountains and flowers.
Most of these people had enough money to do whatever they
wanted, but they were choosing to come to Alaska and give up
amenities they were accustomed to so they could lay claim to
conquering this last frontier.

The groups that had come in so far had been a little shocked
at how "primitive" the Alaska Territory was compared to the
city life they knew. No real cities to speak of. Not much devel-
opment. Very few roads; only the railroad connected Fairbanks

to Seward. People living without electricity and running water. Leaning shacks were labeled as hotels or roadhouses. The list could go on and on—all the interesting facts about this land that surprised the tourists.

But how he loved this land. This had been a great dream for him to come and be the expedition guide for the hotel.

Then Allan had arrived. Only God could have orchestrated that one—to bring the very son of the man he'd lost on Denali to his doorstep. And not just to the hotel, but to work for him. John hadn't been the same since. All those emotions roiled each day when he saw Allan.

But it had to stop. Allan might never truly forgive him. And John needed to be all right with that. He wasn't doing his job as well as he should with this weight pressing down on him every day, and in Alaska that could turn deadly. Cassidy worried about him, even though he'd tried to convince her he was fine.

At this point, he was just surviving from day to day. That wasn't good enough.

Allan was eager to learn, even though things were often strained between them, and John couldn't blame the young man for that. But his apprentice needed the Lord. Plain and simple.

John's heart ached for him—not just for the loss of his father, but for Allan's eternity—and he prayed for wisdom, but God seemed to be silent on this one.

As his steps took him past the water tower and to the very edge of Curry, the churning in his thoughts increased and John cried out to the Lord.

*It's too much, Father. This burden. I can't carry it any longer, but I know You can. Please take this from me. Show me what I need to do, because I'm lost in this shadow of grief. Grief for the Brennan family's loss, but also for the loss of my dreams through it. I've admitted to Allan that I take full responsibility, but for all these years, I didn't want to. I didn't want to think that I had failed in any way. Please forgive me, Father.*

John found himself at the river's edge, tears streaming down his face. He hadn't even realized he'd been crying. But a new peace flooded him. And the weight was gone. Why hadn't he given this over to the Lord weeks ago?

A memory came to mind—a pleasant one of the wife he'd lost so many years ago. Eliza had been wise beyond her years. Perhaps that was due to being the child of a preacher or from living on the mission field, but whatever it was, she seemed to have unusual insight for one so young.

John wanted to please Eliza's parents, and when he heard her mother say she'd like to have her walkway rocked, John saw it as the perfect opportunity to win her over. That night while everyone slept, John dug and carried load after load of rock in sacks on his back to the worn dirt paths that constituted the walkways. The sacks rubbed blisters on his back, and the strain on his muscles left him miserable the next day. However, the walkway had its rock and Eliza's mother seemed pleased, although she never said so. At least not to him.

The next day, John saw Eliza watching him as he struggled to tend to his chores. Surely she knew that he'd been responsible for the improvement to the walk. With his shirt off, he also knew she could see the sores on his back, yet she chided him rather than offer praise.

"You bore a burden no one asked you to bear, John Ivanoff, and now yer sufferin' for it."

And here he was doing it again decades later.

"Well, that seems to be the way with me." He glanced heavenward and smiled. "It's all Yours, Lord."

With a new lightness and determination to his step, John

headed back to the hotel. He had excursions to plan and an apprentice to guide. The rest he would leave in God's hands.

The morning passed in a blur of activities. John and Allan sat together at one of the section gang tables in the basement, planning day-trips. Papers and maps were strewn across the length of the eight-foot table.

"Mr. Ivanoff!" Thomas came down the stairs and missed the bottom step but caught himself before he fell. "Here's a telegram for you." He straightened his tray. "I've got to get back to the kitchen, but Mrs. McGovern asked me to bring it to you straightaway."

"Thank you, Thomas." John took the envelope and tried to cover his smile. He glanced at Allan, who also appeared to be struggling to keep a straight face.

"You're welcome, but I have to get right back. Mrs. Johnson will have my hide if I don't see to the trash." With that Thomas darted back up the stairs.

"It's amazing he hasn't broken a leg or an arm, isn't it?"

Allan nodded. "I remember being clumsy as a kid, but I've never seen the likes of it. I'm surprised Mrs. Johnson allowed him to come back to the kitchen."

"Cassidy said she wasn't overly keen on it, but they needed the help. A kitchen that big requires a lot of hands to get things done."

Smiling, Allan gave a shrug. "It can't be all that helpful if you have to redo things because someone makes a mess of them the first time through."

The smile on his face proved to John that the younger man was working through his issues. Perhaps they were both learning to lay their demons to rest.

"So I take it that must be another request?"

John turned the envelope over. "Most likely." He opened it with a sigh. The summer schedule kept getting busier and busier. Eventually, they would be so full that they'd have to turn people away. He'd heard rumors that the railroad already planned to expand the Curry Hotel.

Unfolding the missive, he glanced it over:

```
23 July 1923
Group of twenty experienced riders wish to trek
into new N.P. (stop)Will pay top dollar for
horses and supplies (stop)Hear you are the expert
(stop)Wish to see glaciers and Denali up close
(stop)Arriving 25 July (stop)
George Barker and company
```

"Good grief, they don't want much, do they?" Allan stretched his arms behind his head.

John pulled out the large calendar they'd been working on, and Allan lowered his arms and leaned forward. He pointed to the schedule. "Even if we leave on the twenty-sixth, that only allows four days before our next major commitments. With the new signs we just put up and the trails trimmed, there's other staff who could handle a few of the nature walks without us. Even Cassidy could do it if Mrs. Johnson would spare her."

He pointed to one of the date squares with a star on it. "We've got to be back for the thirty-first. It's a good fifteen miles to the Ruth Glacier, which would be the only logical place to take them. But we'll have to get a boat to take us and the horses across the Susitna River. Once across, we'll climb the ridge and cross Troublesome Creek and then the Chulitna River."

"Even with mountainous terrain, the fifteen miles *could* be accomplished in a day." Allan studied the map.

John nodded. "Yes, but I'm not sure about how 'experienced'

these riders truly are. We could definitely tell them that is the goal for the first day. Then again, they might make that first ridge and see everything they want to see and decide to head back. I suppose we should just be grateful they aren't asking to climb one of the mountains in the range. I'm always amazed at the people who show up here thinking they can just launch into a full-scale mountaineering experience. I wish they'd seek information about these things prior to showing up." The words were no sooner out of his mouth than John wished he could take them back. He hadn't meant to give any reminders to the past.

The room was silent for several seconds. John looked up but couldn't read the young man's expression.

"Wouldn't that be nice?" Allan's words were clipped as he tapped the table. "Excuse me, I think I need some fresh air."

John didn't have to guess at what caused Allan's sudden distress and struggles. No matter the job before them, there was always something between them. Henry Brennan.

Laying the telegram on the table, John placed his palms on either side of the calendar and map. It's a good thing he'd given this over to the Lord because there wasn't any way humanly possible he could carry this burden.

# 12

The busy summer season thrilled Cassidy. While there wasn't a lot of extra time to spend with her father, she did enjoy the hustle and bustle. Pulling the deboned chickens she'd worked on that morning from the icebox, Cassidy went to work on the stuffing. The kitchen was busy, but no more so than usual. Quiet conversations between the staff echoed off the walls.

Every day newspapers from around the country would arrive at the hotel detailing the President's visit, the completion of the railroad, and tall tales about gold, mountains, and an untamed land.

Dad told her about a group coming in that he planned to take to the Ruth Glacier. She wished she could go along, but gone were the days of Cassidy getting to follow her dad around on one of his jaunts. She had a job of her own now. And one she loved.

Now that she'd mastered Mrs. Johnson's soufflé recipe, she'd been given a new recipe each day to learn and conquer. Cassidy loved that the head cook trusted her and relied upon her. It made her feel . . . special.

Now if she could just break through the older woman's tough shell. They'd worked together for months and while

Mrs. Johnson seemed to trust her more than anyone else, the woman stayed distant from everyone. Did she ever feel lonely like Cassidy? Did she even have any friends?

Cassidy wondered the same about herself. Could she say that she truly had any friends in Curry? They all knew each other well enough, but she wasn't ever invited to any of the young women's get-togethers because she was above most of them as assistant cook. And truth be told, most of the kitchen maids her age were interested in things Cassidy didn't even want to think about or consider.

Secretly, she blamed it on the lack of church. If these young people just knew what they were missing, they wouldn't be caught up in all the worldly nonsense, right?

With the stuffing made, she grabbed the twine to stitch the birds back up before they were roasted. The tangy sweet smell of the stuffing with onions, celery, and sage made her mouth water.

Thoughts of church and their church family back in Tanana made her weepy and even more hungry. Oh, how she missed the days of church socials, Sunday morning services, Wednesday evening Bible studies, and the occasional song service on a Saturday afternoon where everyone brought instruments and picnics and they went from one song to another for hours. They didn't even have any church services in Curry. Her dad led a small Bible study with a few others on Sunday afternoons, but other than that, they had no other fellowship. What was the world coming to?

"Cassidy Faith," Mrs. Johnson's fiery voice broke through. "Are you day-dreaming again?"

Cassidy blinked and looked at her supervisor, then down at the large needle threaded with twine in her hand. "Um, yes, ma'am. I guess I was."

"I should say so." The woman had her hands on her hips. "You've been standing there with that needle in the air for nigh unto two minutes."

"I'm sorry, Mrs. Johnson. But this is the last one. I'll have it ready in a jiffy."

"See that you do." The woman barked and walked out of the kitchen into the dining room.

Cassidy finished up the chickens and looked down the list at her next task. Dessert. She could handle that without too much thought. But something bothered her about Mrs. Johnson's demeanor. Granted the woman was never the friendliest of people, but something didn't seem right today.

Taking a quick glance at the clock, Cassidy washed her hands and went in search of her boss.

She didn't have to go far. Mrs. Johnson stood in the dining room, hands still on her hips.

Cassidy cleared her throat. "I'm sorry to bother you, but I wanted to check on you."

"No need. I'm fine." She didn't even turn around. "Just get on with your work."

"Well, the chickens are done and I was about to start on the dessert." Cassidy shifted her weight from one foot to the other. "It seems like something is bothering you, and I wanted to see if I could help."

The older woman turned, tears at the edges of her eyes. "Help? You can't help me, Cassidy Ivanoff. With your sunny attitude, your smiles, and your laughter. No, you can't help me. Especially not today."

What did that mean? "Why not today? I don't understand. I really do want to help and want to be here for you."

The woman huffed and shook her head. "You just can't let it be, can you? Well, all right then, I'll tell you why. Today would have been my brother Larry's birthday—but he's dead. I don't expect you to understand since you think the world is covered in gumdrops and rainbows, and while I appreciate your positive attitude, it doesn't do me any good today."

The words stung, but Cassidy couldn't allow the woman to hurt and feel she was alone. "But I do understand. And more importantly God understands—"

"Don't give me that God understands nonsense. Because He doesn't. If He did, my entire family—all of them—wouldn't have died of the influenza five years ago."

Cassidy gasped. The flu outbreak of 1918? It had killed millions of people around the world. Tears sprang to her eyes. This dear woman had lost everyone? How devastating!

Mrs. Johnson huffed again. "Don't get all teary-eyed on me, we have work to do. This is exactly why I didn't want to say anything to begin with, and you just need to let me be."

"But I can't." She wiped her face and took a deep breath. This was her chance to share her faith and she couldn't miss it. "God doesn't want you to carry this burden any longer. He hates to see you suffer."

"I find that all balderdash." Mrs. Johnson pointed her finger in Cassidy's face. "If He hates seeing me suffer, then He would have spared my mother and father, my brother, his wife, their three children, my sister, and her son. No, I'd say God rather enjoyed seeing me suffer, don't you? Either that, or He simply doesn't care how I feel." Her last words were full of anguish and anger. She marched back toward the kitchen. "Now, I won't have any more of this nonsense. We have dinner to prepare and I don't want to hear another word."

Cassidy thought to comment but held back. She walked to the kitchen with Mrs. Johnson's comments churning through her head.

*"But I don't expect you to understand since you think the world is covered in gumdrops and rainbows. . . ."*

Did Mrs. Johnson really think that was how Cassidy saw the world? All she'd ever wanted to do was present a positive spirit. There was enough sadness and bitterness in the world to go around, and Cassidy wanted only to offer a smile and an encouraging word. But Mrs. Johnson sounded as if she thought Cassidy foolishly naïve.

She frowned and felt her brows knit together. "Perhaps I am."

• • • • •

There was only an hour before Allan needed to be back in the lobby to help John with the next fishing group. He'd paced his room for almost thirty minutes trying to form a response to Frank, but nothing came. And it needed to get in the mail today. He couldn't wait any longer, or who knew what Frank would do.

The battle raged inside his mind. He'd been watching John day in and day out. More than anything, he wanted to know the truth about the man.

"Looks can be deceiving and few people are the sum total of their appearance," his father had once said. "Their actions are far more important."

Allan had taken that advice to heart in dealing with people all of his life. Why should he handle things any different with John?

Making a mental list, Allan began to assess John Ivanoff. First the positives. John seemed to care about each person. And no matter how great or small the expedition ended up being, he arranged it all with great care and structure. No room for slacking or careless mistakes. No detail left undone. No request unimportant. The man honestly knew his stuff and Allan had to admit—John Ivanoff was an expert.

The negatives? Frank believed John responsible for Henry Brennan's death.

But the depth of his internal war was so much more than John. And if Allan were to be honest, he'd have to admit that it wasn't just John who held his thoughts. He needed to know the truth about the man because of his daughter. The employees of the Curry Hotel couldn't avoid each other. Whether it was meals or staff meetings or just bumping into one another on the stairs or in the lobby—Allan couldn't avoid her. And he wasn't even really sure he wanted to anymore. In fact, he'd sought her out every day to talk to her. Even if it was only for a few minutes. He'd told himself it was just to be friendly. But who was he kidding?

As the past few years had rolled past, Allan felt the growing need for a companion—a wife to come alongside him. His father never failed to praise Allan's mother for being the one person to stand with him through his darkest hours. There had been too many dark hours for Allan since the war.

*"One day, son, you will find a woman who strikes your interest and then without realizing exactly when it happens, you'll find that she's the part of you that was missing and you can't be whole without her,"* his father had told him once.

Was that how it would be with Cassidy? Already he found himself thinking about her all the time. At first he'd tried to convince himself that it was just because she was John's daughter, but he couldn't pretend that any longer.

Frank admonished him to have nothing to do with John Ivanoff, but Allan couldn't just walk away. He couldn't avoid John because he still needed answers about his father, and he couldn't avoid Cassidy because he needed answers for his heart. Marching over to the chair at the desk, he determined to get the response written.

Frank was used to getting his way after all these years, and Allan had allowed the man to boss him around after Henry Brennan's death. But no more. It's not that he didn't respect Frank anymore; it was just time for Allan to show that he no longer needed anyone telling him what to do. He was twenty-eight years old and had a college education and a good head on his shoulders. The company was part his—he probably needed to start acting like it. He came to Alaska to follow in his father's footsteps and to find answers.

And find answers he would. Right now things didn't add up.

Perhaps the only way to find out what had really happened to his father would be to climb the mountain himself. If so, that's what he'd do.

Frank would just have to deal with it until Allan was satisfied.

• • • • •

Heat from the oven blasted Cassidy's face when she opened the door to the big range. The intensity took her breath away. As she stocked the oven with all the loaves of bread ready to bake, it reminded her of Shadrach, Meshach, and Abednego from the book of Daniel. What had the heat been like when they'd been thrown into the fiery furnace? Much worse than this hot oven, and it was more than Cassidy could stand for a few seconds.

Closing the oven, she thought of her chat with Mrs. Johnson the other day. Things had been stiff between them ever since and Cassidy hated it. The older cook was the closest thing Cassidy had to a friend.

But even more than that. Cassidy realized something big that day. Bigger than just being seen as a naïve girl who thought the world a beautiful, happy place. She'd never really been challenged in her faith. Not to stand strong, or to defend it, or to even really witness in the way she should. Oh, she'd shared the gospel with lots of people. John 3:16 was her favorite verse. But it had never gotten as intimate as it had with Mrs. Johnson. Hadn't that been what she'd prayed for? Ever since her chat with Thomas on Deadhorse Hill, she'd prayed for opportunities to be like Daniel and to share her faith no matter the cost.

Was this her chance? The even bigger question—would Mrs. Johnson listen?

And for that answer, Cassidy knew she'd have to wait. She understood now why the head cook was closed off. She even understood that almost impenetrable exterior around the woman was in place to protect her from further pain. Unfortunately, it also blocked out the opportunity to take in love. It would take a miracle to break through that armor.

Good thing she knew Someone in the miracle business.

She'd just have to wait for the right time. God had a plan for Cassidy here at the hotel. She knew it. And maybe she did look at the world through rose-colored glasses, but that didn't mean that being positive was wrong. God had blessed Cassidy with so much that she couldn't help but praise Him for it, and part of that praise was to have a merry heart, even in times of adversity. After all, the Bible said that "a merry heart doeth good like a medicine." Cassidy paused for a moment, remembering the latter half of that proverb.

"But a broken spirit drieth the bones." She barely whispered the words. Both her father and Mrs. Johnson were broken in spirit right now. Allan Brennan too. Cassidy shook her head and sighed. "But what can I do to help them?"

Mrs. Johnson entered the kitchen and approached Cassidy. "Miss Ivanoff, I owe you an apology for the other day." Her voice was low and raspy.

Cassidy was a bit shocked. The head cook never apologized for anything.

"I'm sorry for taking out my hurt and anger on you."

She swallowed. "I'm sorry for pushing, Mrs. Johnson. You were having a day of grief and I butted in."

The older woman gave a hint of a smile. "The truth is, you've grown on me. And I haven't allowed anyone to do that for a very long time. We always hurt the ones we love the most, don't we?"

Tears sprang to Cassidy's eyes. "Yes, ma'am. We do." She reached over and hugged the woman.

Mrs. Johnson gasped and then squeezed Cassidy back. As she pulled away, she wiped a tear from her eye. "Now, we mustn't let anyone see us like this."

"No, ma'am." Cassidy glanced around the room. She knew others had seen the display of affection, but all heads were down and it was eerily quiet. Maybe now was her chance to stand up for what she believed. "You know, Mrs. Johnson, what you said about God the other day really got me to thinking."

"Oh?" She went to the other side of the table and began kneading more dough.

"You see, to me, God is loving and comforting. He's always there for me. Even when I'm the most down."

Mrs. Johnson shook her head. "But you're rarely down, are you? How could you be when your life has been so sweet?"

"It *hasn't* always been 'sweet.' And I really don't see the world as all gumdrops and rainbows."

A frown lined the older woman's face. "I was wrong to say that."

"But it did make me think. I haven't always considered how others regard me. Being happy was important to me because my father always told me it would benefit me far more than being sad. But it doesn't mean I don't feel pain or realize that there is a great deal of tragedy in the world. But God has always been there as my loving heavenly Father." Cassidy grabbed a ball of dough and starting kneading it as well.

*Thunk.* The dough hit the table with a puff of flour as Mrs. Johnson stared at it. "I don't see God that way, I'm sorry to say."

"But why?"

"He's more like a harsh taskmaster to me. Just sitting up there waiting to punish His children for wrongdoing."

Cassidy's dough hit the surface with an even louder *plunk.* "But how could you think that? He's not like that at all."

"Life experience, my dear. Life experience."

"No, what you're talking about isn't life experience, it's circumstances. We live in a sin-filled world, and that's what causes all the bad things around us to happen."

"Humph." She slapped her dough down again. "So now you're saying all the bad has happened because of my sin? That I caused my family to all die from influenza?"

Cassidy let her dough rest. With all the thudding and slapping and plunking, the rest of the staff were beginning to stare. "No, that's not what I'm saying at all. Bad things do happen in this world because of man's sin—but that's only because we messed up the perfect world we had by sinning in the first place. As soon as we let it in, it ate away at the very fabric of joy-filled life. I couldn't live without my faith, Mrs. Johnson."

"That's the difference between us. I could. And I do."

"But maybe that's why you're so unhappy!" Cassidy regretted the words as soon as she said them. She covered her mouth with a flour-covered hand. "I'm sorry. I shouldn't have said that."

A few moments passed as Mrs. Johnson worked on the dough. "It's all right, I know you didn't mean it spitefully. And it's not like I don't want to be happy. Doesn't everyone want to be happy? But the difference is this: your life has always been a fairy tale.

Mine has not. You've never been truly hurt. I have. More times than I care to remember." She sighed. "And each time, I've asked, 'Where is God?'"

Cassidy watched the woman for several seconds. If only her dad weren't off on the expedition to the glacier. She could really use his advice right now. All she could do was shoot a prayer heavenward and forge on ahead. "That's a valid question, and one I'm sure many people have asked, long before you and me." She lowered her voice. "But I've asked it too, Mrs. Johnson. That's something you need to understand."

"No, I doubt that. Not you, Miss Sunshine." Cook shook her head.

Emotions she'd buried long ago came back. Dare she tell the truth? "Yes. Me." She leaned forward and whispered. "My mother died soon after she gave birth to me. I never knew her. And then my grandparents abandoned my father and me because of my father's native heritage. They disowned me. And they never knew me." Cassidy took a deep breath. "And deep down inside, I have to admit that it hurt worse than anything I could have imagined. Why didn't they want me? Their daughter was their only child! I'm angry at the prejudice and hate toward people's heritage and skin color. I'm angry that I never got to hear stories of how my mother grew up or what she was like as a child. I'm angry that my mother died and left me. But I've put it to good use. I've always had compassion for the little guy—the ones left behind, the ones not chosen, the awkward, the less fortunate."

"Because you think that if you can help someone else not feel rejected, then you will feel better about yourself too?"

"No, because I know that's what God has called me to do."

"I don't understand what you mean sometimes, Cassidy."

"It's simple. As believers, we're all chosen to share the gospel and show God's love to everyone. No matter their station in life or the color of their skin."

Mrs. Johnson shaped loaves out of her mound of dough. "While I appreciate your words, Cassidy, it still doesn't help me understand God. But I give you a gold star for trying."

"Well, that's a start." Cassidy smiled.

"Of course, you would think that." She shook her head. "Always the optimist."

"No one ever died from optimism, Mrs. Johnson."

# 13

The day had not gone as planned.

Frank eyed the papers in front of him. He had created all the documentation he needed to frame Louis Brewster—Henry's son-in-law—for the embezzling. Now he just needed a signature from the man. But that proved more difficult than he'd originally thought. Especially since he didn't want him reading any of the documents.

Maybe he could get him to sign off on something else and then have a forgery made?

It was a possibility. Frank tapped his chin with his pen. Why couldn't the whole Brennan clan just disappear? He was tired of having to do all the work for only part of the reward.

A swift knock preceded Lucy's entrance into his office. She handed him an envelope with one hand and then finished putting on her sweater. "Sorry to barge in, but this just arrived and I've stayed much too late as it is tonight, Mr. Irving."

He grunted at her in response and she rushed out the door, closing it behind her. Whatever happened to help who stayed as long as the boss did? He shook his head. Terrible society they lived in nowadays. Perhaps he should go back to having a man as a secretary. Men were so much easier to handle.

He opened the envelope and read the contents:

*25 July 1923*
*Dear Frank,*
*Thank you for your note. I appreciate your staunch dedication to my family and the memory of my father, but rest assured, I've got the situation under control. John Ivanoff is a wealth of information, and I'm certain that over time I will find out the truth of what happened to my father.*

*My mother and sisters are aware of my location. Thank you for your concern for their welfare. Please continue to look after them in my absence. On my return, I think it's time that I stepped up into a new role at the company. It's what my father would have wished.*

*As soon as I have any word, I will get the information to you.*

*Sincerely,*
*Allan Brennan*

Wadding the paper into a ball, Frank threw it against the wall. Stupid boy! Who did he think he was dealing with?

Interference with his plans wouldn't be tolerated. He'd worked too long and hard to accomplish what he had. He began to pace.

He went to the locked cabinet where he kept his liquor. Fumbling with his keys, he finally found the right one. Nothing could be simple. He unlocked the door and opened it to reveal his choices. Picking the bottle of Scotch, he poured himself a generous portion.

He tossed back the drink, then poured another.

He thought of the ridiculous magic show he'd been forced to attend a few nights earlier. The tricks were accomplished by distraction—sleight of hand. Along with that, the magician had the help of a few props and an assistant.

Frank took the drink with him to his desk. He sank to the chair and studied the amber liquid in his glass. Perhaps with a few props and an assistant he could accomplish his desires—perform his own magic.

With any luck at all he might well rid himself of the Brennan interference in the business.

There might even be an opportunity to rid himself of not just Henry's son, but of John Ivanoff as well. Maybe murder was required after all.

He smiled, then downed the scotch. Only time would tell.

• • • • •

All the staff gathered in the lobby as Mr. Bradley worked to quiet them.

Cassidy leaned up against the banister of the staircase. Her feet were killing her. It'd been such a long day.

"All right, all right." The manager rubbed his hands together. "Today, we found a station that will be broadcasting news in just a few minutes. There's a slight crackle, so we ask that everyone remain quiet so we can all hear."

The staff quieted. Cassidy noticed that several of the guests of the hotel had joined them in the lobby as well. Mr. Bradley had made the announcement at dinner regarding the radio, but few had even seemed interested. Radio broadcasts were most likely the norm for them anyway.

A touch on her shoulder brought her attention around. Allan held a chair for her. It was from the dining room; he must have carried it all the way over. "Would you like to sit? You look done in."

She sighed. "Thank you. That's very kind. Will you sit with me?"

He nodded and left for a moment, bringing another chair back with him.

The radio man and Mr. Bradley fiddled with knobs as they all waited. Crackling and sizzling was heard, and then a long hiss.

"It's supposed to start in about two minutes, so please be patient." Mr. Bradley nodded at the man.

Allan leaned toward her and whispered, "Your lemon soufflé the other night was delicious."

"Thank you. How did you know I made it?"

"Mrs. Johnson made an announcement—she's very proud of you."

How had she missed that? Warmth spread through her. Maybe she was finally getting through to the older woman.

"So is your dad. He talks about you all the time."

"Of course he does. I'm his only child. But it is nice to hear." She studied him for a moment. If only they had the time to talk all evening. This man beside her definitely gave her mixed emotions. "He speaks very highly of you as well."

"I'm glad to hear it. He's been very patient with me as I learn and work through everything since my father's passing."

"He's a good man." She straightened in the hardback chair. Did Allan truly see that now? More than anything, she wanted to trust this man beside her. She also wanted to know the truth about what had happened. Maybe as much as he did. Cassidy felt almost certain that until then, neither of them would be free to move forward.

She glanced at Allan to find him watching her. He offered her a slight nod as if having read her thoughts. Cassidy lowered her head, feeling her cheeks grow warm. She was glad to be sitting, as she was almost certain her knees would have given way at the rush of emotions that washed over her.

Allan made her feel things she'd never felt before. Was that a good thing?

The radio hissed and crackled to life. "We open our broadcast tonight with sad news for our nation. At 7:30 p.m. last night, August the second, President Warren Harding died suddenly in his hotel room in San Francisco."

Gasps were heard throughout the room, and Mr. Bradley quickly shushed them.

Everyone leaned forward.

"His countrywide trip—'The Voyage of Understanding'—was drawing near to the end and he hadn't felt well for several days. Mere weeks ago, on June twentieth, the President gave one of the first presidential speeches to be broadcast live by radio. Just recently, he hammered in the golden spike to complete the Alaska Railroad and enjoyed a tour of the Alaska Territory as the first President to visit the Far North. Last week, he gave a speech predicting that Alaska would become one of the United States. And now today, we mourn his passing. We will take a moment of silence to remember President Warren Harding, the twenty-ninth President of the United States."

Music played in the background as Cassidy sat there in shock. Hadn't they just served the man a couple of weeks ago? How could this be?

While she wasn't really sure she liked him, she did have a lot of respect for the leader of the country. Of course, there were the rumors that he had a mistress, and the staff noted arguments behind closed doors. But Cassidy had been taught all of her life to ignore rumors. The President had been gracious and kind to her and the staff . . . and he'd come all the way to Alaska when no other President had.

The hissing returned to the radio in the middle of the song.

"We must have lost the signal." The man fiddling with the radio furrowed his brows.

Conversations started all over the room in a gentle hum.

"This wasn't at all what I expected to hear the first time I listened to the radio." Cassidy wrung her hands. "How very sad."

Allan sat next to her in silence, shaking his head

"He didn't look at all like he was that ill, did he?"

"No, I can't say that he did." He shifted in his seat. "He looked a bit tired after we'd climbed up the hill a ways, but the schedule they had kept up to that point was ridiculously full."

Much of the staff dispersed as Mr. Bradley turned off the radio. No one seemed to be in a mood to socialize after the word they'd just received.

Allan turned in his chair to face her. "Do you think, perhaps, you'd like to take a walk with me? The fresh air might do us some good after such news."

She nodded. "Yes, I'd like that very much." Cassidy stood and smoothed her apron. As Allan picked up their chairs and returned them to the dining room, she watched him and tried to calm her insides. They'd indeed had a rough start—that was for certain—but she couldn't deny the way she felt drawn to him.

He returned and offered his arm. Placing her hand in the crook of his elbow, she allowed him to lead her out the front door and onto the large wooden platform.

"How about we walk down to the roundhouse? There's a trail we could take from there if you'd like to walk farther." His brow was furrowed again.

"That sounds fine."

"My sisters would want to know everything about you if they knew I'd asked you on a walk."

The thought made her laugh. "Well, there's not much to know. I'm just me."

"I beg to differ. You are fascinating, Cassidy."

"I'm glad you think so, but you do realize I'm pretty simple, right?"

"Maybe in your tastes and expectations, but I don't think there's anything simple about you."

His words made her stomach flip. "And you're no longer angry with my father?"

"You keep asking me that, so it must be very important to you." He sighed. "Your father has proven over and over again to me that he's not the kind of man to leave my father to die." He stopped and turned to look into her eyes. "I still want to know what happened up there, but I don't blame your father anymore. I just don't know what to think."

The fire in his green eyes blazed through her. "I can understand that. And I really do appreciate your honesty. I can't imagine what you've had to go through. Have you had a chance to tell my father that you . . . forgive him?"

Allan looked at her oddly. "No, because until just now I wasn't sure I had. But now, talking to you, I realize he doesn't need to be forgiven. He did nothing wrong."

She smiled. "Still, I know it would mean the world to him to hear those words."

He turned forward again and started walking. For several minutes neither one said anything, and Cassidy worried that she'd once again pushed too hard. When would she ever learn a balance?

"The thing is, Cassidy, I've never met anyone like you." Allan's words came without warning. "And even though I'm still struggling with the death of my father, I want to know you . . . and your father better."

What exactly did that mean for her? She didn't quite have the gumption to ask. At least not yet. She had to change the subject. "Speaking of my father, what did you think of the glacier?"

Allan studied her face for a moment. "It was beautiful. More beautiful than anything I'd ever seen." He seemed momentarily to have lost his thoughts. Finally, he continued. "I was quite amazed to learn the glaciers are always moving. It seems strange to imagine."

"Ruth Glacier is one of my favorites. But I think I like the Kahiltna Glacier better. Maybe because of the view you get between Denali and Sultana. Snowshoeing is beautiful there."

"You've been there?" His jaw dropped.

She laughed again at his expression and squeezed his arm with her other hand. "Of course. You forget I was born and raised up here. Those mountains are home to me."

"Have you climbed McKinley?"

"Gracious, no. I'm not up for that. Dad says one of the most important things about life in Alaska is to recognize your limitations, otherwise you'll get hurt. But you never know . . . maybe one day."

"Your dad and I are planning a climb for next year. We wanted to keep it a secret to start with, since it will take much planning and preparation, but I'm excited. It will be a dream come true."

"That's wonderful. Even though it scares me a little." It scared her a lot. Who was she fooling? The last time her father climbed that mountain, one of the men didn't return. What if that happened this time? She didn't even want to think of losing her father. And what about Allan? Was he up to the challenge?

"Cassidy?"

He'd caught her lost in her thoughts. She smiled and pressed on, changing the subject to a safer topic. "Were your clients up for the challenge? I didn't hear too many complaints from my father. That's always a good sign. It always upsets him when people bite off more than they can chew."

"The group was interesting. They were very experienced riders and had obviously done other excursions, but probably not anywhere so remote. There were a few odd glances and questions at times, but for the most part, they were good sports and good travelers. I admit it made the trip that much easier." Allan's brow furrowed again. "So why is the Ruth Glacier named that? I meant to ask your father and I forgot. I like the other glacier name you said. What was it? It sounded so much more . . . Alaskan."

"The Kahiltna is the other one I mentioned. It's the longest glacier in all of the Alaska Range, I think. Stretches for miles and miles and miles. And as to the Ruth Glacier, Frederick Cook named it after his stepdaughter Ruth Hunt when I was a child. Apparently, the name stuck."

"I've heard a lot of controversy surrounding Cook."

"Dad says there will always be men who will actually accomplish what they set out to do and others who won't. Then there will be those who speak for and against those men. Every one of them will have their own reasons and motivations. If Cook didn't actually summit Denali, the loss is ultimately his."

"Yes, but he claims to have been the first, and that was important to a great many people."

Cassidy shrugged. "There are a lot of unimportant things that people call important. I think the measure of a man is his honesty. I don't abide anyone lying about their exploits, but neither am I inclined to give such matters more attention than they deserve. It's just not how I want to spend my time—my life."

They walked in silence for a few moments, and Cassidy enjoyed holding on to Allan's strong arm. She felt safe. And comfortable.

"So what is it that you really want to do with your life, Cassidy? What dreams do you have?"

She continued to hold his arm with both hands and took her time, but gave him a smile. "You're the only person other than my father who's ever asked me that question." She took a few more steps. "More than anything, I want to serve the Lord. Whatever that might look like. I know He's got a great plan. I would love to have a family of my own one day. And, of course, I want to stay in Alaska. But I also really love to cook. It'd be fun to be head chef one day. Maybe." She bit her lip. "Although it is a lot of work. While I'm young, it might be fun, but I can't imagine doing it at Mrs. Johnson's age. I think I'd be plumb worn out. But she doesn't have a family to take care of, so maybe she pours everything into her work. I know it gives her satisfaction and she loves it."

Allan laughed out loud at that one. "She's a tough woman, Mrs. Johnson. How is it, working for her?"

"Oh, we get along just fine. Underneath all her bluster is a tender heart." She grew thoughtful. "A wounded one, but tender with love as well."

"I think you're probably the only person who would say as much."

She shrugged. "Sometimes you just need to look deeper. People have commented that you are rude and think yourself too good to associate with the rest of us. I've paid it no more attention than what they say about Mrs. Johnson."

Allan looked stunned. "People have said that about me?"

"Well, you have to admit you have very little to do with anyone other than Dad. Even then, you don't say a whole lot—unless, of course, it has to do with work."

"But that doesn't mean I think myself better than others."

She looked deep into his eyes and shook her head. "No. It

means you're just as wounded as Mrs. Johnson, and you've built a wall up to keep others out. For some reason you both think that if you keep that wall in place, you won't be hurt again. But what's really sad is that you're still wounded. Never mind getting hurt again."

For a moment he said nothing, and Cassidy thought she'd offended him just as she'd done with Mrs. Johnson. Why couldn't she learn to keep her opinion to herself?

"You know," he said after a few more moments of silence. "I think you're right."

"I didn't mean to cause you pain."

He shook his head. "I needed to hear it, and coming from you . . . well . . . it didn't seem harsh at all. You are about the most optimistic and inspiring person I think I've ever met." He stopped and looked at her. "You simply amaze me."

She breathed a sigh of relief. "Well, I will take that as a compliment."

"You're good for me, Cassidy . . ." He paused. "What's your middle name, if you don't mind my asking?"

"Faith."

"I should have known. How appropriate. As I was saying, you're good for me, Cassidy Faith Ivanoff. I need more positive influences in my life." The brooding look was back on his face. "Now, if I can just figure out how to tear down the wall and let them in."

She wished more than anything she could take away his pain. If he'd been Mrs. Johnson, she might have given him a hug. But if he'd been Mrs. Johnson, she wouldn't be dealing with the war of emotions that threatened to betray her at any moment.

"Well, it is getting late, even though it's still plenty light. Deceiving this time of year, isn't it? I better get you back before your father sends out a search party." He smiled again, that half smile that made his face even more handsome.

She frowned. She hadn't seen her father since before the radio broadcast. "Allan, did you know where my father was going after dinner?"

"He wanted to check on the trail for the hiking group to-morrow."

"He should've been back by now, wouldn't you think?"

"I would have thought so." Allan looked off toward the trail. "Don't worry. You go on in and I'll go check. I'm sure he's fine."

# 14

The evening light in Alaska never ceased to amaze Allan. It looked like it was still only five or six o'clock and yet it was pushing 11:00 p.m.

He hadn't wanted to say anything in front of Cassidy, but he'd forgotten about John. And the man should've been back before they ever left for their walk.

Guilt gnawed at his gut. He should have paid closer attention to the time. Instead, he'd been absorbed by Cassidy's presence. What if something had happened to his boss, and Allan was the only one who even knew the experienced guide had gone out to do what he always did—double-and-triple check everything. All for the care and safety of others.

A mile up the trail, Allan spotted a waving red bandana. He couldn't see John, which meant the man was down. He ran ahead. If only he'd been more observant. Had he been more vigilant . . . had he been more like John . . . maybe this wouldn't have happened.

He came upon his mentor and wanted to retch. Blood stained his shirt and left trouser leg.

John lowered his bandana, his other arm tight about his middle and rasped, "I knew you'd find me."

"John, I'm so sorry it took me so long. What happened?"

He shook his head. "You couldn't have known, son. It's all right." He took a deep breath, which looked like it exhausted him. "I came upon a mama moose and her two calves. There wasn't any time to react; I just rounded this bend and there they were." He leaned his head back on the ground. "I backed up quietly, trying to put some space between us, but the mama probably thought I was after her babies, and she came after me with her hooves. She got in a couple of swift kicks and knocked me down. Then she left. Thankfully, she didn't stay to trample me some more."

Allan went into survivor mode. John had lost a lot of blood and it was more than a mile back to the hotel. He quickly took off his jacket and button-up shirt.

"Here." John lifted his jacket to Allan. "Use this too."

Tearing the bottom of his shirt into long strips, Allan used the material to bind John's leg. Then he folded John's jacket and pressed it against the wound in his abdomen and used the top of his shirt with the long sleeves to wrap around John's midsection as a bandage and tied it as tight as he could. "This will have to do for now, but maybe it will help us get back to the hotel."

"Thank you." John's words were weak.

"Stay with me, John. I need you to stay awake."

"I'll do my best."

Allan assessed the situation. He was going to have to carry him down the trail. John had lost too much blood to leave and come back with help. "This isn't going to be comfortable, but I'm going to have to lift you like a sack of potatoes over my shoulder if we're going to make it back. Hopefully that jacket will give the wound in your abdomen some padding, but I don't know how else to do it."

"Do what you have to do. I'll make it."

Helping John to his feet, Allan hoped he'd have the strength to make it back. His boss was a solid, muscular, and tall man. He crouched down and let John lean over his shoulders and back. Allan grabbed John's right arm and right leg and lifted. As he balanced the man's weight on his shoulders, John moaned.

"I'm sorry, John."

"It's all right. Now that I'm up, I'm okay."

Brave words. But Allan knew they weren't true. Now he just needed to make it back to the hotel in time.

Step after step down the trail, Allan tried not to jostle his cargo too much. John had long since passed out. Probably from the pain or the loss of blood. It didn't matter. Just made it all the more urgent.

Allan's thoughts returned to Cassidy and their conversation earlier. A realization hit him square in the face. He cared about these people. A lot. Somewhere along the way they had managed to find a hole in his wall.

John was more than just his boss. He'd become his friend. Allan respected him and wanted to learn all he could from him. The more he thought about it, the more he realized that John reminded him of his father. All the best parts of him.

And then there was Cassidy. With her dark, inquisitive eyes. And her constantly positive outlook.

He couldn't deny it. He wanted their friendship to grow.

"Mr. Brennan! Mr. Brennan!"

Allan couldn't see anyone yet, but that sure did sound like Thomas—and what a beautiful sound it was.

Footsteps got closer and then he could see the young man running up the path.

"Mr. Brennan, is Mr. Ivanoff all right?"

Allan kept moving down the trail, afraid to stop and lose

the steady momentum. "He's been kicked by a moose. I need you to run back and tell Mr. Bradley. Ask him to get the medic and to prepare a room in the hotel for John. It's not pretty."

"Yes, sir." Thomas nodded and took off at a sprint.

The sight of Thomas renewed Allan's energy. They would be ready to help John as soon as he made it to the hotel, so he simply needed to place one foot in front of the other and make his way down the trail.

\* \* \* \*

Cassidy paced the lobby of the hotel while a few of the other men went out to help Allan the rest of the way.

When they entered the front door, Allan had her father over his shoulders. He looked exhausted, but his eyes found hers and pierced her heart. He nodded to her and went down to his knees, while three other men lifted her father off of him.

She followed them down the hallway but looked back at Allan, still kneeling in the lobby. His white undershirt was soaked in blood. Her father's blood.

Cassidy's voice choked. "Thank you." She didn't wait for his response but hurried to join her father.

The medic wouldn't let her in the room and had placed Mr. Bradley as guard at the door. "This isn't something your father would want you to see. Right now he needs the medic's full attention and you would be a distraction. I'll come get you as soon as we know anything."

"I'm not going anywhere, Mr. Bradley. I'll just wait out here."

He nodded and closed the door.

She leaned against the wall and then slid down it, pulling her knees up to her chest. She couldn't hold the tears back any longer. *Lord, please don't let him die. He's all I have.*

All the conversations from the past few days sprang into her mind. That she was little Miss Sunshine, had lived a fairy-tale life, and was always positive.

She didn't feel so optimistic right now. Instead, loneliness gripped her again. What would she do if she lost her father? He'd always been there.

Sobs shook her shoulders and she buried her face in her apron.

An arm wrapped around her shoulder. "Cassidy, shhh, it's okay. I'm here." Mrs. Johnson's voice sounded almost lyrical. "Allan came and got me. He thought you might need a shoulder."

Lifting her head, she sobbed harder and threw herself into the woman's arms. They sat on the floor rocking for what seemed like hours. She owed Allan so much. He knew . . . somehow he knew that she'd need comfort from a motherly figure. And even though Mrs. Johnson could be all prickles and rough edges, she was the only one Cassidy wanted right now. Other than her father.

A tap on her shoulder brought her awake in a snap. Cassidy sat up. "Dad?" The medic stood before her, blood on his jacket.

"He's all right. And he'll mend. Took quite a beating and lost a lot of blood, but I've got him stitched up. I don't think there's severe internal damage, but we'll keep an eye out for swelling in the abdomen and blood in his urine. There will be a lot of bruising, and we'll have to watch him for infection, but I think in a few weeks, he'll be back to full strength."

She nodded. "Thank you . . . ?" It hit her that she didn't even know the man's name.

"It's Larry. And you're welcome."

She scrubbed her face with her hands and looked at Mrs. Johnson. How appropriate that the medic's name was Larry.

Mrs. Johnson was all smiles.

Cassidy looked back at Larry. "Thank you. May I see him?"

"Yes. He was asking for you earlier, but he's sleeping pretty hard now."

"That doesn't matter. I just want to see him."

The medic nodded and walked away.

Mr. Bradley greeted her at the door. "Your father is a strong man, Miss Ivanoff. I'm sure he'll have a full recovery."

"Thank you, Mr. Bradley. For everything."

"Not a problem, my dear. He's the best man I've got. We'll take good care of him. Barring any complications to his condition, he should be able to get up and around in about a week and then he'll have to take it slow for a week or two after that."

She nodded and looked at her father. He'd always been so strong. The vision of health. Now he looked pale and tired.

Leaning over his bed, she kissed his forehead. "I love you, Daddy. Now you just concentrate on getting better. I'll be praying for you."

"It's probably best you just let him sleep." The manager patted her shoulder. "Looks like you could use some sleep as well. We'll make sure someone comes to get you as soon as he's awake again. Never fear, someone will be with him throughout the night."

"All right." Cassidy headed for the door and saw Mrs. Johnson and Allan both waiting for her outside.

Mrs. Johnson came forward and grabbed her hands. "Go get some sleep. I don't even want to see you before noon."

"But—"

"Don't argue with me, Cassidy Faith. You sleep and get some time in with your father. There will be plenty of work to do later."

Cassidy couldn't help but smile at the glint in the woman's eye. "Yes, ma'am."

Mrs. Johnson waved and walked away. "Not before noon!"

Cassidy looked at Allan for a moment. There was so much she wanted to say to him, but there were no words. Without even thinking about it, she went straight into his arms. She hugged him for all she was worth. "Thank you."

It only took a moment before his strong arms wrapped around her. She'd never been held by a man other than her father, and she didn't know if it was the emotion and relief of the moment, or simply that it was Allan who held her. But she never wanted to leave.

# 15

Six o'clock in the morning came all too soon after such a long night. Allan hadn't gotten much sleep between his thoughts of Cassidy and John. With his boss laid up, the full schedule of excursions would fall on his shoulders. But mainly his thoughts were of Cassidy.

As he went over the schedule for the next few days, his thoughts wouldn't stay on task. It was hard to imagine he'd only known the Ivanoffs a month. And even though he hadn't treated them very well, they'd shown him nothing but kindness. It didn't make sense.

His walk with Cassidy last night had opened up his heart, but he never could have prepared himself for what his heart would do when she hugged him. He wanted to treasure her and protect her, but he didn't have that right. At least not before he made things right—truly right—with her father.

Allan felt so convicted for the thoughts he'd held toward John. Now that he knew the man, and had seen his true character over and over again, he couldn't imagine how he ever believed the man had been responsible for his father's death. But how could he have known? And why did Frank hate John so much? Because he needed someone to blame for the loss of his friend? Or was there something else to it?

He didn't want to go there—but there had been things over the years that made Allan doubt Frank's loyalty to the Brennan family.

*Dad, what do I do?*

He stared at the ceiling. No answer came. But oh, how he wished one would. Since he'd lost his father, he didn't have anyone to talk to about the tough decisions. Allan had relied on his father for guidance and wisdom in every aspect of his life. Henry Brennan often scolded him for it. Told him that he should be relying on God. Not man. But Allan idolized his father.

As for God . . . he shook his head. For the longest time he'd worked to convince himself that he didn't need God anymore.

During the war, after learning of his father's death, he'd often considered his father's faith. He knew his dad would have been disappointed—crushed more like it—that his death would drive his son away from God. Of course, Allan didn't allow himself those thoughts. Not in the trenches. His commanding officer was fond of quoting the old French poet Jean de La Fontaine, who said, "Death never takes the wise man by surprise, he is always ready to go."

His commander had been a Christian, and would usually add that a man could only be truly ready when his spirit was at peace with God.

At the time, Allan forced himself to be logical about it. His father was dead and eventually he would die as well. Whether here or in his bed as an old man. Death was death.

But even now his father's words whispered in his ear.

*"For to me to live is Christ, to die is gain."*

His father didn't fear death, nor did he dread life. He'd been completely at peace with both, and Allan wanted the same.

Shaking off the regret and the endless void that dogged him, Allan headed out to the equipment shed. In time he would speak to John and tell him the truth—that he did forgive him. For now, however, he needed to focus on the job at hand. That's all. John was injured—lucky to be alive, but that meant Allan would need to put all his energy into performing his duties, as well as John's.

The morning passed in a wild-flower hike with city ladies who found the beauty inspirational and the dangers thrilling. They walked in their dainty fashion with their very pretty dresses and thin-soled shoes and marveled that anything so rustic still existed in the modern world. At noon he delivered them back to the hotel safe and sound, with each of the ladies speaking in animated excitement about how they'd faced the dangers of the wild frontier and survived.

What would they have thought if they'd truly had to face all that Alaska had to offer? Allan's growling stomach reminded him that he'd forgotten breakfast. Not a smart thing to do. Especially when he had to spend the afternoon taking a group out fishing. He pulled out his pocket watch—just enough time to check on John and get his advice if he was awake, and to eat a quick lunch.

As he headed to John's room, one of the kitchen boys caught him by the sleeve.

"Mr. Brennan, here's a telegram for you."

"Thank you."

The boy dashed off.

Opening the envelope, Allan stayed in the hall. He hoped it wasn't anything too urgent—especially not another group requesting anything, but John received most of those requests.

4 August 1923
Concerned about Brennan/Irving (stop)Not all appears as it should (stop)Anna believes Frank
involved in shady dealings (stop)Please advise
(stop)
Louis

Allan leaned against the wall and reread it. His sister Anna was the quietest out of all of them, but also the most observant. Whenever she brought something to their attention, she was correct.

For Louis to send the telegram also gave a strong hint. Louis was capable and independent. He never communicated unless it was necessary. Things must be very bad indeed.

But how could Allan deal with the matter from here?

Shoving the paper back in the envelope, he strode the rest of the way to John's room. He knocked softly.

"Come in." Cassidy's sweet voice called out.

When he opened the door, he was overjoyed to see John sitting up and with color in his face. "You look a hundred times better than you did last night."

John reached out a hand.

Allan took it in a firm grip and shook it.

"Thank you for finding me."

"You would've done the same for me." Allan sat in a chair on the other side of John's bed. Not only could he see his boss, but he had a good view of Cassidy as well. However, with her there, Allan didn't feel he could speak to John about forgiveness. That was still too personal.

"I wanted your advice about the fishing expedition this afternoon."

John smiled. "Just take them to Deadhorse Creek. The salmon are starting to run, and they will be so stacked in there that no one should have a problem catching at least one."

"Yes, sir. I knew you would know exactly where to go." He looked down at the envelope in his hand.

"Something bothering you, Allan?"

His head shot up. Just like Dad. The man could read him. "Well, yes, sir. As a matter of fact there is."

"Since I've got nothing else to do, would you like a listening ear?"

Allan looked at John and then at Cassidy. Compassion shone in both their eyes. They really cared about him. The thought struck him. He didn't deserve their friendship, but he was thankful for it. He nodded. "I would appreciate your insight, John." He pulled the telegram out and handed it over.

John read it and sighed. "Not the news you wanted to hear." He handed the paper back.

"No, sir."

"Do you trust Louis? He's your brother-in-law, correct?"

"Yes, sir. On both accounts. And my father loved Louis. Knew he could rely on him for anything. He's always been honest to a fault."

Cassidy leaned forward. "Is this something about your father's company?"

Allan nodded. "Yes, and it's my company now—along with Frank. My eldest sister, Ada, and her husband, Stanley Meyers, helped out a lot while I was at war. But Stanley's family owns a grocery business, and a few years ago it came time for Stanley to step up into his role there managing the stores. Anna is married to Louis and he's worked at Brennan/Irving for years. Dad trusted all of them implicitly. Louis is a good man. But I haven't really taken ownership like I should have. I guess I was grieving the loss of my father too much and just left Frank to do what he pleased." He handed the telegram to Cassidy.

She read it. "Oh my." She turned to her father. "Frank is the other man from the expedition, isn't he?"

"Yes." John frowned and shifted a bit on his bed. He closed his eyes and grimaced. "Sorry, gotta get used to the pain."

Cassidy stood and leaned over her father. She looked at Allan and then back at John. "Don't you think he deserves to know your insight?"

Allan puzzled over that statement. He leaned toward John. "Yes, please, John. Tell me."

"I'm not one to tarnish a man's reputation. Especially since I know how being wrongly judged feels." His eyes opened and he fixed his gaze on Allan. "I don't want to cause problems where none should exist."

"I know that, sir. But if there's something you know that could give me guidance here, I'd greatly appreciate it."

John shook his head. "I don't really know anything. It's just a gut instinct."

"I'd still like to hear it."

"I never felt like I could trust Frank on that mountain. And that frightened me. There was something . . . shifty about him that I couldn't put my finger on." John breathed heavily. "Completely different than your father. I would have put my life in Henry's hands and felt totally comfortable."

"But you didn't feel that way about Frank?" Allan pressed.

"No. I'm sorry to say." John held a hand up. "Now, I'm not saying that I saw him do anything wrong. He just always went for the easy way out. I'd ask him to do things—important things— and he'd only do them halfway. He always seemed distracted, like he was deep in his own little world. I got the feeling the most important person in Frank Irving's world was Frank Irving. Seemed like a weasel to me, to be honest. Always manipulating things. But your father trusted him."

Allan stood up and walked over to the window. "Frank is definitely a manipulator. We all know that. And he likes to have his way. But Dad always had a system with him. Could handle him." He turned back to John and Cassidy. "As to the trust. Well, that goes back to when they were kids. Dad fell out of a tree and broke his arm. Frank gave Dad his coat and ran all the way home to get help." He thought about it for a minute. "You know, Frank was the whiner, the doubter, while Dad was the positive, always optimistic dreamer. Whenever Frank would get down and needed affirmation, Dad would always remind him of that good deed he did. Almost like he knew Frank needed the encouragement to stay on the up and up."

"Sounds like Henry." John nodded. "Your father was encouraging him every step up the mountain. I doubt Frank would have made the summit if not for your father's determination to see him there."

"So now I need to ask for your advice. What do you think I should do?"

John and Cassidy looked at each other. Then John spoke. "Well, I think you need to follow your own gut. And if you have full trust in Louis and know he wouldn't contact you unless he absolutely had to, then you need to find out what's going on. The only caution I have is that Frank is a smart cookie. He probably already has a plan." His mentor sighed. "It could just be that Frank never recovered from Henry's death. People do strange things when they've lost someone they love."

Allan clenched his jaw. But he had a feeling Frank knew exactly what he was doing. And maybe had been all along. "I'll see to it after the fishing trip."

He got up, then remembered what he wanted to say to John, and decided to forge ahead even with Cassidy in the room. He opened his mouth to share his heart just as Mr. Bradley bustled into the room.

"I've come to see our patient."

"As you can see I'm on the mend," John announced.

Allan slipped from the room. There would be another time.

• • • • •

The fishing trip only took two hours because the men were so excited to catch so many fish, they couldn't wait to get them all back to the hotel. One man even pulled out two with his bare hands.

But even the cheers and pats on the back couldn't rid Allan of the black cloud he felt covered him. He didn't want to think Frank could turn his back on the Brennan family, but maybe that is what happened. Maybe he had turned on them that day back in 1917 when his father was lost on the mountain. Maybe he was the reason his father died. It was a terrible thing to consider, but after listening to John, Allan knew he had no other choice. Frank very well could have the answers that Allan needed.

As he stowed the fishing gear in the shed, Allan thought through his response to Louis. How should he advise his brother-in-law?

Maybe he just needed to return home. But would that solve anything? It's not like he'd been highly involved in the business at any point of his life. But how could he leave now? John needed him.

Shutting the door, he realized he just wanted to talk to John again.

Thomas rounded the corner. "Mr. Brennan, there's a telegram for you."

Another one? "Thank you, Thomas. Did it just arrive?"

"Yes, sir."

Allan watched him run back to the main building. The young man's eagerness to please was apparent. It'd been a decade since Allan was that age, but he couldn't imagine going through those tough years without parents. It was hard enough to not have his dad now, and he was twenty-eight.

He opened the envelope and read the second telegram for that day.

```
4 August 1923
Received letter (stop)Anxious for you to be a
part of your father's legacy (stop)Sad news to
report (stop) Louis embezzling (stop)Fired him
today (stop)No other way (stop)
Frank
```

Fury burned in his gut. None of it added up, and Allan *would* find out the truth. No matter what.

He marched straight to the front desk. "I need to send a couple of telegrams."

"Certainly, Mr. Brennan." Mr. Clark, the railroad clerk, stood behind the desk and passed two slips of paper and a pencil toward him. "Write them out here, and I'll get them out straightaway."

"Thank you."

He penned the first one to his mother's brother—an accountant.

```
4 August 1923
In need of your assistance (stop)Embezzling at
Brennan/Irving (stop)Need an audit of company
books (stop)Rush (stop)
Allan Brennan
```

The second one, he took a bit more care writing. Frank needed to know that Allan was serious about taking on a more substantial role, and that he wouldn't be taking Frank's word as truth. Not anymore.

# 16

Thomas watched for Cassidy down the hallway. She had to be coming out soon. Mrs. Johnson would have his hide if he didn't get back to the kitchen, and he didn't want to risk her anger just when she'd finally agreed to let him work for her full-time again.

But he wanted to be there for Cassidy. She was the only one who smiled and encouraged him no matter what blunder he made. Not only that, but she made him feel special, and no other girl had ever done that.

He brushed a dirt smudge off his pants and propped his foot up against the wall behind him. He wanted to tell her how he felt, but every time he tried it felt like he had a mouth full of cotton. If only he could talk to someone and get advice on how to court a lady. The only one he could talk to, though, was Mr. Ivanoff, and he was Cassidy's father. So that made the situation impossible.

A door closed and it brought his attention up. There she was. Carrying a tray, she blew a strand of hair out of her face.

He raced toward her, doing his best not to get his feet tangled. "Here. Let me take that for you, Miss Cassidy."

"Why, thank you, Thomas." She handed him the tray and smoothed her hair back with her hands. "My hair was making my nose itch and I best get it back under control before we reach the kitchen. There's lots of food to prepare, and I don't think the guests would like my hair to be in it."

They laughed together as they walked. She always could make him laugh. That was one of his favorite things about Cassidy. It didn't hurt that she was so pretty. He loved her dark eyes and hair. He didn't even think he'd mind if her hair got in his food.

"Uhh . . . how's your . . . dad doing?"

"A little better. He makes a poor patient. He wants to be up and back to work. It's hard on him not being able to do what he loves."

"At least he knows what he loves." Thomas felt his face flush and hurried to change the subject. "I know the guests have asked about him."

"I know. I've had several ask me as well. He's definitely missed."

She worked on winding her hair around and around, and Thomas forgot what he was going to say and just stared. Was her hair as soft as it looked? When they reached the kitchen, he was so fascinated with the knot she'd made at the back of her head that he must not have been paying attention, because all of a sudden, she turned around.

"Thomas, I—"

Too late he realized his mistake and the tray slammed into the front of Cassidy. The rest of Mr. Ivanoff's soup and fruit now covered the front of Cassidy's apron and dripped off her face.

· · · · ·

Allan knocked on John's door.

"Come in."

He turned the knob and entered the room where his boss was recuperating. "Sorry to bother you, John."

"Not at all."

"I was hoping you might have a few minutes to talk."

John pushed up with his fists. "No matter how hard I try, I keep sinking down into this bed."

"Here, let me help." Allan moved forward and lifted a pillow up while John situated himself.

"I didn't realize how sore my muscles would be." John rubbed his midsection.

"That mama landed quite a kick, so you better follow the doctor's orders."

He took a sip of water. "All right, now what can I help with?"

"It's Thomas."

John raised his eyebrows.

"I just came from a meeting with Mrs. Johnson and Mr. Bradley. Apparently, he had another clumsy moment and spilled a tray all over Cassidy. So Mr. Bradley thought he should assign Thomas to me, since you are laid up and I could use the help."

John chuckled. "Go on."

"Well, last time you took him on when Mrs. Johnson had had enough of him, and while we weren't without mishap, he did do so much better for you. That's why I need your advice. I don't want to lose my patience with him."

"Ah, I understand."

"So?"

"So what?"

"How did you do it?"

His mentor looked out the window and then smiled at him. "You might not like hearing this, but I try to look at Thomas like God looks at me."

"What exactly is that supposed to mean?" He scratched his head. Maybe this wasn't such a good idea.

"It means that I know I'm a messed-up sinner. I make lots

and lots of mistakes. And yet God loves me so much, He looks past all of that and sees what I am underneath—washed clean. Without any of those mistakes."

"I'm not sure you've hit on all sixes today, John. Has that medic given you some medication that's made you a bit . . ." He lifted his eyebrows and wiggled them.

John laughed. "Oh, don't do that. Don't make me laugh, that hurts too much." He patted his middle again. "No, this isn't any medication talking. It's just plain ol' truth. The point is, how dare I think that I'm better than anyone else? No matter if I'm clumsy or beautiful and graceful, no matter the color of my skin or where I was raised. No matter if I have lots of money, or if I have none. God loves us all. Exactly the same. Not one of us can earn our way into heaven."

"I remember hearing my dad say the same thing. But how do you not get frustrated with him?"

John smiled. "With God or with Thomas?"

Allan shook his head and couldn't help but smile. John seemed to be able to read his mind. "Well, both, but for now—Thomas. It's hard to have patience when someone is making another mess while you're still busy trying to clean up the last one."

"We make a mess of things from time to time. When I err, when I make a mess of things, I want to be forgiven. I figure others feel the same way."

The words hit Allan and he knew he could no longer avoid the topic of forgiveness. Not that he even wanted to.

"John . . . I've been wrong to hold Dad's death against you." He looked down at his hands, uncertain he could continue. "I was . . . angry. When I heard about Dad, I was angrier than I'd ever been. I was angry that the war had kept me from going with him on the climb. I was angry that you had somehow failed to keep him alive, and I was angry at God for taking Dad away from me."

When John said nothing, Allan forced himself to look up. There were tears in John's eyes. "I want to do the right thing regarding my family and the business, but I'm almost afraid that what I'll uncover will be worse than what I ever imagined." Allan drew in a deep breath. "But I want you to know that I don't hold you responsible for anything that happened. And . . . I hope that you'll forgive me."

John smiled and wiped at his tears. "Son, you've always had my forgiveness."

"I appreciate that—even if I don't deserve it."

Allan got to his feet, but John wasn't finished with him. "You know, you've got God's forgiveness too. You just need to seek it."

Allan looked past John to the open window. This man was so full of knowledge. Just like his father. And he missed his father. More than he could even say. But John was asking for more than Allan could give. He was asking for Allan to say it was okay for God to take away his father. And to admit that he couldn't handle any of this on his own. Ever since coming home from the war, he'd done a pretty good job of taking care of himself—at least he'd built a pretty good fortress to hide inside.

He drew a deep breath and let it go. "I know."

• • • • •

So young Allan Brennan was getting wise.

Frank was livid. He'd done everything he could to gain complete control of the business—the business that was *his*. His! Henry had been the one in the way, but he'd gotten rid of him. Then that stupid will had to show up. He'd never forgive himself for that giant mistake. Then the son-in-law, Louis, started poking around and meddling. Like he had any say whatsoever.

And now Allan thought he could just defend his family and take sides with John Ivanoff. Who knew what stories that man had planted?

Frank threw the glass bottle in his hand up against the wall and watched it shatter and fall. He glanced back down at the telegram. No doubt, the kid had hired his uncle's firm to audit. But Frank had another card up his sleeve. All he had to do was make a phone call.

"Two can play at this game." The words drifted on the air.

# 17

The crème brulées were just about done. Cassidy prepared to take the water baths out of the oven so the custards could finish cooling and setting. Then they would have several hours to chill before dinner.

Checking the clock, she realized she had just enough time to pull them out and then to whip the dressing for the salad before luncheon.

Mrs. Johnson strode into the kitchen. "Cassidy, those custards look lovely."

She couldn't help smiling under the praise. "Thank you, Mrs. Johnson."

"I wanted to speak to you a bit before lunch."

"Yes, ma'am?" The rest of the kitchen staff might have been afraid of the head cook starting off with that statement, but Cassidy had gotten to know the woman little by little.

"First, I think you probably need to have a conversation with Thomas soon."

"Oh? About what?"

"I'm pretty sure the poor lad has a crush on you. And the sooner you nip it in the bud, the easier it will be for him to recover."

That was unexpected. Cassidy blinked. "I had no idea."

"Of course you didn't. Which makes you even more likeable. But you should be aware, half the male staff has a crush on you, my dear. And with you smiling and encouraging and laughing with everyone, they all probably think they have a chance to win your heart." Mrs. Johnson looked at her. "That doesn't mean you've done anything wrong. It just means your sunny personality is attractive."

"Oh."

"And I'm thinking that you're okay with the thought of one Mr. Allan Brennan being one of your admirers?" She tossed some flour onto the worktable and went to work on her roll of dough.

Cassidy bit her lip. Was she okay with that? She liked Allan very much. But there was still so much he needed to resolve. "Allan is a very nice man."

Mrs. Johnson laughed out loud, which was a rare occurrence. "Oh, Cassidy Faith, you do beat all."

"Yes, ma'am. I'm sure I do." She tried her best not to smile.

The head cook took a pinch of flour and blew it toward Cassidy's face. "And you're ornery too."

"Yes, ma'am." She wiped the flour off her face and continued whipping the dressing. "I'm sure I have learned that from the very best."

"If you are insinuating that I have taught you to be ornery . . . well . . . I really don't have any room to talk, now do I?" Mrs. Johnson winked at her and folded the dough in thirds. "I have to admit that I wanted to speak with you on another matter." Her voice lowered in volume.

"Yes?"

Mrs. Johnson's expression took on a look of discomfort and her mouth tightened. Whatever it was she wanted to say it wouldn't come easily. Cassidy wondered if she should say something to ease the tension, but it seemed waiting for the older to woman to speak was best. Finally the words came.

"How did you not lose faith yesterday?"

"What do you mean?" Cassidy's heart skipped a beat. Mrs. Johnson was actually initiating a conversation about God and she didn't want to do anything to discourage her.

"Last night, when your father was found injured. We spent hours together sitting on that floor waiting for news. And even though you were devastated and crying, you kept talking to God like He was right there. You never lost hope."

Cassidy stopped the whisking. She wiped her hands on her apron and prayed for wisdom. "I didn't lose hope, Mrs. Johnson, because my hope is in the Lord. No matter what might happen. But that doesn't mean that I didn't worry about losing my father. I was almost sick with worry over him—wondering what would happen if I lost him. I was a newborn when my mother died, so although the hurt of losing her is quite real, I never knew her. But with my dad, it's hard to imagine my life without him. That was a hurt unlike anything I'd ever experienced.

"And when you said I talked to God like He was right there—well, that's because He was. And still is. I didn't realize I'd been praying out loud, but I do that a lot, so I'm not surprised."

Mrs. Johnson didn't look at her but pinched off pieces of dough to be shaped. "And you believe that He hears you? And wants to hear from you?"

"All the time. Yes, ma'am."

"The way you view God is so very different than anything I've ever known."

Cassidy smiled. "My relationship with God is unlike anything else I've ever known."

Mrs. Johnson nodded. "I'm not saying I'm ready to buy into

what you believe, but I do know that I admire you for how you handled the situation. And . . . if I'm honest, I have to admit that I often want what you have. The light that shines out of you all the time. It's refreshing. And makes me want it too."

Cassidy smiled at her boss. It was a step in the right direction, and she praised the Lord in her heart for that.

The intimacy of the moment was obviously a little too overwhelming for the older woman. She hurried to the counter on the opposite side of the room. "Now, let me get a tray fixed for you and your father. I want you to take at least an hour to spend with him." She held up a hand before Cassidy could even respond. "No arguments. It's an order."

· · · · ·

The group of tourists who requested a hike up Deadhorse Hill were likely to be Allan's undoing. Women with inappropriate footwear, men with bellies too stout to balance on the side of a hill, and then there were the three boys. Their parents were part of the group, but Allan couldn't say who they actually belonged to, since the adults seemed too preoccupied with their blathering conversations about this and that.

In fact, Allan wondered if there was a lick of sense found among the whole group.

Thomas led the way up the hill, since the three youngsters had way more energy than the adults in the group, and Allan wanted to be prepared to catch whoever would fall next. He hated giving such a huge responsibility to Thomas, but the lad seemed excited to take on a challenge.

And a challenge it was. The boys ranged in age from eleven to fifteen—or so he'd been told—but frankly, they acted like five-year-olds. Pushing, shoving, tripping each other. And covered in dirt. Each one of them from head to toe.

Allan just hoped that none of them had any brilliant ideas of jumping off cliffs.

"Mr. Brennan, did you say that we might see moose?" The stoutest man of them all stopped for a moment. Probably to catch his breath.

"It's a strong possibility, sir, but with all the ruckus we're making, I doubt the moose will venture anywhere near us."

"Oh, well, that's too bad. I hear they're awfully cute and awkward-looking." One of the ladies adjusted her parasol and huffed.

Allan knew he should bite his tongue, but he couldn't contain it. "Actually, ma'am, it's better if we don't see them. They are very dangerous animals."

"Well . . ." she huffed again. "That's not what I've heard." She strutted up the hill, wobbling on her silly shoes.

How did John do this? Day in and day out. The man had the patience of a saint. Of course, what was he thinking? John *was* a saint. The man's forgiving spirit and patient endurance was a credit to him. He saw the good in everyone—at least if there was good to be found. Apparently there hadn't been much of that when it came to Frank Irving. Allan had been so blinded by his sense of injustice and need to blame someone that he'd very nearly missed the deception and underhanded actions of his father's former partner.

Whoops and hollers echoed down from above and brought Allan's attention back to the distasteful task at hand.

While the other adults seemed content to meander their way up the hill, Allan began to worry about Thomas and those boys. And what they could get into.

"If you all believe that you are doing all right, I'd like to check on the youngsters, so I'll go on ahead."

"Oh, please do. That Billy of mine can be quite a prankster."

Another of the ladies plopped down in the grass. "And I'm quite worn out already and these mosquitoes are pesky and annoying."

*Great. A prankster.*

With nods and murmurs from the rest of the group, Allan headed up at a faster clip. While the fresh air invigorated him, the steepness of the trail made it slower going than he'd hoped.

The last twenty yards or so, Allan heard voices.

"Come on, Thomas! Don't you want to try it? Everybody else is . . ." one of the boys' voices squeaked.

"No, and neither should you." Thomas sounded so much older than before.

"It ain't hurtin' nobody. Don't be such a killjoy."

"Hand 'em over, Billy."

Allan was impressed. When push came to shove, it looked like Thomas was made of sterner stuff than he'd given him credit for. Creeping up the hill, he listened and tried not to be noticed.

"No way! My parents gave 'em to me."

"That's a bunch of baloney and you know it." Thomas's voice deepened even more, but his tone was even. "I will speak to them about this as soon as they get here."

The younger boys all seemed to be laughing.

"They won't make it up here. They just want to pretend to be adventurous. Besides, why would they listen to you? You're nothing but the help—a worker. They'd never believe you over their own son. And it's three against one."

"Come on, fellas, we need to smoke these while we have the chance." Billy seemed to be the ringleader. He pulled a matchbook out of his pocket and lit his cigarette. He puffed and didn't even choke on it.

The other two clambered forward and lit matches and then their cigarettes.

Thomas walked in the other direction. What was he doing? After standing up to them, now he was just going to walk away?

Allan waited and watched.

Then the coughing began. First, the shortest kid, then Billy. He actually looked a little green now. Then the last one succumbed to a coughing fit and dropped his smoke.

Before they knew what was happening, the grass was on fire as well as Billy's pant leg. The boys all started screaming like little girls.

"I'm on fire! Do something!" Billy looked toward Thomas.

Allan jumped up but saw Thomas racing toward them. He reached the boys and dumped water from his hat and an entire canteen onto the small fire, effectively quenching it.

So that's where he'd gone. To the creek. To fill the canteen and his hat with water.

That moment was as good as any for him to appear, so Allan walked the rest of the way to the boys. The three troublemakers looked up at him with fear in their eyes.

"How's your leg, Billy? Did it get burned?"

"A little, sir." A single tear slipped down his cheek. "So . . . you saw?"

"Yup. I sure did." Allan checked the boy's leg. The hair was singed, but no other damage except to his pants. He held out his hand. "I'll take the rest of those cigarettes and matches."

"Aw, man. You and your stupid ideas, Billy." The older of the two boys kicked the dirt.

Once he had checked all their pockets, Allan gave them a speech about fire safety, especially in the wilderness, and told them to sit right where they were until the adults joined them. Then he told them if they moved, he'd tell their parents everything.

Surprisingly, the threat worked.

Allan turned to Thomas. "I'm proud of you. That was awfully brave standing up to them."

"It was the right thing to do."

"And when you walked away?"

"My plan was to just dump water over their heads to teach them a lesson. I didn't know they'd be dumb enough to catch themselves on fire."

He slapped the young man on the back while he laughed. "You did good, Thomas."

"Thank you, sir." He straightened his shoulders and stood even taller. "I don't know if I would have before I learned about Daniel."

"Daniel?"

"You know, from the Bible? Cassidy told me about him a while back. So then I asked Mr. Ivanoff about him, and we've been studying together, since he can't do much else. Cassidy inspired me when she said she wanted to be like Daniel." Thomas puffed his chest out. "I want to be like Daniel too." He walked away and stood over the boys.

A tinge of jealousy sparked through Allan. The seventeen-year-old had bested him. He wondered if maybe John had space in his Bible study to include a rather wayward twenty-eight-year-old.

# 18

John shifted in his bed and moaned. Good thing Cassidy wasn't in there to hear him. He'd tried not to let her see how much the bruising affected him, but he had a feeling she knew anyway. And he had to admit, he wasn't getting any younger. Two kicks from a moose had done a number on him. It had been three days and still he hadn't been able to stand up yet. The first few days were to be the worst. He knew that.

A knock sounded at the door. "Mr. Ivanoff?" Thomas's voice preceded his head as he peeked around the door. "You've got a letter."

"Thank you, son."

Thomas handed him the letter and nodded. "I'll be back later to check on ya, but I need to help Mr. Brennan."

The postmark caught John's attention as Thomas left.

Ireland.

It had been twenty-three years since he'd seen that on an envelope.

Tearing it open, he held his breath. Only one page. But as he read it, it packed a wallop.

Eliza's parents were reaching out from the other side of the world.

And they were asking for forgiveness.

• • • • •

John awoke later with tears dried at the corners of his eyes. Wiping away the crusty remains, he took one more look at the letter. He'd waited for so long to hear from them, it pleased him to no end to hear they'd had a change of heart. But could he put his daughter through the ups and downs of hope and possible rejection?

His body ached. Confounded bed. He hated being stuck in it.

Tucking the letter back in its envelope, he put it under his pillow. Best to just let this one sit on the back burner for a while. He had more important things to worry about. Like getting through the summer lineup and planning an expedition up Denali.

But first, he had to heal. And quick.

He wanted to be back out there. Not just to be with his daughter, but he felt an urgency to help Allan.

His apprentice could do the job—of that John was certain. But something else in his heart prodded him on. Ever since Allan's appearance in July, John's mind had churned with the details of the trip up Denali, the loss of Henry, and Frank's demeanor. None of it added up. So what had he missed?

And then there was Allan. He was still struggling and seeking to fill the void in his heart with remembrances of his father. But John knew—better than most—that the void could only be filled by God.

"Lord, I'm not sure why You've got me laid up in this bed right now, but I'm betting it's for a good reason. Maybe it's because I needed to spend more time talking to You. Well, here I am. Allan needs You, Father. And I feel inadequate in leading him. So I need Your direction and Your words. Then there's Cassidy. I know You love her more than I do and want the best for her. I've had this feeling in my gut that You brought Allan here for her. If that's Your will, Lord, let it be done. Bring Allan back to You, Father. Keep Cassidy strong through all of this. And Father God, I know it's asking a lot, but I'd appreciate Your help in healing this flesh of mine—"

"—because You know he's not a very good patient." Cassidy's voice cut in.

John chuckled. "Yes, Lord, You know it's true. In Jesus' name I pray, amen."

"Amen." Cassidy set down the tray she'd brought in and held out a hand to him. "Sorry to intrude on your prayer, but I came to see how you are doing."

He grabbed her hand and squeezed. "Other than feeling my age with these bruises, I'm doing all right." The letter popped into his brain. Should he tell her? No. Now was not the time.

"Liar." She squinted at him. "And you're only forty-five. That's never slowed you down before, so I don't think you can use age as an excuse."

"Okay, okay. I'm hurting a lot. And sick of being in this bed."

"But it won't be too long now. Didn't they say that the first few days would be the worst? Everything on your insides is bruised. Let it heal."

"Prayerfully it won't be long now. I'd like to get back to walking pretty soon."

"Well, that leg is pretty beat up too. Doc said no real walking for a week—just a few more days. Then after that, I'm sure it won't be any time at all before you're up and at 'em again." She laid a napkin across his lap. "Now, it's time to eat so you can build up your strength, and if you eat everything, then you may have dessert." She brought him a plate with a sandwich and beamed him a smile. "I want to hear about all the stories Allan has shared."

"Poor man. He's had his fill of tourists for the summer, I think."

"I can only imagine. Thomas came into the kitchen and told us about the fire the other day." She poured them both a glass of lemonade. "We were all so proud of him. You know, it's amazing, he hasn't had an accident or fallen down once since then."

John picked up half of his sandwich. "He's a good lad. And he's got a knack for tracking as well, I've noticed." He ate a bite and then took a sip of lemonade. "He also seems to be a bit smitten with you, daughter."

She cringed and laid her own sandwich down. "I was afraid you were going to say that. Mrs. Johnson said as much."

"And?"

"Well, I'll talk to him. I don't want to hurt his feelings, though. I like Thomas a lot."

He reached over and patted his daughter's hand. "I know. We all do. But from the first time he came to me to talk about studying Daniel and said you inspired him, I could tell by the gleam in his eyes that he was over the moon. Not that you're not worth being over the moon for, but I have an inkling that your feelings tend to drift toward a certain blond-haired gentleman."

Cassidy was silent for several moments as she chewed. John hoped he hadn't overstepped with his precious daughter.

After a long look out the window, Cassidy turned back to him. "I admit I'm drawn to Allan, Dad. But I know that nothing can come out of it—at least not for the time. He has so much he needs to figure out. I want to be his friend, and of course I'm praying for him." She fell silent for a moment. "I didn't think it would be so hard."

"What?"

"Seeing his pain and knowing I can't make it better. I'm praying for him, but it seems so little to do for someone I've come to care for. It hurts me as well. And it's not just where Allan's concerned, but Mrs. Johnson as well."

John's heart overflowed with love and admiration for this girl the Lord had so graciously given him. "Your mother would be so proud of you. As am I. The Lord has given you a tender heart for those who are hurting and lost. He'll also give you the wisdom and strength to bear up under the burden. Remember, He never asks you to bear anything alone."

Cassidy smiled. "I know, but I'm glad you are reminding me. It's easy to forget when my heart gets all tied up in knots."

He winked at her. "Your mother used to tie my heart up in knots, so I know how that is. I think Allan is a wonderful man, and I know God isn't done with him yet—in fact, I've seen some mighty important changes. Just give him time."

Cassidy scrunched up her nose like she used to as a little girl when she didn't like something. "If he wasn't such a brooder . . ."

"A little brooding can actually do the soul good," John countered.

"And his smile. He's such a handsome man, but his smile never quite reaches his eyes. Like he's guarded about something. I think my one wish is to see a real smile on his face. One that makes his green eyes sparkle."

He just about spewed lemonade on that one. "Well, I don't know, anything about his sparkling eyes, but let's keep praying for him, shall we? God's the only one who can fill the void in Allan."

"Deal." Cassidy stuck out her hand.

He shook it.

"Thanks, Dad."

"For what?"

"For always being there and always listening."

"Anytime, Cass." He hadn't used her nickname in a long time. She'd grown up so fast and into such a beautiful and delightful woman. Eliza would be proud indeed. "Now, did I hear something about dessert?"

She giggled. "You and your sweet tooth . . ."

A knock sounded at the door.

"Come in." Father and daughter spoke at the same time. Cassidy laughed again and walked over to the tray.

Allan peeked in and smiled. "I just wanted to see how you were doing and if I could keep you company for a while, but I see you already have a better visitor than me."

"Nonsense." Cassidy handed John a spoon. "Please stay. In fact, Dad would probably love to hear how your morning went while he eats his dessert." Her eyes had a new sparkle in them. One John couldn't miss.

John smiled to himself. Oh, to be young again.

"Don't go getting all spoiled on me, but I admit I made your favorite—chocolate mousse." She handed him a bowl. She turned to Allan. "And I have another one right here, if you'd like it, Allan."

John raised his eyebrows as he took the first bite. To separate Cassidy from her chocolate was quite an ordeal. The fact that she offered it up freely spoke boatloads to him. He looked from one to the other.

Allan accepted the dish with a nod. "It's one of my favorites as well, so I won't pass it up." He glanced at the tray. "But what about you? Isn't this yours?"

Cassidy took her fork and pointed toward John's bowl. "Nope. You go ahead. I'll just steal a bite or two from Dad."

John enjoyed the lively conversation about the guests and the fun things Cassidy was concocting in the kitchen, but after a few minutes, she gathered up the dishes.

"I've got to get back." She leaned over and kissed him on the forehead. "You and Allan have a nice visit, and then I think you need a nap. You look tired."

He shook his head. "Only because I am."

She smiled and left the room.

John looked at Allan. "What's on your mind, son?"

"I was wondering if once you are recovered, we could continue the plan to climb up McKinley—Denali." Allan cleared his throat. "I know we have plenty of time, but I had an idea. I was hoping we could work at two different routes to see which one would be best suited for other climbers in the future."

"That's an excellent idea."

"I know you understand that I want to climb the mountain myself for personal reasons, but I've had three other men— guests from the hotel—ask if expeditions up the mountain would be offered in the future."

John nodded. What he'd always hoped for, in fact. "We don't need to wait for me to recover to plan. We can start now." He tried to sit up straighter, the adrenaline and excitement pushing past the pain. "I'll need you to go to my room and on the shelf above my desk, there's a dark brown leather book next to my mother's Bible. Go get that and bring it back." He rubbed his hands together. "This is just what I need to get my mind off being laid up."

•••••

The hour with John had been exhilarating. After he'd grabbed the book, they'd pored over John's notes together. The man was meticulous and had research from every angle of the great mountain. The maps were glorious. And Allan could taste it. He would finally, truly follow in his father's footsteps. He imagined his father sitting with John and going over the same details. He could almost feel his presence when John described the dangers of climbing on the glaciers. Had his father felt the same surge of excitement when John showed him the best places to make their camps?

Allan gave a sigh. *Dad, I wish I could have been there with you. Maybe then you'd be here now, with me.*

Their dream of climbing Mount McKinley together would never come to fruition, but at least he could honor his father by climbing it in memory of him. When he'd first talked to John about planning an expedition, his heart hadn't been right—and he didn't feel the true excitement that he felt now. But something else had changed too. While he couldn't pinpoint the reasons, it didn't matter.

"No matter how much planning goes into the climb and the equipment needed," John said as he absent-mindedly rubbed his abdomen, "things always go wrong. Harry Karstens would tell you that himself. You try your best to plan for the worst, but sometimes the worst isn't at all what you thought it would be."

"How so?"

John continued to rub his stomach. "Well, for me, and I think Harry would tell you the same was true on his climb, you think of things like how to deal with the storms and wind. You know there are certain problems you'll face, like crevasses opening up where you least expect it or avalanches. You're less expectant of tent seams ripping and having no way to repair them or of oil stoves clogging—even setting the tent on fire. Then there are the bodily things. Fingers and toes that never quite seem to thaw out."

"You lost two toes, I recall Cassidy mentioning." Allan couldn't imagine how difficult that must have been.

"I did, but it's not unusual. Frostbite will do damage to your face and extremities and in some cases you could lose a finger or toe. You try to take care of those things, but it's difficult to master some of the day-to-day work with heavy gloves and mitts on your hands. You soon learn that even ordinary things like relieving yourself becomes an exercise not without its dangers."

Allan stretched his arms. "You're right, those are things I honestly hadn't given a lot of thought. Dad and I did several mountain climbs together, but never were they as high or isolated as this."

"And that's the danger I think we'll find with so many of the folks who come here to climb. I fear that it won't be long before throngs of people will make their way up here and just climb without much planning or a guide. They'll figure it to be no more dangerous than their other climbs."

"You really should work with Superintendent Karstens and create some kind of a guidebook, John. Then even if the people do come without bothering to check in with Mr. Karstens or seek to hire someone to guide them, at least they'd have the book."

John gave several slow nods as he seemed to consider this. "You know, that isn't at all a bad idea. In fact, it's something you could even sell along with your outdoor gear."

"I like that idea. Maybe a series of books based on various climbs."

"Why limit it there? You could create books that would give detailed listings for hiking trails and let the reader know the degree of difficulty and what amenities are available—you know, like fresh water, sheltered camping, paths to accommodate horses or pack animals. Those kind of details might very well save lives."

Allan slapped his leg, getting caught up in the excitement. "My father used to say that with all the modern conveniences, a lot of folks no longer know how to live off the land or survive in bad situations where there's no one else to help them, and very little in the way of equipment. We could teach folks how to make a shelter out of nothing but pine boughs and how to find dry wood and kindling in a rainstorm. We could detail how to

set up a fire to benefit them the best for cooking and heating."
He had to admit the ideas were coming faster than he could
share them. "I remember my dad telling me that starting and
maintaining a good campfire was paramount to deeming the
success or failure of survival. We could even teach folks how
to start a fire when matches aren't available."

"And then how to make certain the fire is extinguished before leaving the area. I've seen some sorry situations arise from
carelessness in that area," John admitted.

"You know, I really think we have something here. Especially
where Denali is concerned. Most would be unaware the tree
line is at one thousand feet. So the lack of wood for fires and
shelter will make for even harsher conditions. There aren't very
many men who could offer true wisdom regarding the climb
and what's needed to make it successful. Even if we start small
and just create a booklet, I think this would be a very useful
thing. We could work on it throughout the winter."

"Then you plan to stay?" John raised his eyebrows.

His question caught Allan by surprise. He hadn't really considered that possibility. He knew at some point he would have
to go back to Seattle and deal with the problems at hand. Not
only that, but there was the matter of his personal possessions
and other things he'd need to start a new life in Alaska.

He couldn't help but grin. "You know what, John? I just
might."

"Well, may I offer a bit of advice?"

Allan was taken aback. "Of course you can. I think you know
that by now. Next to my father, you're the only man I respect
enough to listen to." He smiled. "What is it?"

"Pray about it." John held up his hand as if expecting a protest
from Allan. "I know you've had some rough waters where the
Almighty is concerned, but, Allan, you will never be happy until

you put those matters to rest. Allow for the fact that even though you don't understand Him or still have questions regarding why He allowed your father to die, He still knows best and is quite willing to show you what's best."

"But . . . well . . . I'm still so angry with Him." Allan surprised himself by being willing to speak the words aloud.

"Then forgive Him."

Allan shook his head. "Forgive God?"

John smiled. "Well, not exactly. God doesn't need our forgiveness, after all. But since we're human and think in such ways, it might help you to consider it. See, forgiving is all about letting go—about giving over our right to retribution. It isn't approval, like some folks think, and therefore won't offer it. It's a release." A weariness came to John's expression. "And until you find a way to let it go—you'll always be stuck in the same place."

As Allan walked back to the equipment shed to prepare for this afternoon's hike, his thoughts drifted to Cassidy and of staying in Alaska. Mostly, however, he thought of John's words regarding forgiveness. John was wise—like Dad. Dad always stressed the importance of forgiveness. Over the years since losing his father and enduring the war, Allan had truly given little thought to forgiveness. Now since coming to Alaska, it seemed that issue was all he could think on. And while he'd learned to forgive John—even seek his forgiveness—Allan wasn't sure how to go about making things truly right between himself and God.

If Cassidy were here, she'd no doubt tell him it was simple. Just do what needed to be done. Life seemed very straightforward for her—and John. He envied them that and the love they shared.

The relationship Cassidy had with her father was special—just like Allan's with his father had been. But the Ivanoffs had something different. Perhaps it was due to the death of Cassidy's mother or maybe because they lived in such an isolated location.

Their love for one another seemed so easy and sure. And their laughter, happiness, and sunshine really did seem to radiate out of Cassidy's skin. The more he got to know her, the more he realized that her optimistic and shining outer shell truly was a reflection of her inside. She wasn't offering up pretense. She spoke her mind and shared her feelings without being overly concerned about how someone might take it. It wasn't that she sought to be cruel either. She just wanted the truth on the table, as his father might have once said.

John and Cassidy hadn't known that he'd been outside the cracked door listening to their earlier conversation about him. Or how their words had affected him. Was God really the only person who could fill the void inside of him? Allan would have adamantly said no a few months ago. Now he wasn't so sure. Especially after witnessing the strength in John. And in Cassidy as well.

She attracted him like no one else ever had. But she thought he was a brooding man. That didn't conjure up images of romance.

But even so . . . it was apparent she liked him. But found him lacking.

He looked up to the brilliant blue sky for guidance.

Maybe he needed to learn how to let his smile reach his eyes.

# 19

The summer sun of August in Alaska beat down on Cassidy's head. Even in the evening hours, the heat could be brutal. She fanned herself as she walked next to Allan, both to cool her face and to keep the mosquitoes from it.

How could it already be the twenty-second of August? In the past two weeks, a lot of things had changed at the Curry. The Annex behind the T-shaped building of the hotel was now housing overflow. The night cook and his staff were having to increase their preparations so the kitchen would be ready for the following day. Mr. Bradley was even talking about the need for additional cooks for the next summer, much to Mrs. Johnson's protests. He assured her she'd still be in charge, but the woman had only harrumphed and exited the room. Cassidy couldn't help but smile at the memory. Mrs. Johnson might put up a fight, but in the long run she'd come around.

Besides the endless hours of work required in the kitchen, there was the laundry and its problems. The laundry now serviced up to thirteen thousand pieces a month between the railroad dining cars, the Anchorage and Nenana hospitals, and the hotel. The hotel alone accounted for half that number of fresh linens. There wasn't just bedding to consider, but kitchen and serving towels, cleaning and polishing rags, aprons, tablecloths, and linen napkins. There were also the staff's clothes and of course the towels and washcloths for all of the bathrooms. Cassidy knew the laundry worked round the clock to meet the needs, and Mr. Bradley felt additional staff was needed there as well.

The differences at the hotel weren't the only changes. Cassidy and Allan spent more time together visiting with her dad in his room while he recovered. Then they began taking him for short walks once he was up to it. The last few days, Dad was walking without a limp but still tired easily. And as he would head back to his room in the evenings, she and Allan would continue their walk together. They fell into the new routine easily, and Cassidy marveled at the ease in conversation.

Allan smiled more often now too. Especially when he talked about their plans for a Denali expedition and the guidebooks they were working on. The more time she spent with him, the more she liked him, and the greater urge she felt to pray for his heart. What had been a dear friendship to her was already becoming much more than that. She couldn't be certain, but Cassidy feared she'd already fallen in love with him.

Could she lose her heart to Allan Brennan?

"Your dad was telling me about 'Cassidy Lane' this afternoon." Allan's steps were slow down the path. He looked at her with such warmth. "How does it feel to have a dangerous cliff named after you?"

That was another thing. He made her laugh quite often, and she loved it. "I guess I could take it a couple of different ways, but I'd like to think that it's endearing rather than ominous."

"I agree. I thought the story was quite charming. Apparently, my father did too." He clasped his hands behind his back as he walked and his smile faded a bit.

"Your father sounds like he was an amazing man." This topic always threw Cassidy for a loop. Her own father loved to talk about Henry now—but in a positive and almost joyous tone. It always seemed the opposite for Allan. His memories were fraught with sadness and pain. But maybe that was because no one ever encouraged it to be otherwise.

"That he was." Allan turned toward her again. "I wonder if there's some ridgeline up there that I can name in my father's memory?"

"You never know. You might get up there and find the perfect spot. There are many places that have been named by those who've gone before. I'd bet my father would remember someplace where your dad was particularly happy or in awe of the scenery."

"That's a good idea," Allan responded. "I hadn't considered that possibility."

Cassidy drew a deep breath and let it out slowly. "You must have been quite special to your father."

Allan cocked his head to one side. "Why do you say that?"

"Dad told me you were the only son in your family. Sons have a special place in their father's hearts."

"Daughters do too." He smiled. "My dad was always doting on my two sisters."

"Oh, I agree, but you must allow that there is something unique between a father and son. I always wished Dad could have had a son."

Allan surprised her by laughing. "I think he's more than content with what he has in you. You light up his world."

"But I'm sure he misses having a son."

"How can he miss what he's never had?"

"I miss my mother and I never had her." Cassidy saw him wince and wished she could have taken the words back. She began walking again, uncertain what to say.

Allan easily caught up with her. "I'm sorry, Cassidy. I didn't think before speaking. Of course you miss your mother, but don't you see—she existed. The memories of her were able to be shared with you, and even though you didn't have a chance to know her personally, you've learned to know her through the hearts of others."

"I never thought of it that way."

"It makes a big difference. Not that a person can't long for something. I'm not saying that at all. I long for a great many things. I'm sure your father would have loved a son, but when I watch him with others—even in how he deals with me—I think he has found great purpose with the sons of other men."

"He does love people. He always has. He's always been so generous with his time and love. There isn't a person back in our village who didn't love him." She smiled at a memory. "In fact, my father could have remarried many times over. There were always women who tried to win his affection."

"Why didn't he take another wife?"

She stopped and met his gentle expression. "He said he could never love anyone as much as he loved my mother. He didn't think it was fair to make another woman live in her shadow."

Allan nodded. "Your father is indeed a very wise man."

"I like to think so. He's given me great insight and wisdom over the years. He's always encouraged me—like with my cooking. He knows how much I enjoy it and he helped me get the job here. He's always telling me to seek the desires of my heart."

"And what are those desires?" Allan asked in a barely audible voice. She wasn't sure, but she thought he also might have moved just a little closer.

She longed to change the subject, but wasn't sure how. Her knees seemed to weaken as she stood there so close to him, gazing into his eyes. The thought of sharing a kiss came to mind and Cassidy felt her face flush.

Footsteps behind them broke the moment as they both turned to look.

Thomas ran up waving an envelope. "A telegram just came in for you, Mr. Brennan."

"Thank you, Thomas."

The young man ran back to the hotel while Cassidy waited for Allan to open it.

He stared at it.

"Would you like me to give you some space? I can head back by myself."

"No." Allan tore the envelope. "I'd like for you to stay." He read the contents quickly and then grimaced and sighed. He handed it to Cassidy. "Here, read it."

```
22 August 1923
Coming to Alaska (stop)Need to discuss business
(stop)Expect me on the 28th (stop)
Frank
```

She handed it back to him. "What do you think it means?"

"I have no idea." Allan looked at the river. "I haven't heard anything about the audit, and Louis hasn't sent anything either." He tapped the paper against his palm. "It makes me wonder what Frank is up to."

●●●●●

The heat of the kitchen drained the life out of a person. Cassidy couldn't remember the last time she had perspired so much. And it wasn't a pleasant thought. She wiped sweat off her neck with a towel and went back to assembling the puff pastry stuffed with asparagus and lemon zest. The buttery pastry was one of her favorites. It made her mouth water to think of the glorious flavors melding together.

But the heat. Goodness, it was almost enough to make her wilt. If they didn't need the ovens on, it sure would help with the temperature. But the ovens ran day and night to simply keep up with the bread needs for the hotel.

Mrs. Johnson was red-faced and dripping herself, but the woman kept everything going like clockwork. No one could ever complain about the food at the Curry. It was always, *always* delicious and on time.

Her thoughts drifted to Allan and their walk. Ever since that telegram from Frank, he'd been quiet. And had gone back to brooding. She missed her friend, but she also prayed for him in a new way. The weight of taking care of his family rested firmly on his shoulders. And no matter what she did or thought, something about Frank didn't sit well with her.

*Lord, only You know our hearts. I don't want to judge Frank without knowing the truth, but my heart aches for Allan and his family. Something scares me about Frank coming here, but I don't know what it is. Please help to calm my heart. Draw Allan to You. And help me to show Your love to Frank as well.*

"Cassidy, you're looking mighty warm." Mrs. Johnson came to her station.

"Yes, ma'am. It's hot today." She didn't dare comment on how warm the head cook appeared.

"Well, I know I'm about to melt into a great big puddle, so I imagine you're pretty uncomfortable yourself." The woman pulled out a fan and leaned closer. "You're doing a fabulous job. Especially considering the heat. Thank you."

Compliments from her boss were few and far between. Cassidy smiled up at her. "If it gets any worse, though, I'm going to want to jump in the frigid Susitna."

Mrs. Johnson chuckled. "You and the rest of us! Wouldn't that be a sight? The kitchen staff all floating down the river."

She fanned herself some more. "I wonder what they would do about dinner." Raising an eyebrow, the older woman smirked. "They would never make it without you, Mrs. Johnson."

The rest of the staff seemed busy across the kitchen, so Cassidy decided to brave a question. "I've thought about what you said regarding Thomas. I want to say something to him, but I don't know how to go about it. He's so sweet and I don't want to hurt him. I thought maybe you could advise me on what to do—what to say."

Mrs. Johnson grew quite serious. "Honesty is always the best. Of course, don't embarrass him by speaking to him in front of others. That wouldn't be right."

"Of course not."

"You might not believe this, but I had my share of young men who I had to disappoint."

Cassidy smiled imagining a younger, but just as fierce, Margaret Johnson. "I certainly can believe it."

"Letting others down gently isn't easily done, that's to be sure. Even so, it is always best to just explain the situation and move on. Find a time when you can be alone with Thomas. Start with a kindness and then explain the truth of the matter."

"What do you mean?"

Mrs. Johnson frowned. "Tell him he's a nice young man or that you admire the way he's worked hard to change his everlasting clumsy ways. I don't know. Just say something nice so that it's easier when something not so nice follows."

"Do you suppose that will really make it any easier?"

Mrs. Johnson shook her head. "No, I doubt it. He's quite batty over you, and nothing will make it any easier when he hears that you don't feel the same way." She reached over and patted Cassidy's arm. "Just be gentle and kind. Don't give him any reason to think you're looking down on him or making light of his feelings."

Cassidy nodded. "I would never do that. Thomas is such a fragile soul in so many ways. He told me how hard things were growing up in the orphanage. How the missionaries there forced God upon the children but taught them very little about His love. I'm sure Thomas longs for love more than anything else in his life."

"We all do," Mrs. Johnson admitted. Then as if she'd said too much, she turned away and took on her gruff, bossy façade. "Now, I want everyone to pick up their pace. These meals don't prepare themselves!"

• • • • •

The platform outside the hotel wasn't any cooler than anywhere else. Allan paced the length of the hotel and back, but nothing could get rid of the gnawing in his gut. He'd telegrammed Louis but had no response. What was going on? And why on earth was Frank coming here?

His long strides ate up the boards but did nothing to ease the anguish.

"Thomas said I'd find you out here." John stood under the awning, his arms across his chest. "Here, this letter came for you." He held out an envelope.

Allan walked over and took it. He checked the postmark—Seattle, and nearly two weeks past. Flipping it over, he saw Louis's name. "Thanks, John. Let's hope this has some answers in it."

"Anything I can do to help, or do you just need to read?"

"I'd like it if you would stick around while I read it. I might need your advice."

"I'll be here." John walked over to a bench, took off his hat, and sat down, fanning himself.

Opening the letter, Allan prepared for the worst.

*14 August 1923*
    *Dear Allan,*
    *I'm sorry to say that the news I must share with you is grave.*
    *I've been fired from Brennan/Irving for embezzlement. Frank actually accused me of stealing. But it's worse than that. He has accused the whole family of being in on it, stating that we were unhappy with Henry's will (that Frank inherited half of Henry's stake in the company). Your mother slapped Frank and ordered him from the house.*
    *Before I go any further, I must tell you, emphatically, that I have never stolen from the company. The accusations from Frank are untrue.*
    *But the story doesn't end there. Frank has told Mother that he is going to sue if she takes one more penny from the company. He says that he's been terribly hurt by the unkind treatment and doesn't understand how we could do this to him. Even worse, he's been telling the story to other business relations in Seattle. He has tarnished the Brennan name. Your mother says it wouldn't be right for us to try to defend ourselves right now—it would just feed into the story Frank has told. But this has crushed her. She trusted Frank like a brother all these years.*
    *Uncle Melvin's firm did indeed do a thorough audit. I'm sorry to be the bearer of more bad news, but somehow the books have been swapped. (I know this for certain because the books presented at the auditor's findings were NOT the ones that we used day in and day out.) I don't even know where to begin to find the real ones, and now*

*my hands are tied, since I am not allowed anywhere at the company.*

*We brought in Josiah Biedermeier to attempt to straighten out the mess, but he's hit a major roadblock. The audit was done by a family firm that we hired. The man who Uncle Melvin put in charge of the audit was a Mr. Ephraim Henderson. Uncle Melvin assured us he trusted the man. But now Mr. Henderson has disappeared. Along with all of the files from his office.*

*I know this must be terrible to hear, but it was too much to put in a telegram. I've decided to assist a man our lawyer has hired in the search for Mr. Henderson. Somehow, Mr. Henderson must be the missing link to all this confusion.*

*Through it all, your mother and sisters are well. Emotionally this has devastated them, but they have bucked up under the weight of it and are ready to carry on. We believe that we must be united. There is sufficient money set aside for the running of the household and day-to-day needs. Your father, as you know, was not one to invest all of his money in one place. I will continue to oversee the finances, unless of course you feel me unworthy in light of what has happened. You must think of your mother and sisters first. However, I pledge you and them my loyalty.*

*As to Frank, he played the martyr well, or perhaps he truly is hurt thinking that we have wronged him. But rest assured, we will continue to seek the truth.*

*Your mother, Anna, and Ada all send their love and prayers. They had a prayer vigil for you last night, knowing that the receipt of this letter would be difficult.*

*I will, most likely, not be available for a few weeks as we search.*

*As to the company, I will leave that up to you to decide
what is best. We will do our part to ascertain the facts, and
if I have any news, I will telegram immediately.*

*Your brother-in-law,*
*Louis*

Allan growled and crumpled the paper in his hand. "That man is lower than a snake."

"Let me guess. You're talking about Frank Irving."

Allan met John's knowing gaze. "None other. The man has treated my family abominably. He has accused the entire family of robbing him blind. And he has ordered them to stay away from the business, fired my brother-in-law, accusing him of embezzlement, and told my mother she is not to have any more proceeds from the company."

"Are they left destitute?"

Allan shook his head. "No, thank God."

John smiled. "Do you mean that?"

"Mean what?"

"That you're thankful to God they aren't destitute?"

For a moment Allan considered the question. Then he nodded. "I am. It will take God's intervention to make this right. Frank Irving is quite astute, and it's obvious he's the one responsible. I'm willing to bet that if money is missing—he's the one who has it. Or who had it. Dad said that while Frank had a head for books and the overall running of the office, he was a poor steward of his money. It seemed Dad was always loaning him money or allowing him to draw from the profits, even though they paid themselves a reasonable dividend every quarter. My brother-in-law has brought in the family lawyer to help, so that should afford me an edge."

"Are you to return to Seattle, then?"

"I don't know what I'm going to do. My brother-in-law says things are under control and that my mother and sisters are fine. As he points out, my father was good to diversify his holdings so the loss of Brennan/Irving would be hard, but would not leave my family in financial ruin."

"So Frank would steal the company out from under you? Would you allow for that?" John watched Allan the entire time.

"It's not the company that matters. I only have a fourth interest in it anyway. And there's no reason I can't start up my own company and do it bigger and better. Dad was the one who had the ideas for new gear, and between you and me, I'm certain we could continue along those lines."

John smiled but said nothing. Allan knew he'd presumed upon the older man's willingness to participate, but at the moment that was the least of his concerns.

"What matters is my father's good name. I won't have the likes of Frank Irving running it into the ground the way he has the company."

"And how will you stop him?"

Allan let out a heavy sigh. "I don't know. He'll be here soon, however, and I need to have a plan in place."

"I'd like to help if that's possible."

"I appreciate that you would help me. I'm afraid I'm at a complete loss as to how to handle this. I've known Frank all of my life, but I don't think I really know him at all. I can't help but wonder if Dad knew how underhanded and deceptive he was."

"Well, it's possible that even Frank is being duped."

Allan's eyes narrowed. "What are you saying? Do you think my brother-in-law is lying? That he's really responsible for embezzlement?"

"No, not at all. I'm merely suggesting it is possible that someone else in the company could have done it."

The idea wasn't without merit. It was possible that someone could be working behind the scenes to frame Louis. Perhaps he had an enemy at the company—one who was envious of his position. Perhaps wanted his job.

"You're right. There I go jumping to conclusions again. I trust Louis implicitly, so it seemed obvious to find Frank at fault."

John shifted and stretched his legs out in front of him. "I'm not saying Frank isn't to blame, but I think you should consider all the possibilities. Frank isn't stupid. If this is his doing, he will have planned it out and had a whole lot more time to consider all the details. If he's set this up to blame your brother-in-law, as you suspect, then he's no doubt created the necessary proof. You're going to have to find some way to reveal the truth."

"Well, Frank's going to be here in a matter of days. That means he won't be at the office. I could arrange for someone to go through everything. Everyone makes mistakes and Frank is no exception. I'm going to get word to Louis. He was well liked, and he's bound to have friends in the company who would be happy to help him get the information we need."

"That's a good idea. Perhaps that lawyer might arrange for some legal papers that would help. I'm sure there is probably something that a judge could do."

"You're right, John." Allan felt a glimmer of hope. "I appreciate talking to you. It's helped more than you know." He unclenched his fist and looked at the wadded-up letter. "I just want to make sure I do all I can to make this right."

"Well, there is one more thing I would advise."

Allan looked up and met John's smile. "What's that?"

"Pray. We all need to pray on this and ask God to reveal the truth."

# 20

Cassidy couldn't stop thinking about that moment with Allan before Thomas interrupted them and how she thought Allan might kiss her—and how she'd hoped he would. Her thoughts had been a jumble ever since. She knew Allan was gradually working through his issues with God and that he'd asked her father for forgiveness. The two were, in fact, becoming quite close.

The two most important men in her life had become friends. Her father commented just the night before about how he had seen great changes in Allan spiritually and felt certain he was finally on his way to working things out with the Almighty.

That, of course, gave Cassidy great joy. She couldn't allow herself to fall in love with a man who didn't love and serve God. Nor would her father ever sanction any such union. No, if she were to marry anyone, he would have to put God first.

Marriage. Where had that thought come from? She didn't even know for sure that she was in love, although she highly suspected that was the reason for her confusion and sense of elation. Goodness, but was it like this for everyone? It didn't seem a minute went by without some thought of Allan going through her mind.

"Cassidy Faith, what in the world is wrong with you?" Mrs.

Johnson came and forced the measuring cup from Cassidy's hand. "That's salt—not sugar."

"Oh my." Cassidy looked at the cup and then to Mrs. Johnson. "I'm sorry. I guess my mind was elsewhere."

"Why don't you go work on the hollandaise—you've never had any trouble with that."

"I don't know what's wrong with me." Cassidy quickly moved away to do as Mrs. Johnson requested. Whirling around, however, caused her to collide with several newly washed pots. They went flying off in several directions, crashing to the floor in a loud metallic clatter.

"Cassidy!" Mrs. Johnson shook her head. "Have you been taking lessons from Thomas?"

Two of the young women who helped in the kitchen came running to see what the problem was. They stood in amusement, pointing at the pans and Cassidy, giggling all the while.

"And you two . . ." Mrs. Johnson stalked to where the girls now stood, trying to compose themselves. "You have potatoes to peel and vegetables to cut up. I'm almost certain you couldn't possibly have completed it in the few minutes you've been at work."

"No, ma'am," one of the girls replied. The other cast her head down.

"Then get to work! I won't have you dawdling about my kitchen."

Cassidy had just retrieved one of the pans by the time Mrs. Johnson turned back to address her. "I want a word with you. In the other room. Now."

She swallowed the lump in her throat and put the pot aside. Following Mrs. Johnson, Cassidy knew she'd have to explain herself.

"You've been making mistakes all morning. First it was dropping that crock of cream. Then it was burning the rolls. I've never seen the likes."

"I am sorry." Cassidy forced herself to meet Mrs. Johnson's displeased gaze. "I haven't been myself."

"I should say not. What in the world is wrong with you? You weren't even this distracted when your father got hurt. Now he's up and on his feet again, but you seem completely daft."

Cassidy folded her hands. "Mrs. Johnson, have you ever been in love?"

The older woman's mouth dropped open, but no words came.

"I'm sorry if that was an inappropriate thing to ask, but . . . well . . . you see . . ."

"You fancy yourself in love." It was more statement than question. Mrs. Johnson led Cassidy by the hand to a chair. "Sit and tell me everything."

They each took a seat and Cassidy cleared her throat. "I don't know if I'm in love. I think it's very possible, but I've never had anyone around to tell me what a girl feels when she's in love."

"And what do you feel?" It looked as if Mrs. Johnson was trying to keep from smiling.

"Confused, mostly."

"Sounds about right." This time Mrs. Johnson did smile. "Go on."

Cassidy shook her head. "I find myself thinking about him . . . Allan. I think about him all the time. I find myself wondering what his favorite food is and what he thinks about. I wonder if he ever thinks about me and if maybe he feels the same way.

"One minute I think I have a good grasp on it—on my thinking and my heart, but then I see him and find myself quite overwhelmed. Sometimes when we walk together I'm so nervous I can't even speak. My knees get all weak, and my hands get sweaty. Then just as I get control of that, he says something and I find myself feeling quite . . . well . . . I don't even know what to call it. I don't know what I'm feeling."

Mrs. Johnson nodded. "It sounds like love all right. Never felt quite as useless as when I was in love. I couldn't seem to do anything right until I accepted I'd contracted the fever and gave in to it."

"You make it sound like a disease." Cassidy laughed. "But I suppose it does feel like that. I feel like I've come down with something. I wasn't even this bad off when I had the measles."

"Falling in love is never easy."

"Do you think Allan knows how I feel?"

Mrs. Johnson snorted. "He's too blinded by his own feelings to know much of anything."

"What do you mean?" Cassidy frowned.

"I mean he's batty for you. Even more so than Thomas. I've seen the way he looks at you. He watches you all of the time. I feel quite certain he is just as caught up in this sickness as you are."

Cassidy felt a surge of joy at Mrs. Johnson's declaration. "So what do I do? Do I just go and tell him how I feel?"

"I have no advice on that matter. You see, love is a very individual thing. Much like your measles. Some folks take a light case and others fight for their lives. It all depends on the people involved." She looked past Cassidy and seemed to forget she was even there.

"When I fell in love, it was all I could do to keep food down. Like I said, I wasn't any good to anyone until I gave in to it. But in my case, he was very vocal. He wooed and courted me in spite of my initial disinterest. He proposed several times, and I laughed at him and told him I wasn't of a mind to marry. The darn fool wouldn't take no for an answer, though. He told me that sooner or later I would be his bride."

"It sounds very romantic to me."

Mrs. Johnson looked back at her with a sad smile. "It was. And I miss him very much."

Cassidy reached over and took hold of the older woman's hand. "But do you regret it—love, that is? Do you regret having fallen in love?"

The look on her face changed to one of pure joy. "No, Miss Cassidy Faith. I do not regret it. Falling in love was the best thing that ever happened to me."

●●●●●

The deck of the steamship was crowded as Frank edged his way to the bow. Now that the seas had calmed, everyone wanted fresh air.

He just wanted them all out of his way.

A plan had formulated in his mind over the last week. He could play the martyr—and a changed man all at the same time. The Brennans were all churchy, Bible-thumping, give-everyone-a-second-chance type of people. Frank could use that to his benefit. The devastation of the family embezzlement drove him to God. And there, he'd changed. Now he only wanted forgiveness and to offer forgiveness. Oh, he would make them feel so guilty that they wouldn't challenge his legal rights. All would be right with the world.

Let them think that anyway.

The years of patiently waiting for his due were over. This time, there wouldn't be any mistakes.

Little by little he'd let various men know about his plight. Men he felt certain were and would remain on his side. Sympathy had poured in for him from business associates across Seattle when they'd heard the news about the embezzlement. Frank had to admit, he liked the attention, even if he had to keep playing the wounded victim for a time.

He'd paid a reporter to put a story in the paper. Nothing that shared any real detail, but instead gave just a hint of scandal and the question of responsibility. This brought other reporters to his doorstep and allowed Frank to portray himself as the wronged individual who refused to point the finger at any one party, but felt unfairly taken advantage of by some betraying source.

The only pieces of the puzzle standing in his way were Allan and John. Frank had thought he could have what he wanted in spite of them, but that wasn't proving true. Allan wasn't as easily manipulated as he had been at first. Given time, he would no doubt conspire with Ivanoff—if he hadn't already done that. Ivanoff had never liked Frank—it was almost as if he could read his thoughts and knew the darkness in his soul. All the time on their descent from the mountain, Frank had been certain John was suspicious. Frank had been sick and played it to the hilt to avoid John's endless questions about what had happened. However, he hadn't been too sick to realize John suspected him of foul play. Once they were back in Anchorage, Frank rallied from his illness to point the finger at John. He had heaped copious amounts of blame on the man—condemning his leadership skills and calling him negligent. He hoped it might even lead to John's arrest, but it seemed there was no real law in Alaska. People dying on a mountaintop didn't seem all that unusual. He laughed in spite of himself.

People dying anywhere in the wilds of Alaska didn't seem all that unusual. In fact, it was expected. After all, death was around every corner for the trained and untrained alike. With any luck at all, Frank would use this to his benefit. With any luck at all, he'd soon be free of any entanglements. John Ivanoff and Allan Brennan would no longer be a problem.

●●●●●

The hike for the morning had been canceled due to rain, and Allan was glad for the respite. He and John planned to meet in the basement reading room of the hotel to plan a little more for their Mount McKinley expeditions and guidebooks. Allan realized over all the talks he'd had with John that he preferred the native name, Denali. It rolled off the tongue and sounded regal and fitting for such a mountain as the High One.

Even though he knew that John was using the distraction of planning the climb to keep his mind off Frank's arrival, thoughts bombarded him hourly. He still had no idea how to learn the truth about what had happened to his father, nor what was happening back in Seattle. John had been right about one thing: Frank was crafty.

Allan took the stairs down at a brisk clip and shuffled the papers in his hands. While John had several maps of the Alaska Range, there was still so much unknown about each mountain. Glaciers were everywhere, icefalls and sheer granite walls were prevalent. And the crevasses. They were mostly unseen until upon them. Or falling into them.

Every other expedition that they knew of had come into the Alaska Range from the north. The successful summit in 1913 and his father's own summit in 1917 had both taken the Muldrow Glacier up. And that was after the serious trek into the national park all the way from Nenana.

Even the entrance to the national park was far north of where they were in Curry. If they journeyed by train up there, it would only be wasted time and energy. Whereas at Curry they had the prime location to start.

As he laid the papers out on the table, excitement built in Allan. Curry's location was not only perfect for the railroad as a needed stop between Seward and Fairbanks, but once the ridge to the west was crested, the views of the Alaska Range were incomparable. And they were so close. In fact, Curry was only forty miles away from Denali "as the crow flies." Wouldn't it be wondrous to one day open up the Curry Hotel as the premier location to venture into the national park and climb the tallest mountain in North America?

Thoughts of staying in Curry long-term appealed to him. More than he'd ever imagined they would. He enjoyed working with John and knew the man's dream would be to lead expeditions up the mountains. He thought it more than a little exciting to be a part of that. Even plans to create and publish guidebooks gave him a sense of satisfaction that had long been missing in his life.

Then there was Cassidy. Just the thought of spending time with her thrilled him. He had to admit it. There were feelings present.

But she held back. And with good reason. Allan had come here under different pretenses. Granted, he still wanted to find out what happened to his father, but before, he'd thought John was responsible. And he'd blamed God. Admittedly, he still did. Allan hadn't quite come to terms with that, but at least now he actually wanted to. He also knew he'd have to figure that out before he could advance his relationship with Cassidy.

He shook his head. One step at a time.

"Just wait until you see this latest map." John entered with a huge smile on his face holding a long roll of paper. "Karstens has been working on it for the government and he allowed me to copy it. It took a while, but I believe I was able to duplicate it correctly."

"Let's open it up." Allan felt like a little boy planning his first tree house.

"Now, if you look here"—John pointed with his pen—"I believe that for our first ascent we could take the Ruth Glacier up to the east side of the buttress. From there it would be very steep, but the south summit is doable, depending on the icefalls and crevasses. Since we already have a decent trail blazed from here to the Ruth, we would just need snowshoes and a dogsled team to go up the glacier for about thirty or so miles and then our climbing equipment from the wall here. Base camp could be here, in the northwest fork of the glacier that climbs up."

Allan studied the idea John had. "This looks outstanding. The most distance will be covered on the glacier, correct?"

"Yes, but the most time-consuming will be above ten thousand feet. And that's after we reach the wall here."

"I like it. So for the second ascent, what were your ideas?"

"I haven't studied it enough, but the Kahiltna Glacier seems to be the next logical step. I'm familiar with the glacier, but not with that side of Denali."

Allan nodded and studied the map a bit more. "Well, then, I think you're right. We should start with what we know and go from there. There's bound to be more than one good way to reach the summit, right?"

John laughed. "Yes, but sometimes, you find several other ways that do not reach it at all. I've explored the possibilities and discussed it at length with Karstens. I've even read things written by others who attempted to explore the area."

"I've climbed a few fourteen-thousand-foot peaks in the States with my father. But that's been years and, of course, not this far north. Should we attempt a smaller peak in the range first, for training purposes?"

"That would actually be very wise. We could try for the Child first if you would like. That would get you used to the sleds, snowshoes, and other climbing apparatus. As well as the weather."

"When should we plan?"

"I'd say March or April for the smaller mountain. And then aim for a June expedition on Denali."

"That will give us plenty of time to put away more stores of food."

John brought over another piece of paper and a pen. "Karstens wrote this down for me—it's how they sustained themselves in 1913. Granted, they had to take lots of time away from the expedition to hunt and then prepare it, but we have the upper hand. We can start on it now and preserve it to take with us."

Studying the paper, Allan was fascinated. Rather than taking cans of pemmican with them, they made their own. He read aloud. ". . . A fifty-pound lard can, three parts filled with water, was set on the stove and kept supplied with joints of meat. As a batch was cooked we took it out and put more into the same water, removed the flesh from the bones, and minced it. Then we melted a can of butter, added pepper and salt to it, and rolled a handful of the minced meat in the butter and moulded it with the hands into a ball about as large as a baseball. We made a couple of hundred of such balls and froze them, and they kept perfectly. When all the boiling was done we put in the hocks of the animals and boiled down the liquor into five pounds of the thickest, richest meat-extract jelly, adding the marrow from the bones. With this pemmican and this extract of caribou, a package of erbswurst, and a cupful of rice, we concocted every night the stew which was our main food in the higher regions."

Putting the paper down, Allan looked back to John. "I've had the canned store-bought pemmican on other expeditions with my father, and it wasn't pleasant at all. This actually sounds good. When should we go hunting?"

Another laugh. "As soon as we have another break in the schedule. I don't think Mr. Bradley will mind at all. Especially since he knows that we are doing all of this to expand the experience for future guests of the Curry."

"Mr. Brennan!" Thomas's voice carried down the stairs. He rounded the corner and strode purposefully to Allan. "Another telegram."

"Thank you, Thomas." Allan tore the envelope and muttered, "I swear the telegraph company is the one benefiting from this fiasco."

John patted Thomas on the shoulder. "And thank you for all your hard work lately. We have appreciated you."

"Thanks, Mr. Ivanoff. I'm finding that even though I like kitchen work, I like the outdoors and hiking a lot more. Especially when we go fishing." The boy, who was really almost a man, smiled at them both. "Of course, I don't get to see . . . ah . . . some of the folks in the kitchen when I'm working outside."

Their conversation faded behind Allan as he walked away and read the brief note.

```
26 August 1923
Frank coming to you (stop)Found evidence of foul
play at Henderson's (stop)Police on the case
(stop)Be wary (stop)Best not to tell him you
heard from me (stop)
Louis
```

A thousand questions clamored for attention in his mind. Henderson was the auditor who worked for his uncle. What kind of foul play? Did that mean the man was dead? How did Louis know Frank was coming to Alaska? Or did the police suspect something and they tried to warn the family?

"Allan?" John's voice broke through his thoughts. "Everything all right?"

"I don't think so."

# 21

As he made his way back to the kitchen, Thomas thought about Cassidy. She and Mr. Brennan seemed to be spending a lot of time together lately. And he liked Mr. Brennan a lot. But what if Cassidy did too?

"If she does, it's because I haven't told her how I feel," he murmured. It made perfect sense that Cassidy would want to share her time with someone. Thomas just had to find a way to let her know how he felt.

The object of his thoughts appeared and she jumped back. "Goodness, Thomas." She put a hand near her throat. "I didn't realize you were right there."

"Sorry to startle you, Miss Cassidy. I guess I wasn't paying attention."

"That's all right." She took a deep breath and folded her hands in front of her. "I actually wanted to talk to you."

"Really?" His insides quivered and he couldn't help the smile that covered his face. She'd looked for him! Maybe explaining his feelings wouldn't be so hard after all.

"Yes." Then she gave him one of her beaming smiles that had the potential to melt all the snow on Mount McKinley. "Why don't we go sit in the dining room?"

He nodded and followed her. Anything she wanted. He'd

follow her anywhere. He pulled out a chair for her and then took a seat on the other side of the table so he could look into her expressive eyes. She really did have the most beautiful eyes.

She placed her hands in her lap. "I hope you know I think very highly of you, Thomas. I've seen you work hard to make changes around here and you've borne up under that stress with great dignity." She paused and cleared her throat. "I also want you to know that I like you very much."

"I like you too." More than he could say. In fact, his brain couldn't come up with anything better to say and his mouth felt like it was stuffed with dry bread.

Another brilliant smile. "I just want to make sure that I haven't confused you."

He furrowed his brow. Confused him? She seemed to be the only person who could explain things to him where he actually understood.

"Let me start again." She looked down and then back into his eyes. "It has come to my attention that you might perhaps think of my friendliness toward you as if it's in a romantic way. And it wouldn't be fair for you to keep thinking like that." She drew a deep breath and continued. "Not that you aren't deserving of a girl's romantic feelings toward you—you are a wonderful young man—it's just that I would never have wanted to give you the wrong impression. I'm so sorry if my actions to you have been untoward."

Thomas didn't understand. He blinked several times as his eyes felt dry and then he thought he might burst into tears at any moment. "Are you saying that you *don't* like me in that way, Miss Cassidy?"

She bit her lip for a moment and shook her head. "I'm sorry, Thomas. I never meant to lead you astray. I do like you very much . . . as my friend. And I hope we will remain friends for the rest of our lives."

He looked down at his lap. "Is this because I'm an orphan? Am I not good enough? Too clumsy?"

"Heavens, no! You're wonderful just the way you are. It isn't like you have a sign hanging over your head that you're a bad person because you're an orphan. That's never mattered to me. I grew up without a mother and my grandparents wanted nothing to do with me. People can't help what happens to their folks."

"I didn't know your grandparents didn't want you."

Cassidy nodded. "Sometimes it really bothers me. My mother had no choice, but they did and it hurts to know they walked away." She squared her shoulders. "But enough about that. I just want to assure you that your being an orphan has nothing to do with my feelings for you. As for your abilities, you must remember, I was much clumsier than you at one point."

"I don't think you've ever been clumsy, Miss Cassidy." He felt a growing sadness wash over him. It was like he was all alone again.

"Thomas, I will still be here for you, and there are a great many people here who truly like you." It was as if she'd read his mind. "One day you are going to find the perfect young woman to fall in love with."

*But I already love you.* He left the words unspoken.

"And when you find her, then you'll realize what I'm talking about when I say that our kind of love is more like that of a brother and sister." She squeezed his arm. "Thomas, you are the last person in the world I wanted to hurt. If I was untoward, then please forgive me. I truly do think you are an incredible young man and I am blessed to have you as my friend."

"I'm blessed too, Miss Cassidy. And I don't think you have

been untoward. You've been my friend. And I really appreciate that." He stood up. "I need to go now."

He hurried from the room fighting back tears. There wasn't any way to explain the emotions that surged through him. But he did understand that Cassidy Ivanoff didn't love him like he loved her.

•••••

Cassidy fanned herself on the train platform. She'd agreed to wait with Allan and her dad to greet his father's partner, Frank Irving. But tensions were high. And it wasn't just the heat that seemed to strain everyone's nerves. She didn't know the full extent of problems that existed with Mr. Irving, but it was evident that both Allan and her father were less than pleased to have the man coming to Curry.

The whistle sounded in the distance, which meant the train was almost there. She turned to Allan. "Are you all right?"

"Yep." His lips were a thin line.

"You don't look all right."

"Well, I don't know what to expect."

Dad placed a hand on Allan's shoulder. "I've been praying for you."

Allan's brows knit together. For a moment Cassidy thought he might protest, but then he gave a curt nod. "Thank you, sir." His eyes remained on the tracks.

Dad leaned back behind Allan and caught Cassidy's eyes. His look covered a gamut of thoughts. Allan wasn't ready for this. And he was obviously still angry at God, or at least dismissive of prayer, even with all the healing he'd come through the past few weeks. The arrival of Frank Irving could be disastrous to his tenuous thread of hope.

She took a deep breath and watched the steam engine ease

toward them as it came to a stop. No sense worrying about what was about to happen. She had a front row seat to watch it unfold whether she liked it or not.

The seconds ticked by as if they were minutes. Passengers disembarked. Luggage was gathered.

Then an elegantly dressed man with silver hair showing around his ears descended the steps.

Cassidy felt Allan tense next to her.

The man headed straight for their group. He looked into her eyes, and even though his were a brilliant blue, they made her feel cold even in the insufferable summer heat.

All of a sudden the man smiled. "Allan, my boy! So good to see you." He clapped a hand on his shoulder. Before Allan could reply, he dropped his hold and turned.

"And my, my, if it isn't John Ivanoff?" Frank nodded toward Dad. "How long has it been, John?"

"Six years." Dad took Frank's proffered hand and shook it. "Welcome to Curry."

The man removed his hat and fanned himself. "Thank you. I didn't remember the heat being so intense." He looked at Cassidy. "And you must be Miss Cassidy Ivanoff, of Cassidy Lane fame." The man bowed a bit, took her hand, and kissed it.

"Um, yes. I guess I am." She wasn't quite sure what to make of this man. But he seemed . . . oily, and she immediately wanted to wash her hand.

"Why don't we get you settled in a room, Frank?" Allan extended an arm toward the hotel's entrance.

Dad took that opportunity to take her elbow and lead her toward the door, but she realized she wanted to hear what Frank would say next and so she kept her steps slower than usual and her ear attuned to the men behind her.

"It's so good to see you, son." Frank's voice seemed smooth

as cream. "I have to admit that one of the reasons I wanted to come all this way in person is to make sure you—my partner—were all right. That everything is well between us. Especially after that terrible disaster with Louis." The man *tsk*ed several times. "After all, one can't choose who their family members are, but you can choose who to trust. Business partners need to have the utmost trust, don't you agree?"

"I do." Allan cleared his throat. "Quite adamantly, I must say."

"I also came to tell you that while your family has hurt me deeply, I am a changed man from the Frank Irving of the past. I'm hoping we can move forward into the future with no regrets."

Mr. Bradley allowed for some of the staff to eat with John, Cassidy, Allan, and Frank Irving in the main dining room after the rest of the guests had been served. It had been a lovely dinner Cassidy was quite proud of, but now that she sat down for a few moments, her feet ached, and her head wanted nothing more than to hit her pillow for the night.

But the men continued talking. Hiking, climbing, and the latest gear seemed to be the topics of the evening.

"It appears, Miss Ivanoff, that we have lost your attention." Mr. Irving's comment brought her head back to the conversation at hand.

"I apologize, Mr. Irving. Did I miss something important?"

"We were just discussing your father's plans to find other suitable approaches to climb Mount McKinley." Those cold blue eyes drilled into hers in an almost accusing manner, even though a smile seemed plastered to his lips in contradiction. Something about it made her uncomfortable.

"Well, he is an expert in that area, Mr. Irving." She brought her water glass to her mouth and took a drink.

"That he is. That he is." Frank tapped the table. He leaned

back in the chair as if he owned the place. "I say, why don't we put a climbing expedition together while I'm here?"

Cassidy sputtered on her water. Quickly grabbing a napkin, she dabbed her mouth.

The man turned to Allan and patted his back. "The idea has been on my mind the entire trip north. I suppose because the last time I made this journey, that was the excitement and motivation. As I get older, however, I find it important to act quickly on our desires. None of us knows how much time we have on this earth." He looked around the table. "Not only that, but I've been wanting some good exercise and fresh air. It's been some time since I've gone mountain climbing."

Allan looked to Cassidy, his jaw clenching. "It's a little more than just good exercise. I don't know if that's a very good idea, Frank. It's late in the season and we'd have a lot to do to prepare."

"Seems to me the weather is just fine. The heat today could have melted my hat."

Allan shook his head. "That's all well and good, but it takes a lot of time to plan . . ."

"And my father . . ." Cassidy hated to interrupt, but she had to. "It's only been a few weeks since his accident."

"An accident, you say?" Frank's attention shot to Dad. "John, you look healthy as a horse. What happened, man?"

Her father picked up his own water goblet and swirled the contents. "Nothing too major. Just had a run-in with a moose." His pointed glance at her made her insides jumble. She knew better than to contradict him.

What was going on?

"Well, then?" Frank smiled around the table. "Shall we give it a go? If the weather did turn bad, we could turn back. It's not like we'd have to climb to the top. I've already done that, as have you, John, and Allan . . . well, he'd have plenty of opportunities in the future. No, I think we should just strike out and do as much as the weather and our energy allows."

When no one said anything in response, Frank continued. "Not only that, but such an endeavor would allow me time to make plans. It would give Allan and me time together to discuss business. I could get some good ideas for equipment to supply, and we'd get to build trust together as we planned it."

Murmurs around the table did nothing but encourage Frank. The idea seemed to excite the other staff.

But Cassidy felt a knot growing in her stomach.

Thomas entered the dining room with a tray. "They're already planning a trip. You should see the maps—whooo-eee."

Frank pointed to Thomas. "See? It's meant to be." He slapped Allan on the back. "I've never seen you decline such a wonderful challenge."

"Well, it's just that . . ."

"And it would give us a chance to bond. I know you always wanted to climb it with your father. I could help you accomplish that dream." Frank put a hand over his heart. "And we could talk about what *God* has done in my life."

Why did he sound so fake? The men weren't buying this man's story, were they?

Her dad looked toward Allan. "We have done a lot of the legwork and planning already. If we took a couple weeks to finalize the details, we could leave after the last booked fishing trip. Mr. Bradley has already voiced his support. He won't mind us moving up the timeline, since it will probably help with advertising for next year, and that means next year we'll be available for more trips."

What was her dad saying? He actually agreed with Mr. Irving?

"I don't know . . ." Finally, Allan was being a voice of reason.

Cassidy sat back and crossed her arms. She knew she liked him. "I agree the time is too short . . ." Allan leaned forward. "But it's even more important to stay ahead of the weather. I think we should do it."

She took it back. They were all a bunch of harebrained, ridiculous men. And she didn't want anything to do with them.

# 22

Whatever had possessed him to volunteer to climb that stupid mountain again? Frank paced his room, smoking a cigar.

There wasn't any real logical explanation other than the fact that as soon as Allan and John shared their excitement about their future plans, Frank saw it as a way to get rid of them both. He'd killed Henry that way, hadn't he? It seemed ironic that he should eliminate his other problems the same way.

But he had no desire to go trekking up a mountain again. Sleeping in tents. Eating food that was only worthy for dogs and gutter rats. There had been nothing about that trip six years ago that had been worth the time and money. With exception to Henry's death, of course, and even that didn't satisfy as much as Frank had hoped it would.

As the night escalated with the men's plans, Cassidy left, citing a headache. He was just as glad to see her go. The young woman was rather unnerving. She seemed to gauge that something wasn't quite on the up and up, and Frank didn't need to have to worry about her interference. Especially when there were details to iron out and plans to be made. Way too many plans.

In the end it was concluded that John's Ahtna-Athabaskan tribal people would help. Frank was less than excited when he heard this. The fewer people around the better. It would force Frank to wait on his plans until they were able to leave them all behind at the lower camp. He sighed at the thought of the work that would have to be done. They'd have to do a lot of snowshoeing and use dogsleds again. There would be that ever annoying need to walk hunched over, poking a stick into the ground to make sure that the trail wouldn't give way to some endless glacial hole. And then there was the cold.

Frank shook his head.

He really should stop complaining. He'd provided the perfect scheme. He wouldn't have to climb all the way up. Just once they left base camp with the helpers and dogs behind, he'd have to look for his opportunity.

He walked over to his bag. This time, he'd come even better prepared. Unwrapping a brown paper package, he pulled out a thirty-eight revolver and a brand-spanking-new hunting knife he'd taken from The Brennan/Irving Company. It didn't have to look like an accident, because there wouldn't be any witnesses. And because of the very accommodating nature of the glacier, he'd have no trouble ridding himself of the bodies.

He'd be the only one to come back alive. And of course—he'd be grief stricken.

•••••

Cassidy slammed the pie crust dough down on the worktable. All morning long, the staff had been abuzz about the team climbing Mount McKinley. After she'd snapped poor Marie's head off with her words about the stupidity of the idea, the rest of the group left her alone. No one here had ever seen her in less than a positive spirit. And they definitely hadn't seen her lose her temper. Well, they were getting an eyeful *and* an earful today.

The wooden rolling pin sped across the dough. There wouldn't be any issue getting the crust thin enough today. She was mad enough to roll it out as thin as paper.

"Cassidy Faith." The kitchen was hushed at Mrs. Johnson's voice. "I'd like to see you in the dining room, please."

Cassidy nodded but kept rolling.

"*Now.*" Mrs. Johnson's voice was sharp.

She blew the hair off her forehead, set the wooden pin down, and wiped her hands on her apron. "Yes, ma'am."

In the dining room, Cassidy crossed her arms. Deep down, she knew she was acting like a toddler throwing a tantrum, but her anger ruled out everything else.

Her boss turned to look at her as soon as she shooed everyone else out of the room. "Let's get one thing straight right now, missy. I will not abide you taking out your ill-mannered and uppity temper on the other staff in this hotel. You seem determined to prove to me that you aren't all gumdrops and rainbows, but I assure you there is no need. Nor desire. No matter what, you will treat the others with respect."

"I didn't—"

Mrs. Johnson cut off her protest mid-sentence.

She stepped closer to Cassidy and pointed her finger. "I don't want excuses. For someone who I never thought could have a bad day, you sure do beat them all. Did you know that Mrs. McGovern just had to speak with me because you lit into one of the maids and she hasn't stopped crying since?" The older woman began to pace. "I don't know what has gotten into you, but it needs to stop."

Cassidy bit her lip.

"Well? Do you have anything to say for yourself?"

A few moments passed, but then Cassidy couldn't take it any longer. "I don't think they should go."

"You don't think who should go where?"

She rolled her eyes. Now she knew she was being impertinent. "The men. I don't think they should go up the mountain."

"And they need your permission *why* exactly?"

The woman knew how to stab her where it really hurt. "They don't. But my father is just now healing and last time he went up there, he lost a man coming down—"

"But it's not your decision."

"But neither one of them even thought about me and what I—"

"Aha. So there it is." Mrs. Johnson put her hands on her hips. "You're offended that your dad and Allan didn't consult you before making the decision."

Pretty much.

All her life, her dad had talked things through with her. But now he didn't need her. He talked to Allan instead. And Allan . . . well, he should know better. At least, if he cared about her, he should. Maybe that's what really ate at her. Maybe Allan didn't feel the same way she did.

Mrs. Johnson's arms came around Cassidy and pulled her in for a hug. "It's hard being in love, isn't it?"

•••••

He hadn't seen Cassidy all day, and when Allan asked Mrs. Johnson about her, she gave him a scolding glance and shooed him away.

It didn't seem right. Almost every day now, they walked in the evenings together, but Cassidy was nowhere to be found. And Allan couldn't wait to share everything with her. He paced the spot where they usually met and considered all that was happening.

It had all moved so fast. Once the decision had been made, momentum took off. Sure, their timeline wasn't ideal, but all the pieces were fitting into place nicely. John dug out the equipment he'd had from the last expedition, and they'd spent the day trying on gear, patching the tents, and making lists. Frank wasn't his ideal climbing partner—or business partner for that matter—but Allan was still excited. The man had several stories of how his life was now changed. He was even going to church. Could the conniving Frank of the past be gone? Maybe Louis and his family just didn't know.

Allan's dream of climbing Mount McKinley would finally be realized. Not only that, but Allan had it in the back of his mind that once they were actually on the mountain away from everyone else, he could finally get Frank to tell the truth. The truth about the business and about his father. Especially if the man was being honest about God changing his life.

Allan's questions could be put to rest. His dreams come to fruition. Maybe they could even square away the disaster that happened with the company.

It was funny—although he didn't trust Frank, Allan thought him far less imposing than he'd expected. The man was accommodating and even pleasant. When he made suggestions and John or Allan overruled them, he yielded. Often he was even self-abasing, admitting how little he knew and how grateful he was for their wisdom. Maybe he really had changed.

Allan wasn't entirely sure they were being all that wise, given the way they were advancing their plans. John had always been a very cautious man who gave heavy regard to the details. This time . . . there wasn't that luxury. Now they had to scramble for everything from gloves and mittens to thick woolen socks and backpacks.

It was a good thing John had gotten that info from Karstens regarding the food. Last week's hunt had been prosperous, and they had enough homemade pemmican balls made to make it through the whole trip. Of course they still needed a variety of other stores, but Mr. Bradley had been generous after their promise to repay. They were blessed.

Now if he could just talk to Cassidy, all would be right with the world.

He glanced at his watch. It was well over an hour past the time they usually met. Something must have happened to keep her occupied. It wasn't like they had any promises to meet there. But until now—she had come with regularity.

Allan couldn't help feeling the loss of her company. Cassidy affected him in a way he'd never known. She'd encouraged his love of Alaska and of Denali. The mountain was no longer just the place where his father had died. It had become a steadfast companion, constant and in many ways comforting. Through Cassidy's eyes, Allan had learned to look for the positive things in life—the good in people—joy in the moment. She had a passion and a love for life and Alaska that exceeded anything Allan had ever experienced. He wondered if there would ever be a chance . . . a time when she could love Allan with that same degree of passion.

He looked down at his watch and then once more in the direction Cassidy had always come in the past. Nothing. He put aside his disappointment and headed for the staff sleeping quarters. They had an early morning fishing trip planned with some guests, so he'd better head on to bed. He'd have to find Cassidy at luncheon tomorrow.

For two straight days, she'd managed to avoid him, but Allan couldn't figure out why. Sure, their schedules were jam-packed, but that hadn't stopped them from finding time to chat before. John said that he hadn't spoken to Cassidy either, which was doubly strange. Maybe Mrs. Johnson had some major event coming that the men didn't know about. That would explain it. But he decided to wait in the dining room anyway. Just in case.

Allan sat down with a paper from Seattle and decided to catch up on the news from last month. Between the President's visit, then subsequent death, and everything else at the Curry, Allan had no idea what was going on in the rest of the world. Frank happened upon him shortly after Allen finished with the front page.

"We've had so little time to talk since my arrival," Frank said, taking a chair opposite Allan. "I know there's much to be said between us."

Allan put the paper aside. "Yes, I suppose there is."

"I'm sure you have questions about Louis."

With a nod Allan fixed his gaze on Frank. "Yes. A great many."

"Well, I suppose the temptations were just too great. I've been suspicious of the man for years. I tried to overlook the occasional discrepancy for the sake of the family, but the loss became far too regular."

"And you questioned him about this?"

"It wouldn't have done any good," Frank countered. "He would never have admitted to it. I think the fact that you called for an audit of the books left him trembling in his boots. I was quite grateful that you made the decision for that. It took some of the pressure off of me."

"I would still like to hear what Louis has to say."

"Oh, I'm sure he would have some sort of excuse—if he admitted to any of it. I think for the sake of the family it's probably best to just let bygones be bygones."

Allan knew better than to believe Frank—at least the old Frank. But what about now? "So you don't intend to press charges?"

"Well, I had considered it. I'm not one to treat thievery lightly. I always figure it just encourages others to take advantage.

However, in this circumstance, there are only a handful of people who know the truth. To have him arrested would force your entire family into scandal. Your good name would be dragged through the courts and I fear it would spell disaster for the company."

"I'm not afraid of that." Allan could see his statement caused Frank to squirm. "In fact, I would welcome a trial. I want to get to the bottom of it. I want the truth to be told. If Louis has done what you say he did, he deserves to go to prison."

Allan heard Cassidy's distinctive laugh. He had to speak to her. He turned back to Frank. "If you don't mind, I have some business to attend to."

"As do I." Frank jumped up, seeming only too happy to put an end to the conversation. "I hope you have a productive day, my boy. I find it most difficult to wait for our impending journey." He gave Allan a nod and made his way from the dining room just as Cassidy entered. Allan watched as she stepped aside to let Frank pass. He gave her a nod and then disappeared.

Allan thought she looked relieved. At least until she turned back and saw him. Anxiety mixed with what appeared to be distaste filled her expression.

"What's wrong?" He stood and crossed the room to be near her. She shook her head. "Nothing."

"I don't believe that for one minute, Cassidy." He stepped closer to her. "I thought we'd just been too busy to see each other, but now, by the look on your face, I'm thinking that I've done something to upset you."

Her hands fidgeted in front of her. She looked down for a moment and then looked back into his eyes. "I . . . I . . ."

The hurt he saw there was almost his undoing. For the rest of his days, he never wanted to see her look like that again. He took her hands in his. "Go on. What is it?"

"I'm worried."

Her words took him aback. "Worried about what?"

"You . . . my father . . . the expedition. All of it."

Was that all? He smiled. "Oh, Cassidy, there's nothing to worry about. That's why I was waiting for you. I wanted to talk to you about all the exciting things—"

"That's just it." She pulled away. "It's going to be mid-September when you leave. The temps will still be moderate most likely, but I've seen the snow fly here in early September. Snow down here means major snow up there. And you're heading into the wilderness knowing this! My father used to always say that June, July, and August were the best times to do any climbing in Alaska. I just don't understand. You were planning an expedition for *next* year. And then Frank comes along and says, 'Hey, let's do it now' and you all just think it's a grand plan? Why do you even trust the man?" She placed her hands on her hips.

Allan had never seen her feisty like this. She'd always been so positive and upbeat and now she seemed . . . well, to be honest, she seemed angry. He held up both his hands. "I came up here wanting to climb Mount McKinley eventually. You knew that. I thought you'd be happy for me."

"Happy? How could I be happy? The time of year is a disaster, the time crunch is a disaster, my dad is still healing *from* a disaster, and you stubborn men are dashing around to make all these plans, and you didn't even think to ask how I felt about it when the two men I care most about in all the world—" She slapped her hand over her mouth.

The words were like a punch to the gut. But a good one—if there could be such a thing. She was worried about him and she cared for him. Sweeter words couldn't have ever been said.

Allan took hold of her arms with a new confidence. "Cassidy . . . I'm sorry. It was wrong for us to not include you."

He inched closer to her again, intent on doing what he'd wanted to do for a very long time—kiss her. "Forgive me?"

Tears spilled out of her eyes and without a word she pushed him away so hard that he nearly lost his balance. Allan steadied himself and started to call out to her, but she was already gone.

He thought about going after her, then decided against it. She obviously needed time, and he knew what that felt like. A slow smile formed and Allan couldn't resist whirling on the heel of his boot. She cared about him. In that moment he felt like he could have run straight up the side of Denali.

·····

Cassidy could hardly see for her tears by the time she crested Deadhorse Hill. She found her favorite rock and plopped down to have a good, long cry. Why did things have to be so complicated? Why couldn't Allan and her father understand how hard this was for her?

She buried her face in her hands and sobbed. She had a terrible feeling that something horrendous was going to happen to them on that mountain, but no one cared. No one would listen to anything she had to say about it.

Rustling sounded in the brush behind her. Cassidy stiffened. She'd been foolish to fly up here without her rifle. She drew in a deep breath to force her nerves to calm.

"Cassidy?"

Thomas peeked around the rock, looking apologetic. "I'm sorry, but I saw you come up here and thought you looked upset."

She let down her guard. "Oh, Thomas, you are probably the only one in the world who cares what I feel right now."

He climbed up on the rock. "Why do you say that?"

Cassidy shook her head and straightened out the tangles of

her skirt, then dried her eyes on the hem of her apron. "I don't know. Besides, it's not fair to burden you with my worries."

Thomas shrugged. "You said we were friends—that we'd always be good friends. Don't friends share their burdens?"

She was humbled by his gentle words. "Of course they do. I'm sorry. It's just been so hard these last few days. I'm terribly worried about my father making this climb."

"Don't you think he knows what he's doing?"

The question was asked innocently enough, but hit Cassidy like a slap to the face. Of course her father knew what he was doing. He'd never been one to take unreasonable chances. He was born and raised here, and he knew full well the dangers and how to avoid them.

"Thomas, you are quite amazing." She forced a smile. "Of course my father knows what he's doing. I suppose I'm being childish. He didn't talk to me about it and I felt left out. Then when I tried to talk to Allan about it he . . . well . . . he didn't help matters."

"Your dad is the smartest man I know. He's real careful too. I've learned a lot from him about how to do things so as not to get yourself or someone else hurt. You should trust him."

She nodded. "I do. And I know I shouldn't worry."

"No, you shouldn't." Thomas sounded quite the authority. "In my Bible study with your father he told me worry was a sin. It's like saying that God doesn't care enough to take care of the problem."

Again she received his gentle chastisement with a smile. "And we both know there isn't anything God doesn't care about. I've been such a ninny, Thomas, and you were a good friend to deal with me honestly."

He returned her smile. "I've never really had a friend until you, Miss Cassidy."

"I'm certain you will make many friends as the years go by, Thomas. I'm sure my father already considers you one, and Allan too."

"You like him a lot, don't you? Mr. Brennan, that is."

She was momentarily taken aback. Dare she be honest with him about her feelings for Allan, or would that only serve to reopen his wounded heart?

Thomas seemed to understand. "It's all right, Miss Cassidy. I know you love him."

"You do?" She shook her head. "How can you possibly know that?"

He shrugged. "Because I know what love looks like. You look like you feel things for him that I felt for you."

"Oh, Thomas. . . ." She looked away, afraid she might start crying all over again.

Thomas touched her arm. Cassidy forced herself to look at him. He was such a sweet boy.

"Don't be sad, Miss Cassidy. Love is a good thing to feel."

# 23

The entire staff of the Curry and most if its guests were standing in the grass by the dock on the Susitna River. The day had finally arrived. September the fourteenth, 1923. Allan could hardly believe it. Today, they'd start their journey to Denali.

Frank came up beside him and patted his back. "This takes me back, son. I can't tell you how privileged I am to have shared this with your father and now with you."

"Thanks, Frank." He had an instinct to want to cringe every time Frank called him "son," but he held himself in check.

The past few weeks had been exhausting but worth it. Nothing could put a damper on the joy he felt to be on his way to a dream. Nothing except saying good-bye to Cassidy.

She'd apologized to him for her treatment of him that day in the dining room but hadn't resumed their evening walks. Their conversations had been few and far between the past couple of weeks, but she appeared supportive, and he appreciated that effort. The time away would give them both a chance to really think about their future and what they wanted. Allan was confident that he already knew that he wanted Cassidy for his wife, but first he had to settle things with Frank and finally lay his father to rest.

The boat arrived that would take them downriver and south a bit to a better location to cross the ridge to the west. Frank headed toward the boat. "Guess we better get going." He walked down the dock.

John said good-bye to Thomas and Mr. Bradley and thanked them for their help and support. Then he hugged his daughter good-bye.

Allan couldn't hear their words to each other, but he noticed a long hug. John waved to the crowd and walked down the dock as well.

Then Cassidy came to Allan. He'd been hoping she would spare a moment for him.

"Hi." He had nothing profound to say.

"Hi." She smiled. "Well, this is it, isn't it?" Reaching forward, she grabbed both his hands in hers. Allan forced himself not to show his surprise. "I'll be praying for you every day."

"Thank you. I'm sure we'll need it."

She nodded. "Dad gave me your basic itinerary, so we'll know about where you'll be. Just be safe and don't ever risk the weather."

"Yes, ma'am." He winked at her.

Tears formed in her eyes. "I'll be looking forward to when you get back."

"Me too." There weren't words to describe how he felt, but hopefully she knew. And when he returned, he'd tell her.

"Please watch over Dad. He's . . . well . . . you know."

He smiled. "He'll be just fine. I'll see to it."

She nodded and reached into her apron pocket for a hankie and an envelope fell to the ground. "Oh, goodness! I'm so sorry. I almost forgot. This came for you just before breakfast." She wiped her nose and her eyes and handed over the envelope. "Please be careful."

"I will." He tucked the telegram into his jacket pocket, certain it was something that couldn't wait, but he didn't want Frank to see it. "You too."

He tapped her nose with his finger and headed to the boat. Waving to the crowd, he wondered if Cassidy would think about him as much as he thought about her.

•••••

The first day passed without incident, although Allan was a bit saddlesore from the number of miles they'd covered. And they'd made it all the way across the Susitna by boat and then the Chulitna River and beyond by horse. Their first camp was made without mishap at the base of the Ruth Glacier.

John's friends from the Ahtna tribe had a hot meal waiting for them and told them of the journey for the next few days. They'd be snowshoeing once they made it to the top of the glacier, and the sled teams would carry their supplies.

The thrill that rippled through him now was unlike anything he'd ever felt. Here he was at the base of a glacier, with Denali in his majesty towering in the distance. Allan couldn't take it all in.

Blue ice walls rose from the rock below him in great ripples. Their jagged edges looked sharp and uninviting. He couldn't help wondering what his dad had thought when he'd first seen this sight.

Their team had left the trees much earlier in the day. John had explained that the tree line was at its height at one thousand feet because of the glaciated land around them.

It was all so beautiful and amazing.

Their camp was several hundred yards away from the actual glacier so that just in case the glacier walls calved in the night, they wouldn't be buried in glacial ice.

Allan listened to the native Athabaskan tongue flow off the men. John joined in and laughed. What a beautiful language and what incredible people. These men were tough as nails and yet loved to teach Allan new things. The one Allan questioned the most never seemed to lose patience with him. No wonder John was the amazing man he was.

Frank stood up and stretched. He'd been quiet most of the day and went from friendly to wearing a scowl as soon as they'd met up with the Athabaskan party. "I'm tired. I think I'll hit the hay for the night."

Allan nodded. "All right."

After Frank left, one of the Athabaskan men walked over and sat by Allan. "Your friend isn't very friendly."

"No, he doesn't seem to be."

"But he's not looking forward to this adventure the way you are, is he?" The man's eyes twinkled.

"No, he's not. And you're right, I'm excited about this adventure."

"Anyone who respects the Great One like you do will be blessed." He looked down at the pile at Allan's feet. "Do you need help with those?"

"As a matter of fact, I do. These are different snowshoes than I've used before."

"That's because they're *tsistl'uuni.*"

"Chist-loo-nee? What does that mean? Do I have the wrong ones?"

The man laughed. "No. These are hill snowshoes. What you will need to climb the glacier."

"Oh yes. Thank you." Allan watched intently as the native man demonstrated with grunts. John had told them before they met up with the natives that they would learn the men's names if and only if the men told them. It wasn't polite to ask, and they had to earn each other's trust. Allan found it all fascinating.

The man nodded once Allan finally latched the shoes correctly. "Here." He handed Allan a paper-wrapped packet. "For your journey."

"What is it?" He leaned down and took a whiff.

"*Natsak'i.*"

Allan tried to say it. "Nat-sa-kee."

The man laughed. "Close enough. It's smoked salmon strips. To keep your mind clear as you travel up the mountain."

"Thank you, my friend. This is a wonderful gift."

The native man walked away and went to his tent. Such fascinating people. Hardworking. Giving. Simple.

As Allan placed the packet of salmon into his coat pocket so he could carry his snowshoes to his tent, his hand brushed on the envelope Cassidy had given him that morning. He'd completely forgotten about it.

With everyone else occupied or asleep, he opened it up.

```
13 September 1923
Henderson found dead (stop)Murdered (stop)Witness
and evidence point to Frank (stop)Pray you are
safe (stop)Please let us know update (stop)
Louis
```

He read through it three times as a chill settled over him. Glancing at the tent where Frank had gone, Allan thought momentarily about confronting him with the news. He put that thought aside, however. If he caused a confrontation, there was no telling what Frank might do. Was the man's story about a changed life all a sham?

He glanced around for John and found him on the far side of the camp reloading his backpack. Making his way across the camp, Allan cast a concerned glance at Frank's tent. Had he murdered Henderson, and if so, why? Had the man threatened to expose him? Perhaps he had simply served his purpose and

Frank felt it necessary to get rid of the man. Had that been how he felt about Allan's father?

The thought of Frank being responsible for actually ending his father's life sickened him. He had been fully accepting that negligence or even his father's confusion at high altitude had resulted in Henry Brennan's death—but murder was something entirely different.

John looked up as Allan approached. He gave him one of his customary smiles, but when Allan didn't return it, John's expression sobered.

"Is something wrong?"

Allan prayed for clarity. What was the truth? The Frank of the past, or the jovial story of a changed-life Frank?

Allan squatted down beside John, the weight of the truth hitting him. "We've got a killer in our camp."

# 24

Three days had passed since the men left on their expedition. Everyone still talked about where they were or what might be happening, but for the most part, life just kept going at the Curry Hotel. Trains came in and trains left, bringing with them interesting passengers, miners, and railroad workers. There were fewer tourists, but enough that elaborate meals were still required. Cassidy tried to keep her mind on the task at hand, but it became more difficult with each passing day. She couldn't shake off the feeling that something was very wrong.

She looked to the west several times during the day and prayed. She prayed that the weather would hold and the temperatures remain well above freezing. She prayed that they would be safe from harm and that her father's previous injuries wouldn't put him at risk. Most of all she prayed that time would pass faster and they would all return home safely.

Walking back to the kitchen from her room, Cassidy had to stop suddenly to keep from running into Thomas. "Whoa there. Where are you headed in such a hurry?" She reached back to straighten the bow in her apron.

"Actually, I was coming to fetch you, Miss Cassidy. Mr. Bradley says he needs you right away in his office." He gulped in a few breaths.

"Thank you, Thomas. Would you mind letting Mrs. Johnson know where I am?"

"Sure. I'll go right now."

"But you don't have to run." Cassidy laughed over her shoulder. His retreating steps slowed.

As she headed to the manager's office, she wondered what concoctions Mrs. Johnson planned for the Asian diplomats they expected this weekend. That must be what Mr. Bradley wanted to speak to her about. He'd been all excited to host the dignitaries.

Cassidy reached the manager's office and knocked on the door.

"Come in." Mr. Bradley opened the door.

Immediately, she noticed the older, gray-haired couple sitting in front of the manager's desk. Then she noticed that he closed the door behind her—making both doors to the office shut. Unusual for this time of day.

"Have a seat, Cassidy," Mr. Bradley directed.

She looked to the couple and then to her boss as she took her chair. "Is there something wrong?"

The manager cleared his throat. "Cassidy, this might come as a surprise to you, but I'd like to introduce you to your mother's parents, Mr. and Mrs. Callaghan."

Had she not been seated, she probably would have fallen over. What? Her mother's parents? Here? Words wouldn't form, but she felt her mouth drop open and couldn't do a thing about it.

"I know this is a shock for you." Mrs. Callaghan spoke first. "We sent a letter first, several months ago, but we weren't sure your father had received it."

Had Dad gotten a letter? He hadn't mentioned it.

"We planned to speak with your father first, but Mr. Bradley informed us of his whereabouts, so we felt we had no choice but to come to you." She paused and looked at the old man before continuing. "We've come to make amends." Tears streamed down her cheeks.

Of all the things that could have happened to her on that day, this was the one that Cassidy would never have expected. Her grandparents had never been a part of her life. There had never been so much as a single word from them in twenty-three years. Now here they sat as if those years meant nothing.

"Yer hair and coloring is darker, but ye look like yer mother." Sobs shook the woman.

Dad often told her she was as beautiful as her mother, but Cassidy knew her dark hair and dark eyes were from her father. She looked native Alaskan and she knew it. Still the thought of looking like her mother sent a little thrill through her.

Mr. Callaghan rose from his chair, his hat in his hand, and then slowly knelt in front of Cassidy. "My granddaughter." His voice cracked on the words. "We've wasted too much time, and we've come to apologize."

Cassidy blinked and closed her mouth. "I . . . I don't understand. You left us. You wanted nothing to do with my father or me."

Mrs. Callaghan sniffed and spoke again. "We were missionaries from Ireland. We'd come to this beautiful land to teach the native people. And we shouldn't have been surprised that your mother would fall in love with one of the men, but we were. We were terrified of him as a half-Indian"—she corrected herself—"half-Athabaskan man. All those years we served with our holier-than-thou attitudes, knowing that we had the knowledge of the one true God and how He loved everyone and died for the world. And yet, we didna truly understand.

"We were angry with John for taking away our only daughter. And then when you were born and she died, we could bear it

no longer. We felt we were being punished. We said some very
ugly things to your father. Things that should never have been
thought, much less spoken."

After all these years. She had more family. They were here.
Apologizing. And yet, Cassidy couldn't move.

Mr. Callaghan reached for her hand. "Our attitude and be-
havior toward your father has haunted us these many years.
When God finally got ahold of my stubborn heart, I knew we
had to come and repent to you both as well, but sadly, we lacked
the funds and the courage until now."

Her grandmother—yes, her very own grandmother—stood.
"You see, we're old. It couldn't wait any longer. We wanted to
see you—to know you not only because you're all that remains
of Eliza, but because you are our only grandchild. And . . . we
are hoping that ye'll forgive us and let us be a part of your lives."

Cassidy blinked and looked around the room at each face.
This couldn't be real. Suddenly, she stood, opened the door,
and ran back to the kitchen as fast as she could. She couldn't
imagine what they would think of her, but at the moment she
didn't care.

The clatter of the kitchen was comforting as Cassidy ran in
and found Mrs. Johnson. Before she knew it, she started sob-
bing all over the woman.

Mrs. Johnson's warm arms came around her and guided
her into the dining room. "What on earth is going on? Are
you all right?"

Cassidy pulled her apron up to her face and sobbed into it.
Then she lowered it and started telling Mrs. Johnson everything
that had just transpired.

The cook was stunned as well. "I can say that's one I never
expected." She leaned back in her chair. "And you just left them
and ran in here?"

"I didn't know what to say. The shock was just a bit too much, and then my stomach started flooding with all these nasty feelings. I couldn't believe they'd left us the way they did. The way they'd been prejudiced against the very people they were trying to minister to. And all the hurt from my childhood of growing up without them—without their love—and knowing they were out there just overwhelmed me."

"I see." Mrs. Johnson leaned forward. "And so you don't want them in your life?"

"I didn't say that."

"You *do* want them in your life?"

"I didn't say that either. I'm so confused." The sobs shook her again.

"Cassidy." Mrs. Johnson's hand engulfed hers. "Remember when I told you that I lost my entire family a few years ago?"

"Yes."

"I didn't have a choice to keep them as family or to let them go. I didn't have the choice for them to come back."

"I know. And I'm so sorry to come to you with all this. It's not very sensitive of me."

"Oh, hogwash. My point is this: They're family and you have a chance to start anew. You need to forgive them for the past and leave it there—in the past. Losing them the first time was a loss you couldn't fix. But to lose them again now would be devastating—and your fault. I would give anything to restore relationships with my family if they were still here. . . ."

The words sunk in and Cassidy nodded. Her heart broke looking at Mrs. Johnson's face so full of regret. She threw herself into the older woman's arms. "I hope you know that *you're* my family now too. And I love you." Before the woman could respond, Cassidy kissed her cheek and ran back to the manager's office.

Her grandparents were waiting.

She could see the apprehension on the faces of the two elderly people. No doubt they had been completely surprised by her reaction.

"I want to apologize." She looked first to her grandmother and then to her grandfather. It was funny that their blood flowed in her veins, but they were strangers.

"There's no reason to," her grandmother assured. "We put a terrible shock on you. Please say that you'll forgive us—both for the shock and for all the lost years."

Cassidy sank onto the chair she'd only recently vacated. "Of course I do. I can't tell you how many years I dreamed of a meeting just like this—prayed for it too. I think after a while I gave up hope of it, but God had other plans."

Her grandmother smiled. "I'm glad to hear you speak of God."

"My father raised me on the Bible and taught me the value of hope in God. He also told me stories about my mother, but of course he had so few. I would very much like to hear more about her."

"We would love to tell you."

•••••

John watched the clouds above as they trekked farther up the glacier. The wind had a nasty bite to it. The weather had definitely changed.

Two days ago, they'd all snowshoed in their shirt-sleeves when the sun had been so warm reflecting off the snow and ice. But today, they were bundled up. Of course, they'd also climbed a couple thousand feet in elevation. He didn't like the change from warm to cold.

But he didn't like much right now. After Allan shared the news of the telegram with him, John made it his job to keep a constant watch on Frank's whereabouts. Everything the man did or said was suspect. If Irving knew just how closely he was observed, he didn't show it. Frank was as jovial as ever when it was just the three of them. But when the native men were anywhere around, his mood changed. And two of the Ahtna had told him that they didn't trust Frank.

Not a good sign.

But what reason did they have for turning around and quitting? Unless the weather changed drastically, John realized they couldn't let Frank know that they were suspicious. Irving knew how much Allan wanted to succeed, and he also knew how much they'd paid the native men to help and for all the supplies.

The only way out seemed to be if they hit some weather they couldn't manage.

So John prayed for a storm.

A big one.

# 25

The evening meal passed in relative quiet—at least for a bustling hotel. But Cassidy couldn't wait to spend more time with her grandparents. Nothing could put a damper on the joy she'd felt the last day getting to know them.

As soon as she'd gone back and forgiven them, a beautiful blanket of peace seemed to rest on her shoulders. Now she couldn't wait for Dad to get back so he could share in this joy.

Grandmother Callaghan sat at a table in the dining room with her tea, waiting for Cassidy to be done.

"Grandmother." Cassidy plopped in a chair across from her. "Thank you for waiting for me."

"Not to worry, my dear one. It has been fun to watch you work." She pointed at her bowl with her spoon. "What is this delicious dessert you created?"

"Lemon soufflé. It's Mrs. Johnson's secret recipe."

"It's delightful."

"Thank you." Praise from the woman who gave birth to her own mother gave her more happiness than she could have known. "Where is Grandfather?"

"He's been so tired from the travel and excitement of finding you that he went to bed. He hoped you wouldna mind."

"Not at all." Cassidy smiled and folded her hands. "Would you tell me more about the family?"

"I'd love to." The lines on her face crinkled around her eyes. "Did you know you were named after my family?"

"Yes. My dad told me that my name was the last gift that my mother gave me before she died."

"Cassidy is a good, strong, noble Irish name. It was my family name. My father's name—your great grandfather—was Ewan Cassidy."

"What does it mean?"

Grandmother laughed. "It means 'clever one' or 'one with the twisted locks.' But your mother's hair didn't have a bit of curl, and neither does yours."

Cassidy wondered if that was why dad always called her "Clever Cassidy" as a little girl. The memory brought a smile to her face. "Tell me about my mother, please."

"Oh, she was such a sweet girl. She was our pride and joy. Voice like an angel. She loved to help with church—especially with the children. And the children loved her. She was always so happy. Her father—your grandfather—used to say she was 'as sunny as the day she was born.' Nothing ever seemed to make her sad—unless it was some injustice done to someone she loved." Her grandmother frowned. "Like the way we treated your father."

"Was it really just that Dad was part Athabaskan?" Cassidy hadn't really meant to ask the question aloud, but now that it was out, there was no taking it back.

Grandmother sighed. "No. At least not for me. I think it was more about losing my daughter. You see, we knew we wouldn't stay in Alaska forever, but if Eliza married your father, I knew she would never leave—because I knew your father would never leave. It was clear how much he loved this land.

"I think there was a part of me that was jealous of the affection Eliza held for him." She shook her head. "I was so wrong. I had my piety and my religion, but no charity—no love. I can only pray your father will find forgiveness in his heart."

Cassidy smiled. "I don't think you have to worry about that. I've never seen Dad refuse someone forgiveness."

"Perhaps no one has ever hurt him as much as we have."

Shrugging, Cassidy didn't feel she could countermand the woman's statement. "With Dad it's never been about the degree of wrong done him. He forgives openly and willingly because he wants forgiveness in return. At least that's what he's always telling me. If I know him as I think I do, he'll be seeking your forgiveness."

"Oh, but he doesn't need to. The only thing we ever held against him was loving your mother—and we both know that wasn't a sin or anything that needs to be forgiven."

Now that they were talking about her father, Cassidy couldn't help but let her worries creep to the front of her thoughts. If something happened up there, she wouldn't get word until long after the fact. He could die . . . they could both be killed by an avalanche or lose their footing and fall off the mountain and Cassidy wouldn't know about it until days, even weeks afterward. She truly regretted having spent any time in anger toward Allan and her father.

"I can see you are far away." Grandmother stifled a yawn.

"I was just thinking of my father up there on the mountain." Cassidy stood and forced a smile. "But I've kept you up way too late as it is. Why don't you let me walk you to your room?"

"I'd like that very much."

The frailty of her grandmother's arms couldn't be hidden by the woman's thick sweater. Cassidy slowed her pace and once again sent a prayer heavenward, thanking God for the opportunity to be reunited with family before it was too late.

Once she had her grandmother safely delivered to her room, Cassidy walked outside. The summer days of long light were gone and now the skies were dark. At least here she had the glow of electric lights to mark her way, but on the mountain they had nothing more than their lanterns.

She looked in the direction of Denali and wondered where they were. Were they safe? Wrapping her arms around her body, Cassidy couldn't help the thought that came to mind.

Why didn't she tell Allan that she loved him?

·····

The wind was stronger than any he'd ever felt. Allan bundled up inside the tent he and John shared and drank the tea before it lost all its heat. He also wrestled with his conscience and God. For so long now he had blamed God for his father's death, but now that he was here . . . near to where his father had died, Allan felt he had to make his peace.

*I don't really know where to start.* He tried to imagine God sitting on His throne in His full majesty. *I've been so wrong—so angry. I knew it wasn't right to blame You or John for Dad's death, but I had to blame someone . . . and . . . well, I couldn't blame Dad. Even though he was the one who made the decision to come. He knew all the risks, but came anyway.*

*I think for a long time I've been mad at him more than any-one else, but I couldn't admit it. Not to myself or anyone else, and certainly not to You.* Allan had been considering this for most of the climb that day and now that he'd allowed himself to realize the truth, it was like a dam had burst. His emotions and memories flooded down over the years.

"I need Your forgiveness." The words were barely whispered

but seemed to echo in Allan's head. "Please, God—Father—forgive me." For a moment the wind ceased and there was absolute silence. With it came peace to Allan's weary heart.

Then just as quickly the wind started up again and the tent shook harder than before.

John entered as he tried to shake off all the snow. "It's not good."

Allan nodded. "I guess that storm you prayed for is upon us." He didn't speak very loud, but he knew John heard him.

"Yes. I knew God answered prayers, but I guess I didn't realize what I was asking for." John sat down by the camp stove and extended his hands. "I tried to convince Frank to join us here, but he refused. "

It had been three days since they'd left the native men, sleds, and dogs at a camp on the glacier. Each day, they'd made a little progress, but John and Allan purposefully slowed their pace. Frank had been edgy and irritable, but the weather had been nice, so they'd pushed on. Today, they made it over a towering wall and could no longer see the camp below them. Which meant the men from the camp couldn't see them either. And that made Allan's hackles rise. Up until this point, they'd had other people around them. But now, they were truly alone with Frank. And they didn't know what he had planned.

A strong sense of foreboding filled him.

John sat cross-legged on the floor and then pulled out his notes and a map. "We're in dangerous territory. Not good in the middle of a storm."

"Do you think Frank will suspect if we suggest we turn around?" Allan handed him a tin cup with hot tea. John took it and sipped it before answering. He set the cup aside and returned his attention to his book of notes.

"Probably. At least if we don't wait a few days to let the storm pass. We have enough provisions." John closed his book. "And Frank will remember from the last time that we had to hunker down and wait more than once. There's also the possibility that this storm will last for a week or more. Up here on the mountain it's not at all unusual. Maybe if it continues we can convince him that it's impossible to go on—that we simply waited too late in the season."

Allan nodded. "I think we have grounds to declare that now. It's obvious the snows are going to be heavy. We can remind him how difficult it is to break a path through new snow. I'm sure he must remember that."

John grimaced. "I don't know if you've noticed, but he's miserable up here. He doesn't want to be here."

"Sure, I've noticed."

"Well, that means he came here for an entirely different reason than just to climb. A reason that made him willing to risk his own comfort—possibly his own life. What isn't clear is what he has planned. I think you and I should sleep in shifts so that one of us is always awake. I just don't trust him."

The gravity of the situation before them scared Allan.

"I suggest we pray. It's the only surety we have."

John smiled, seeming to sense the change that had taken place in Allan's heart. "I couldn't agree with you more."

●●●●●

Another day, another train. Cassidy watched the southbound train pull in. No doubt filled with hungry men from the railroad. The workers had been flooding in and heading south the past couple days now that their work was complete up north. A lot of them wanted to get home before the snow started to fall. And she couldn't blame them.

She went back into the kitchen to see what needed to be

finished up for dinner. Time with her grandparents had been wonderful, but she still couldn't wait for the return of Dad. The time with her grandparents had also taught her that time was short—if Allan Brennan came back and told her he cared for her, then she would sit him down and tell him that he needed to let go of his anger toward God before she could give him her heart. No more mincing of words. No more waiting for him to see the light. She cared about him. A lot. Enough to tell him the truth.

The railroad agent, Mr. Fitzgerald, entered the kitchen and called out, "Miss Ivanoff!"

She wiped her hands and went over to him. "Yes, sir."

"We've just gotten terrible news that there's a massive storm sitting over the mountains. Some of the men say the natives told them it was worse than anything else they've seen." He looked down at the floor. "I hate to be the bearer of bad news, but I wanted to tell you personally."

A hand flew to her mouth. Her worst fears had just come true. She'd been so consumed with her grandparents and her own thoughts that she'd hardly given the weather any thought.

After dinner, Cassidy received permission from Mrs. Johnson to take the rest of the evening off.

Racing up Deadhorse Hill in her apron and dress, she didn't care a lick about her attire or any danger that might befall her. She just had to see for herself. Had to get a glimpse of what the men were all talking about around the tables. The light was fading fast, which only made the urgency greater. She stumbled on something and barely righted herself before hugging the ground. Another time, the thought might have amused her.

When she finally reached the top, an icy wind cut across her.

The temperature had dropped considerably since earlier in the day. Cassidy drew in her breath and held it before turning to face the view. Thick, black, swirling clouds to the west told her the story she didn't want to hear. The Great One was completely engulfed, and the storm was moving toward the hotel at a rapid pace. For a moment she was mesmerized and then a blast of cold wind hit her face. She let out the breath she'd been holding and fell to her knees. "Oh, God, please don't take them from me! Please!"

Her mind raced to remember their plan. If they'd followed the itinerary, Dad and Allan . . . and Frank would be close to ten thousand feet up the mountain. This storm could cover them in hours, and they might be buried alive. They might already be! The temperatures would be subzero and there would be no place to take refuge except the tents they'd carried with them. And depending on how quickly the storm came up, they might not even have had time to erect the tents.

"No, Dad would have been more aware of the weather than that," she told herself aloud. It did little to comfort her.

"Miss Cassidy, Miss Cassidy!" Thomas's voice drifted up to her. "Miss Cassidy!"

She tried to collect herself and stood. "I'm here, Thomas."

"Miss Cassidy, we need to get down from here right now. The storm is coming this way. Mrs. Johnson told Mr. Bradley where you went and they sent me to fetch you. They're preparing for a doozy down at the hotel."

She nodded. "I just had to see for myself." She pointed toward the mountains.

When Thomas's gaze followed her finger, he gasped. "Oh no! But I'm sure Mr. Ivanoff and Mr. Brennan are hunkered down and waiting it out. Nobody is as smart as your dad when it comes to that mountain." He grabbed her hand. "But we've got our own problems. We've got to get down."

Sheets of rain began to pelt them with no mercy, and Cassidy half ran, half slid her way down the top part of the hill. The wind was a constant opponent, leaving her exhausted, just fighting to stay upright. Finally, Cassidy gave up and plopped down. She began to work her way down, letting her backside anchor her to the ground. It kept her center of gravity lower, and her feet could at least guide her over rocks. Thomas looked at her like she was crazy, but he soon joined her, offering whatever help he could. He stayed beside her the whole time, making sure she didn't get to going too fast.

By the time they reached the bottom of the hill, the rain had turned to snow. And by the time they made it to the hotel doors, it looked like a full-on blizzard.

If it was this bad down here, how bad was it up on Denali? *Oh, Lord God. Please help them!*

# 26

Morning came without a break in the storm. The howling of the wind did little to offer any hope of an end to the blizzard. Allan nudged John. "Are you awake?"

"I am. I'm just trying to stay warm."

"Should one of us go check on Frank?"

"I was just thinking that, but didn't want to leave my warm blankets." John pushed the warm bedding aside. "Fool of a man. He did this last time we climbed—refused to share a tent with anyone else."

Allan nodded. Frank had always been a bit of a recluse—even a snob. "I don't trust him, but I also don't want to see him die, so maybe we should invite him over here."

John donned his outer gear. "I'll do that. You stay here and heat us up something to drink."

"I can do that."

The wind roared around them and when John opened the flap of the tent, a blast of air took Allan's breath away. "Hold on to the rope!" he yelled, but doubted John could hear him over the noise of the storm.

Several minutes passed and Allan pulled on his coat to go check on the men. But just then John entered the tent with his hands over his head, Frank right behind him.

Frank shoved John to the ground, revealing a gun in his right hand. "I've had about all of this I can take," he shouted. He motioned to Allan. "Do up the flap."

"What are you doing?" Allan shook his head. "Frank, you've lost your mind. Put the gun down." He edged slowly to the opening and grabbed the flap as it beat mercilessly against the tent. With one eye on Frank and the other on what he was doing, Allan managed to reclose the opening.

"You two think I haven't known what you've been up to, but I have. You've been plotting a way to get rid of me, but little did you know I was doing the same."

"We've been doing no such thing, Frank." Allan looked at John. There was a nasty gash on his head. Frank must've hit him with the gun before they came to the tent. "What have you done?"

"What have I done? What have *I* done?" A hideous laugh spewed out of the man's lips. It was clear he'd gone mad. "I'll tell you what I've done. One—I've waited for years to have sole ownership of my company. Your father was supposed to die and I was supposed to get it all. But no . . . he had to leave half of his share to his sniveling brat of a son who wanted nothing to do with it. So I killed him for nothing."

"You killed my father?" Allan lunged.

Frank stuck the gun in his face. "I'm not finished." He hissed. "Yes, I killed your father. When this fool stopped to find our trail marker, it gave me just enough time. I positioned myself in the perfect place, and when your father joined me I held his attention by asking him to help me clear my goggles. While he did that, I untied the rope from around his waist. It almost cost me my fingers because I had to take off the thick mittens in order to work the knot." He laughed in a maniacal manner and waved the gun.

Allan noted that he wore only a thin pair of the woolen gloves they'd brought. With his hand wrapped around the cold metal of the gun, his fingers would have to be extremely stiff.

"Then I shoved him over a cliff. How's that for lifelong friends?" The man's eyes were crazy. "Let's see, where did I leave off? Oh yes . . . Two—I've had to deal with your pious family sticking their nose into everything they shouldn't. Three—I've lost a fortune because I've been waiting for the rest of my money to invest in my other ventures. And four—I had to resort to stealing money from the company to make it all work. Then, of course, your brother-in-law had to get in the middle of all that, and then there was that stupid auditor—"

"How many have you killed, Frank?" Allan couldn't take any more. He pushed forward, but Frank stuck the barrel of the gun on his forehead.

"I don't think you want to press me."

Allan pulled back an inch. Frank had gone over the edge. He was insane. It wouldn't do his family any good for him to allow the man who'd taken his father away to take his life as well. But one question haunted him. "You did it all for money?"

"Of course."

He gritted his teeth. "Why? My father would have given you all the money you wanted."

"I don't care. He didn't deserve it. And he didn't deserve his family and all the respect of the community. He didn't deserve any of it. He made plans and they turned golden. I made plans and they turned to ash. It wasn't fair." His voice took on a shrill, almost screeching tone. "I had plans that were good. I had ideas and dreams."

Out of the corner of his eye, Allan saw John slowly reach for his ice axe. He needed to stall. "Frank. Please. Why don't you let John go and I'll sign over the whole company to you now. It'll be yours. All yours." He held up his hands. "Nobody else needs to get hurt."

He lowered the gun almost as if he'd forgotten all about it. "Do you think I'm stupid? John could just go tell the authorities everything."

"No. He wouldn't. Not if I asked him to promise. We could help each other down the mountain and you'd own the company."

"You're dumber than your father, Brennan—"

John rose up with the axe and took Frank by surprise. The gun fired.

John fell to the ground, a circle of red growing above his knee.

Allan took that moment to lunge at Frank and tackled him to the ground. Wrestling with him, Allan knew that this could be the end. But he had to save John.

For Cassidy.

Another shot fired from the gun.

• • • • •

Three weeks had passed since the expedition team left the Curry Hotel. Cassidy was a bit beside herself. The storm had cleared but had left two feet of snow in its wake.

Now the sun was shining once again and the snow began to melt. Unfortunately her fears would not.

Every day she looked toward the west. Did they survive the storm? Would she ever see her father again? And Allan?

She regretted not sharing her heart with him earlier. Now it might be too late. The thoughts threatened to overwhelm her, but she held on to hope.

Through it all, her grandparents and Mrs. Johnson had been a rock beside her. In fact, Mrs. Johnson seemed to be slowly coming around. Each morning she asked Cassidy to share a

Scripture with her and then asked what it meant. She might have only been doing it to force Cassidy to think on something other than the missing men, but Cassidy knew God's Word would never return void.

Maybe there was hope to break down those seemingly impenetrable walls as well.

Nothing was impossible with God.

Not even sparing her father and the man she loved from a killer storm.

· · · · ·

Allan awoke to a dog licking his face. Where was he?

Every muscle in his body ached as he tried to sit up.

But then spots danced before his eyes. Thoughts of Cassidy surged through his mind. Would he see her again? He never got to tell her that he loved her. Or that he'd gotten himself straight with God. He wanted to see her face when he told her.

But maybe it wasn't meant to be.

The rushing of his own heartbeat filled his ears.

Everything went black.

# 27

Mrs. Johnson and Cassidy spent the morning cleaning sweet Alaskan blueberries and preparing them for jelly. While she appreciated Mrs. Johnson's efforts, she hadn't realized the woman could come up with just about anything to keep them busy—including traversing hills and gullies to pick berries.

But it had kept her mind off the fact that her father and Allan hadn't returned yet.

"Now, you finish with those and then work on this bucket," Mrs. Johnson instructed, hoisting the bucket alongside the first. "I'm going to check on those silly girls and make sure they've properly cleaned the pots and pans." She hurried away before Cassidy could reply.

Once her work was finished, Cassidy planned to talk to Mr. Bradley about letting her ride out with Thomas and maybe a couple of other men to look for her father. She was certain the storm would have ended their ascent and they surely were making their way back. They had to be. They couldn't be dead.

She'd know if they were. Wouldn't she? Tears threatened.

Cassidy straightened for a moment and closed her eyes. Drawing a deep breath, she calmed herself and sighed. God was in control. Not Cassidy Ivanoff.

As she reached for another bucket of berries, hands came over her eyes and she gave a squeal of fright. She immediately recognized the warm chuckle of the man she'd fallen in love with. She turned and found herself in Allan's strong arms.

"What . . . ? How . . . ?" She hugged him tight around the neck and spotted her father behind him.

His leg and head were bandaged, and he leaned on a cane, but he was there. In front of her. "Dad!" She ran to him and hugged him too.

Mrs. Johnson and the others had come to see what the ruckus was all about. They broke into a round of cheers, clapping all the while. There were very few dry eyes.

Cassidy couldn't believe it. She grabbed one of each of their hands and dragged them to the dining room, where she knew everyone would follow to hear the story of their mountain expedition. After she sat her father down, she kissed his cheek. "Tell me everything. I can't wait to hear what happened."

John shook his head. He looked around the room at the anxious gathering. "It's not a pretty story, Cass. But I think Allan should tell you the hardest part first."

She turned to Allan. "The hardest part was waiting for you to come home. I think I can face anything now that you're both here."

His eyes were clear and bright and when he smiled at her, it reached his eyes and melted her all the way down to her toes.

"Go on," Dad prodded.

Allan nodded and his expression sobered. "Frank is dead. He planned to kill us both up there."

Gasps were heard around the room.

As the story unraveled, Cassidy cried and grabbed her father's hand. The fact that he had survived being shot on the side of a mountain was a miracle in and of itself.

". . . After I realized that it wasn't me who was shot, I saw Frank's empty eyes. But there wasn't time to worry about him. I knew your dad was bleeding and I had to get him down the mountain. But we were still in the middle of the storm. So I cleaned his wound and pulled the bullet out. After I had him bandaged up, I prayed the bleeding would stop. And wouldn't you know, it did.

"Then I prayed for the storm to stop so we could get down the mountain. And within the hour everything calmed. So then, I thought, 'As long as I'm praying, I might as well ask for a miracle to get down the mountain.' So I prayed some more. I knew I couldn't carry your dad and too many provisions, so our survival depended upon me getting us down to the base camp as quickly as possible.

"The first day was excruciating. The snow was deep. I was tired and coming to grips with what Frank had done. And then we hit the big wall on the east buttress. John was passed out, no doubt from the pain, and I didn't know if I could go on any farther. And then all of a sudden, I looked down and could see the camp. It was a long ways down, but someone was waving at me. It gave me the encouragement I needed.

"Next thing I knew, I woke up with a dog licking my face and a huge knot on my head with every muscle in my body aching."

John laughed.

Cassidy couldn't stand it. "What do you mean? What happened? How did you get down?"

Allan and her dad shared a look. They both smirked.

Then Dad leaned forward. "Apparently we slid the rest of the way down."

"What?" Cassidy couldn't believe it. "There's no way you could survive that. Could you?" Others murmured around the table.

"Well, let's just say that I shoved the pack with our meager provisions over the edge to see what would happen—and if there were any obstacles or crevasses along the way. It bounced and then rolled and turned into a huge ball of snow but showed me a decent path to take. I started over the edge, but it was steeper than I thought. With your dad over my shoulders, my equilibrium was way off and I was worn out. So I prayed some more—asking God to get us down. About a third of the way, I completely lost my balance and landed on my backside. I slid for a ways, but our combined weight was too much for me to stay upright and not go head over heels, so I leaned back and tried to keep John behind me. But along the way, I must have hit a rock with my head because I don't remember anything after that."

Dad laughed. "Don't look at me. I don't remember anything because I was passed out, but our friends at the bottom said we gave them quite a show."

"And then we had the opportunity to tell them about the power of prayer." Allan patted her father on the back.

The weariness in Dad's eyes made his pale complexion more intense. And Dad wasn't pale. Ever. "Enough storytelling for now. You need to be in bed." She motioned to Thomas. "Please help me."

"What about me?" Allan asked, looking almost hurt.

Cassidy laughed. "I would love to spend more time with you, but you should probably go and rest too." She knew there would be plenty of time to make her declaration of love, and she had no desire to do so in front of a bunch of people. She helped get her father into bed, then asked Thomas to bring him some lunch. The boy smiled and hurried off to do her bidding.

"Once you've rested, there's someone here to see you. In fact, two someones."

Her father eyed her with a raised brow. "Cassidy Faith, what kind of mischief have you been up to?"

She grinned. "Only the very best kind."

With her father settled, Cassidy found her grandparents and shared the joyous news of the men's return. She explained that she hadn't told him of their arrival, only that there were two people who wanted very much to see him. After that, she joined the others for lunch, including the Ahtna men who had escorted them all the way back down the mountain to the hotel. Allan was nowhere to be found. Maybe he'd taken her suggestion to go rest.

"We were just hearing about how your father and Allan were rescued," Mrs. Johnson declared, pulling back a chair at the table for Cassidy.

She took a seat. "I want to hear it all."

Her father's Ahtna friends began filling in the missing details of what had happened. "We had already decided to go after them, but then we saw them on top of the ice. Then before we knew it, they were falling. But it wasn't like any fall I'd ever seen. It was slow—almost like unseen hands were lowering them."

Cassidy felt the hairs on her arm prickle. Unseen hands indeed. God's hands.

"We managed to get to them and get them off the glacier. They were banged up and bruised, and both were unconscious. They slept for days and we figured it was best not to move them."

They continued answering the questions thrown at them by the others, but after about twenty minutes Cassidy had heard enough. She made her excuses to Mrs. Johnson, then slipped from the room eager to find Allan. She didn't have far to go. He stood leaning against the hallway wall as if waiting for her to join him on some prearranged date.

Cassidy smiled. "I was just coming to find you. I have something I need to say."

Allan pushed off the wall. "I have something I need to say to you, as well."

She felt a delicious shiver run through her. Cassidy had little doubt he loved her. He offered her his arm and she took hold of him.

She found herself wanting to pour her heart out to him but not knowing where to start. So she chose to quietly walk beside him as they made their way back to the main lobby. Cassidy was glad to see it deserted.

Allan led her to the fireplace. "I'm afraid it's going to take me a few days to feel warm again."

Cassidy laughed and took his hands. "I'm so glad you're all right." She felt a blush creeping up her neck. "And I need to thank you for saving my father."

"He's a wonderful man." He stepped closer and took her chin in his hand. "One I hope to call father myself, Lord willing."

For a moment his words confused her and then it hit her. "Oh! Do you . . . I mean . . . does this mean . . . that you . . . ?"

He got down on one knee and looked up into her eyes and took hold of her hand. "Cassidy Faith Ivanoff, I've already gotten your father's permission, and so I'd like to ask you if you'd give me the honor of becoming my wife."

"Don't you want to know first whether or not I love you?"

He chuckled and shook his head. "I already know that, you silly goose. I can see it in your eyes. I hear it in your voice." He stroked the back of her hand with his thumb and grew serious. "I knew the only thing left to settle was my anger at God. I did that on the mountain."

She felt tears come to her eyes. "Oh, Allan, I'm so happy."

He gave her a lopsided grin. "Does that mean you're saying yes?"

"Yes!" She pulled him back to standing and jumped into his arms. "Yes, yes, yes!"

**28**

JULY 1924

Cassidy held her father's arm tighter than she intended. Thomas stood in the center of the new suspension bridge over the Susitna waving at her, and she watched the bridge sway.

When Allan told her his idea to get married across the river and up on the ridge, she thought it sounded terribly romantic. But now as she faced crossing the wooden planks in her white wedding gown, she wasn't sure she'd been thinking straight.

But she did love him. More than she'd thought possible. And she'd follow him anywhere. Even across a footbridge and up a mountain so they could stand in the shadow of Denali and take their wedding vows.

"I'm so glad Grandfather and Grandmother could be here for the wedding. It means the world to me that we're all a family again."

Her father nodded. "It would mean the world to your mother as well. I like to think she knows."

Cassidy nodded and squeezed his arm. "I do too."

For several seconds they said nothing more. Then with a smile, her father pulled her forward. "Well, they're all waiting for us. Now, if we can just keep Thomas from bouncing too

much on this thing, we might make it across without mishap."
Dad had a twinkle in his eye.

"It is a bit disconcerting, isn't it? Knowing there's nothing
in the middle holding us up?" Cassidy wasn't sure how she felt
about the gently moving bridge and she leaned over the railing
to look down. "But today of all days, I'd rather not give the
bridge a hug."

Dad laughed heartily. "Me neither, sweetheart. Although
that would be a story you could pass down to your grandkids
one day."

"Oh, there will be plenty of those."

Her dad looked at her. "Grandchildren or stories?"

"Both." She patted his arm. "You can just tell them about
all my clumsiness."

Cassidy took a tentative step. She knew on the other side of
the bridge and up the ridge her groom awaited her with friends
and family who wanted to be a part of their wedding.

With each step, her courage grew. God had indeed blessed her.

The walk up the ridge trail wasn't easy in her pretty dress,
but Cassidy kept reminding herself it was worth it. They had
plenty of time and she enjoyed the conversations she shared
with Dad and Thomas.

Grandmother had sewn her dress—a stylish drop-waist satin
creation, with layers of filmy white chiffon below the wide satin
sash forming a beautiful handkerchief hem. It was the most
beautiful dress Cassidy had ever seen, and she loved it even
more since it was created by her grandmother.

So many memories to cherish today. She didn't want to forget
any of it. Not the sway of the bridge, the smell of the flowers,
the sunlight sparkling off the river, or even the climb up the
ridge. Because she knew, at the top, she'd see Allan.

Thomas raced on ahead to let everyone know they were almost there.

Dad stopped and took her hands. "This is it, my daughter. You have my blessing and I love you with all my heart."

Blinking away tears of joy, Cassidy swallowed hard. "Don't you dare make my cry, Dad." She breathed in deep. "Thank you. For your blessing, and for your love. I love you too." She turned forward again and could see the last twenty steps or so leading to the top of the ridge. "Now, let's get moving. I'm ready to get this shindig under way."

He laughed and held out his elbow to her.

Thomas stood above them, turned, and nodded real big.

As Cassidy took the final steps, she heard the words of the doxology wash over her. The whole wedding party sang it together, and it echoed over the ridge in beautiful harmony. As she reached the top, she looked to her groom. He was all smiles, and it lit up his whole face.

To the west was the most glorious sight. Denali stood in all his majesty—not a cloud in view.

The crowd continued to sing until John brought her to stand beside Allan.

"Who gives this woman to be married?" Their pastor from Tenana had come all this way to perform the ceremony.

"I do," Dad answered with a slight break in his voice.

The pastor continued on.

Her soon-to-be-husband leaned over to whisper to her. "I hope the journey was worth it."

She giggled. "Oh, definitely. And you'll be proud—I didn't hug the ground even once."

Before she knew what was happening, Allan wrapped his arms around her and kissed her with a passion she wasn't expecting. Then he pulled back and chuckled. And then he kissed her again.

The crowd applauded and laughed.

The pastor cleared his throat. "We're not to that part yet, young man."

More laughter surrounded them.

Allan straightened, tucked her hand into his elbow, and pulled her closer. "I'm sorry, sir, I couldn't resist." He breathed in deep. "I'll behave."

Cassidy tried to cover her laughter. She looked at Allan, his face now serious and focused on the pastor. Oh, the joy to be with this man.

She tried to keep a straight face, but she just couldn't help it. Her smile generated from her toes today.

The pastor leaned in, a twinkle in his eyes. "May I continue?"

"Yes. Please do."

Now her dad started chuckling as well. At least it was a joyous occasion. And one they would all remember for the rest of their lives.

"Ladies and gentlemen, we are gathered here today in the sight of God and in the shadow of Denali, to join this man and this woman in holy matrimony . . ."

# Dear Reader

Thank you for joining us for the beginning of THE HEART OF ALASKA series.

Our heroine—Cassidy Faith Ivanoff—is very dear to our hearts, and yes, she has a lot of Cassidy Faith Hale's real personality traits. In fact, the saying, "I guess the floor needed a hug" was a direct quote from this special girl. We hope you enjoyed the light from her legacy.

Curry and the Curry Hotel are fascinating pieces of Alaska's—and our country's—history. For many years, Curry was the heart and hub of not only the railroad but of all who visited the great Territory. There are conflicting reports about the actual layout of the Curry Hotel in 1923. Alaska Rails cites that the kitchen was originally in the basement and then moved, where the original floorplans for the hotel show the main kitchen on the main level and the section gang kitchen in the basement. Alaska Rails also states that the Annex was built in 1923 while other sources claim that it was built later. We've chosen to follow the original floorplans for our story and added the Annex in.

The book *Lavish Silence: A Pictorial Chronicle of Vanished Curry, Alaska* by Kenneth L. Marsh is a fascinating read and provided us with wonderful research for *In the Shadow of Denali*, but there are discrepancies with other sources in some matters of the history, buildings, and layout. Over the years, the Curry Hotel changed. The town changed as many other buildings were constructed. While we tried to be as accurate as possible, we did take a few liberties to fit our story when all the sources didn't line up. We'd like to thank Ken Marsh for all his work and his incredible help sharing his research about Curry.

Today, the only remaining structure is the historic Curry Lookout, sitting high above the Susitna River on Curry Ridge (which, by the way, the lookout was not the President's idea, but we had fun putting that conversation into the story). It's not easily accessible. (We even tried to get in by helicopter, but the weather didn't cooperate.) You can find a couple of pictures at www.alaskarails.org/historical/curry/lookoutview.jpg and www.alaskarails.org/historical/curry/lookout.jpg.

The location where Curry existed can be visited by riding the amazing Alaska Railroad, but since the suspension bridge has been gone for several decades, there's no way across the river to the lookout. Coming in from the west, you can drive the Parks Highway to where the future South Denali Visitor's Center will be (and the preliminary plans show a hiking trail to Curry Lookout), but this is still several miles west of Curry Ridge, and there are no trails to Curry Lookout at this time. At one time there was a snowmobile and ski trail, but it seems to be gone as well. Remember, Alaska is still wild and untamed—and Curry and the Curry Lookout are in the "bush" of Alaska and off the road system. But to know that these pieces of history are still there thrilled us as authors.

For simplicity's sake, we have named the railroad throughout the book as the Alaska Railroad. In actuality, the history of the Alaska Railroad includes the Alaska Central Railroad, the

Alaska Northern Railroad, the Tanana Valley Railroad, and the Alaska Engineering Commission.

The President and First Lady really did visit Curry on their journey to Fairbanks. There are some fascinating pictures and stories of this time. Be sure to check out Kim's blog at http://kimandkaylawoodhouse.com for pictures of the "Presidential Special" railroad car that now resides in Fairbanks at Pioneer Park. To be historically accurate, we spent hours and hours researching President and Mrs. Harding and their cross-country trip. Facts about the formal dedication of Mount McKinley National Park and the presidential visit in 1923 were taken from reports made to the Department of the Interior.

The First Lady's line to Thomas about "If I had a son . . ." would have been accurate for the private lady. Most people are unaware that she had a son before marrying Mr. Harding, and the son died in 1915, long before this story took place. What is fascinating though, is that very few during Harding's presidency ever knew that she even had a son. She never mentioned him either, which gave us an interesting twist to use.

The views from Talkeetna, Curry Ridge, and the South Denali Viewpoint on the Parks Highway are my favorite views of The High One. Even though the entrance to Denali National Park is one hundred miles north of these locations on the highway, Curry had the most ideal location to become a climbing expedition starting point since it was barely forty miles away as the crow flies. Even though Curry didn't survive, the quaint little town of Talkeetna did, and today that is where you find the Park Ranger Headquarters to climb Denali. If you go there, say hi to Missy for me (Kim). She was, once again, an invaluable source of information.

On June 7, 1913, the first ascent of the main summit (the southern peak) of Denali was achieved. The expedition was put together by Howard Stuck, but the first man to reach the summit was a native Alaskan, Walter Harper. The first superintendent of Mount McKinley National Park, Harry Karstens, was also part of this historic group and the real leader. (Harry Karstens is a fascinating man, and you will get to read more about him and his incredible work there in the rest of THE HEART OF ALASKA series.)

After the successful summit of 1913, nineteen years would pass before another known party attempted the climb. So for our story, we obviously took some artistic liberty and thought how fun it would be to have a party attempt the climb after Mount McKinley was officially named a national park. When the *Brooklyn Daily Eagle* delegation went to dedicate the park, it really was a party of seventy, but from what we found in doing research, there's no mention of the staff of the Curry helping in any way. But we had fun adding that into our story since it is a significant part of history.

We also used *The Ascent of Denali* by Hudson Stuck several times in *In the Shadow of Denali*. In chapter twenty, we used the actual description in the book for how they prepared their meat for the expedition. It's hard to imagine the time and preparation it took for their group to tackle the monumental task of climbing North America's tallest mountain. A free e-book of *The Ascent of Denali* by Hudson Stuck is provided by www. gutenberg.org/files/26059/26059-h/26059-h.htm.

In 2016, the national parks across the country celebrated the one hundredth anniversary of the creation of the National Parks Service. And in 2017, Denali National Park will celebrate its one hundredth year. We pray this book honors that in some small way.

A big thank you goes out to Dr. John Smelcer for his invaluable work on the *Ahtna Dictionary and Pronunciation Guide*.

His love for his native people and the desire to preserve a dying language is evident in the care and immense amount of time he's taken over the years to provide this free resource. For this book, we've used the western dialect of Ahtna, the tribe whose native land was the setting of our story.

We've so enjoyed weaving in the people and historical facts that were part of this amazing time, but please remember this is a work of fiction.

Randy and Jackie Hale, thank you for giving us the honor of sharing Cassidy with the world.

As with all our other books, we would be lost without the team at Bethany House Publishers. It is a joy and a privilege to work with the whole team there. From editing to marketing to cover design and everything in between, they are top-notch. Thank you, BHP, for all you do.

Thank you—our readers—for your notes of encouragement and anticipation for each new book. We couldn't do this without you.

Last and ultimately most important, Thank You, Lord for giving us the opportunity to write for You.

Until next time . . .

Let it shine, let it shine, let it shine.

Kim and Tracie

**Tracie Peterson** is the award-winning author of over one hundred novels, both historical and contemporary. Her avid research resonates in her stories, as seen in her bestselling HEIRS OF MONTANA and ALASKAN QUEST series. Tracie and her family make their home in Montana. Visit Tracie's website at www.traciepeterson.com.

**Kimberley Woodhouse** is a multi-published author of fiction and nonfiction. A popular speaker and teacher, she's shared her theme of "Joy Through Trials" with hundreds of thousands of people across the country. She lives, writes, and homeschools with her husband of twenty-plus years and their two awesome teens in Colorado. Connect with Kim at www.kimberleywoodhouse.com.

# Sign up for Tracie's newsletter!

Keep up to date with Tracie's news on book releases, signings, and other events by signing up for her email list at traciepeterson.com.

# Sign up for Kimberley's newsletter!

Keep up to date with Kimberley's news on book releases, signings, and other events by signing up for her email list at kimberleywoodhouse.com.

# You may also enjoy . . .

Nanny Lillian Porter doesn't believe the dark rumors about her new employer. She feels called to help the Colton family. But when dangerous incidents begin to plague the farm, will she find the truth in time to prevent another tragedy?

*Beyond the Silence* by Tracie Peterson, Kimberley Woodhouse
traciepeterson.com, kimberleywoodhouse.com

Dr. Jeremiah Vaughan has come to Alaska in hope of a better future. While working at a rural medical practice, he soon develops an attraction to nurse Gwyn Hillerman, who also grows fond of him. But when rumors begin to surface, will the truth about his past ruin his chance at love?

*All Things Hidden* by Tracie Peterson, Kimberley Woodhouse

Grace Martindale loses her last vestige of security when her husband dies on the grueling trail west. Upon arriving in Oregon Country, she uses her midwifery skills to help the other settlers, including the Cayuse tribe, with the aid of fur trapper Alex Armistead. But peace between the groups is fragile, and Grace soon finds herself in more danger than she ever imagined.

*Treasured Grace* by Tracie Peterson
HEART OF THE FRONTIER #1

# More from
# Tracie Peterson . . .

Within the mountainous regions of Montana in the 1890s lies the promise of sapphires and gold for those who seek it, but danger and deception are also found there. When three women are separately pushed into that world, can they and their hearts survive?

SAPPHIRE BRIDES: *A Treasure Concealed, A Beauty Refined, A Love Transformed*

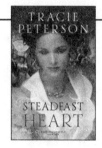

Brought together by the Madison Bridal School in 1888, three young women form a close bond. In time, they learn more about each other—and themselves— as they help one another grow in faith and, eventually, find love.

BRIDES OF SEATTLE: *Steadfast Heart, Refining Fire, Love Everlasting*

◆BETHANYHOUSE